# THE NORTHERN LIGHT

This was Henry's passion, his religion, if you like, his obsession: the England that was, and must one day be again. With quiet sincerity he loved his country, the texture of its earth, the very salt of the sea that washed it. He was not blind to the deterioration which, since the war, had changed the structure of the national life. Yet this could only be, must only be, a temporary aftermath of that Homeric struggle. England would rise again. Her history proved that she had survived even more devastating disasters, when the country lay spent and bloodless, when the outlook seemed clouded beyond hope. Somehow, because she was herself, she had generated fresh life, renewed the cycle of her great tradition and, refusing steadfastly to sink into obscurity, had emerged exultant in the end.

**Also by the same author,
and available from NEL:**

ADVENTURES OF A BLACK BAG
ADVENTURES IN TWO WORLDS
THE CITADEL
CRUSADER'S TOMB
GRACIE LINDSAY
GRAND CANARY
THE GREEN YEARS
HATTER'S CASTLE
THE JUDAS TREE
KEYS OF THE KINGDOM
THE MINSTREL BOY
A POCKETFUL OF RYE
SHANNON'S WAY
A SONG OF SIXPENCE
THE STARS LOOK DOWN

## About the Author

A. J. Cronin, doctor and novelist, was born in
Dunbartonshire in 1896. His many novels
include THE CITADEL, THE STARS LOOK
DOWN, THE KEYS OF THE KINGDOM and
THE SPANISH GARDENER, all of which were
successfully filmed. The collection of short
stories, ADVENTURES OF A BLACK BAG,
became the basis for the TV series, *Dr Finlay's
Casebook*. A. J. Cronin also wrote his
autobiography, ADVENTURES IN TWO
WORLDS. For some years until his death in
1981, A. J. Cronin lived in Switzerland.

# The Northern Light

A. J. Cronin

NEW ENGLISH LIBRARY
Hodder and Stoughton

First published in Great Britain by
Victor Gollancz Ltd., 1958
© A. J. Cronin 1958
First NEL edition 1973
New edition 1978
This impression 1987

ISBN 0-450-03476-3

Printed and bound in Great Britain for
Hodder and Stoughton Paperbacks, a
division of Hodder and Stoughton Ltd.,
Mill Road, Dunton Green, Sevenoaks,
Kent (Editorial Office: 47 Bedford
Square, London WC1B 3DP) by
Robert Hartnoll 1985 Ltd.,
Bodmin, Cornwall

# PART ONE

## I

IT WAS PAST EIGHT on St Mark's church clock that damp
February evening when, in the ordinary way, Henry Page said
goodnight to Maitland, his chief assistant editor, and came
out of the *Northern Light* building. The leading article for
Monday had kept him later than usual – even with twenty
years' experience his composition was not particularly fluent,
and that extraordinary call from Vernon Somerville had
delayed and distracted him.

His wife was using the car and he intended walking home
– lately Dr Bard had been urging him towards more exercise
of a moderate sort – but now, because of the hour, he
decided to take the tram.

As it was Saturday night, not many people were about the
Mealmarket – the old, commercial part of Hedleston, a net-
work of narrow wynds and passages converging on Victoria
Square where Page's offices and printing plant occupied part
of an Adam terrace that betrayed its eighteenth-century origin
in a patina of ancient smoke and weather. Free of traffic, its
cobbled streets for once so muted that his footsteps echoed
down the alleyway behind him, the ancient quarter seemed to
Henry, more than ever at this hour, the steady heart of this
royal Northumbrian borough where for five generations his
family had lived and worked. Instinctively he drew a deep
breath of the moist and slightly acrid air.

A short cut through Dean's Close took him to the main
thoroughfare. At the stopping place there was no queue, the
Wooton tram was half empty, yet when Henry counted the

*Lights* – a lifetime habit – there were four on view. An artisan with a tool kit at his feet, a man of about sixty, was reading his current editorial through steel-rimmed spectacles, holding it up to the dim electric bulb in the corner, his lips moving on the words. He had actually missed the football match to work overtime, and Henry thought: The old ones are the best. Although he had no illusions about his style – his son David was inclined to smile at his *pronouncements* – he found a comforting warmth in the thought that he did occasionally manage to reach, and influence, the ordinary people of the town, towards whom he had a troubling sense of responsibility.

At Hanley Drive he got off. The villas in this road, all built of red sandstone from the Eldon quarries, had few distinguishing features beyond a common aspiration to half-timbered gables, but the entrance to his house was defaced by two heavily convoluted cast-iron lampposts embossed in gilt with the Hedleston coat of arms, three silver martlets on an azure shield. Page was a man who disliked show of any kind; however, having twice been mayor of the town, he had felt obliged to conform to custom and accept these formidable reminders of his years of office.

The garden in which, with enjoyment, pottering around, he spent most of his spare moments, was beginning to show encouraging signs of spring. Taking the front steps rather slowly, he felt for his latchkey. In the hall, as he hung up his coat, he listened for a moment and was reassured by the absence of sounds of social activities. He went into the dining room, where his place had been left set, and, feeling along the carpet with his foot, pressed the bell. Presently a tall bony woman with a scoured complexion and red, chapped hands, dressed severely in black, brought in some sliced mutton, potatoes, and cabbage, standing, her head a little to one side, before remarking with a slight elevation of the corner of her mouth and the tart understatement that for twenty years had been the feature of her service:

'I'm afraid it's a trifle overlong in the oven, Mr Page.'

'I'll have a go at it,' Henry said.

'I could poach you a couple of eggs,' she suggested, after a pause.

'Don't bother, Hannah. But bring me some biscuits and cheese, in case.'

Unseen, she directed towards him a glance of ironic sympathy, the look of a privileged servant recognizing that the household owes everything to her discretion, prudence, economy, and hard work, and expressing, between affection and admonition, an exact assessment of her employer's character.

Yet for this desiccated repast Henry held himself entirely to blame – no one, he felt, could cope with a timetable so irregular as his, and he had long ago agreed that seven sharp should be the fixed hour for dinner. In any case, he was not particularly hungry tonight; he managed fairly well with the Cheddar and biscuits and when Hannah had fetched his slippers he went into the library, as he usually did, before going up to work in his study at the top of the house.

Alice, his wife, still wearing her bridge-party hat with the bunch of cherries – she had the habit of sitting absently just as she came in from the street, sometimes even holding her tightly rolled umbrella in one gloved hand – was on the sofa with Dorothy. They were doing the crossword. It pleased Page to see his daughter at home: since she had started travelling to her art classes in Tynecastle, she had been out rather too often and too late for a sixteen-year-old just free of school.

'Dad,' she complained without looking up, as he entered, 'your crosswords are strictly non-U.'

'They're meant for moderately intelligent people.' Stooping Page made up the fire, which had been allowed to go down. 'What's your trouble?'

'The South Sea name of Robert Louis Stevenson.'

'Try Tusitala . . . and if you read a book occasionally you might know more about him.'

She tossed her hair, tied in an exaggerated pony-tail.

'I bet you looked at the answers in the office. And I did see his movie – *Treasure of the Island*.'

7

Henry was silent, wondering, as he often did, how his children could be so totally opposite – David so brilliant and studious, Dorothy a perfect scatterbrain. He had been optimistic, too, in assuming that she had suddenly become domesticated, for his wife remarked:

'Dorrie has an invitation tonight – a television party at the Wellsbys'.' In a well-bred manner Alice gave the name its due value – Sir Archibald Wellsby, banker and boot manufacturer, was Hedleston's local knight, and Eleanor, his wife, Alice's chosen intimate.

'But surely . . .' Henry looked at his watch. 'It's nearly ten already.'

'Don't be a stick, Henry. If you won't let the child have a television set in the house you can't stop her going out to look at one.'

Dorothy was already on her way to the door. When she had gone, he couldn't help protesting.

'She's getting out of hand. Why in heaven's name you let her go to that confounded art school . . . These kids do nothing but sit in the Tynecastle cafés, gossip and drink coffee, when they're not idling their time away at the cinema. . . . You know she hasn't a grain of talent.'

'Perhaps not. But she meets *nice* young people there . . . some of them from the best country families. Lady Allerton's son is in Dorrie's section . . . and the de Cressy girl. That's quite important. After all, we don't want another disaster, do we dear?'

As Henry gave no answer she put aside the crossword and took up her needle-point. Presently, between stitches, she began an account of the afternoon party she had attended, describing those present, the dresses, the hats, gloves, and varying hair-dos, an epic to which, through long experience, Page was able to close his ears while giving the appearance of a sympathetic auditor. The business of that telephone call from Vernon Somerville still lay on his mind. It puzzled him. He had been briefly introduced to Somerville at a publishers' dinner in London – it was for the Associated Newsvendors Charities three years ago – yet he had never

8

imagined that so prominent a personality would remember an unimportant provincial editor like himself nor, for that matter, that his opinion of the *Light* should be so favourable. The owner of the *Morning Gazette* ought surely to hold an opposite view.

'Henry, are you listening?'

Page started. 'Sorry, my dear.'

'Really . . . you are very unkind.'

'The truth is,' he apologized, 'there's something on my mind tonight.'

'Your mind? Good gracious . . . what?'

As a rule, Henry never discussed the affairs of the paper at home. In the early days of his marriage he had done so with the weirdest consequences, but this evening he felt a need to confide in someone.

He looked across at Alice, spare and stylish in figure, with the fair, sligtly freckled complexion, faded yet still good, that goes with sand-coloured hair.Her vague blue eyes, set in a narrow head under brows arched as though in permanent surprise, were directed towards him with questioning interest, the look of a woman, who by an effort, maintains a qualified forbearance towards her husband despite the trials and disappointments which, during twenty years of marriage, she is convinced he has imposed on her.

'As a matter of fact, I had an offer for the paper today.'

'An offer? To buy it?' She sat up, her cherries quivering, the party forgotten. 'But how exciting! Who was it?'

'Somerville of the *Gazette*.'

'Vernon Somerville. His wife was Blanche Gilliflower . . . they separated last year.' Versed in the genealogy, relationships, and intimate doings of the great, Alice reflected for a moment, then said, in the superior accents of her native Morningside – the best part of Edinburgh – which at her most social moments she always intensified, 'Henry, this is rather thrilling. Was the offer . . . ?'

She broke off discreetly.

'My dear, since I did not accept, I have no objection to your knowing. It was fifty thousand pounds.'

'Goodness! What an amount!' Her eyes became ingenuously remote. 'Just think what one could do with that . . . travel . . . see the world. Oh, Henry, you know I've always wanted to see Hawaii.'

'I'm sorry, my dear. Hawaii will have to wait.'

'You mean, you won't accept.'

'Somerville already has three publications – that raffish weekly of his and the *Sunday Argus* in addition to the *Morning Gazette*. I can't see he has any need of another. Besides, he'd' – he checked himself – 'be rather too go-ahead for our little property.'

There was a pause.

'But it seems such a chance,' she resumed, re-threading her needle and taking on a light, persuasive air. 'You know you haven't been well lately. And Dr Bard keeps telling you that high pressure and irregular hours don't suit you.'

'You'd like me to retire. To a villa in Torquay perhaps? I'd be unutterably miserable.'

'I don't mean that at all. You're still a comparatively young man, and we oughtn't to be stuck all our days in the provinces. With influence you could easily get a post . . . say with the United Nations.'

'Shut myself in that Tower of Babel? Never.'

'But, Henry . . . I'm not thinking of myself, although you know I'm frightfully tired of Hedleston and everyone in it. Isn't it worth considering . . . a chance? You know you never make the most of your opportunities.'

Page shook his head, ignoring this reference to a familiar and indeed justifiable plaint that 'if he had really tried' he might have secured a knighthood at the end of his second term of office as mayor.

'My whole life is in the paper, Alice. And I've made it something, too.'

'David could take over.'

'Don't be absurd, Alice. If Somerville brought? He wouldn't have a look in. And you know how I've built on him . . . once he's fit again.'

'But . . . fifty thousand pounds . . .'

10

'My dear, if that amount dazzles you, let me assure you the property is worth at least double.'

Momentarily she was startled.

'Well,' she said, after a pause, during which her look of disappointment gave way to a knowing expression, faint image of that shrewdness with which her father had summed up evidence in the Edinburgh High Court, but which in Alice was so naïve it touched Henry. 'Perhaps if you hold off he'll offer more.'

'No, Alice,' he said mildly. 'I told him positively I would never sell.'

After this she was silent. She resumed her needle-point, turning the news over and over in her mind. While as yet she did not quite know what to make of it, she was both excited and displeased by the attitude Henry had taken up. The length and stiffness of her silence – strange in one so voluble – the piqued glances she occasionally darted towards him, the appearance of having withdrawn from something of which she could not approve were, as always, the signs of her disaffection.

Page was annoyed with himself. Surely experience should have taught him the futility of opening his heart to Alice. Yet some unfulfilled need in his nature drove him to it, and always with the same result, a lack of understanding and accord, so that he emerged unsatisfied and chagrined, like a bather who, thinking to refresh himself in cool water, finds that he has plunged into a shallow pond.

At last she said, rather shortly:

'Are you going to Sleedon tomorrow?'

'Of course . . . it's the end of the month. Do you want to come?'

She shook her head. He had known that she would refuse. David's marriage had not satisfied her; there remained a smarting sense of disappointment, the aftermath of frustrated ambition, at what she referred to privately as the 'disaster.' It was one of her good qualities that she had always wanted the best for her chidren, and Cora, who, in Henry's view, was most things that a woman should be, did not fulfil those

11

exacting requirements which she had looked for in the wife of her son. The shock of that first meeting, when David appeared, unexpectedly, with a strange young woman, tall, pale, and a little frightened, on his arm, had passed, but there still were difficulties and objections – the word 'common', in particular, although never spoken, seemed held back only by an effort that demanded all of Alice's ladylike restraint. Now indeed, the irritation of her mood, for which Henry was responsible, made her suddenly exclaim:

'I wish you'd try and get them into town a little oftener. Let them come to a dance, or a concert. Be seen with us. People do talk, you know. It's so unnatural, living out there in the wilds. What our friends make of it all I shudder to think.'

Wisely, he checked the obvious answer.

'Very well, my dear,' he said, 'I'll mention it.'

II

NEXT DAY CAME FINE and fresh with only a few clouds streaking the blue sky – invigorating weather. Although Page's forebears were strongly evangelical in their beliefs he was not a regular churchgoer. Whenever his wife and Dorothy set off for eleven-o'clock service, he cut some early flowers from the back lawn for Cora, picked up a book that had come in for review that he thought would interest David, and got into the car. Driving quietly out of the garage, along the lane behind the houses, so as not to scandalize the neighbours, he nevertheless failed to escape the eye of Mrs Harbottle, widow of Bob Harbottle, who had been a close friend of his father's, and the old lady, proceeding slowly to St Mark's in her Sunday grandeur, acknowledged Henry's greeting with a glance of reproof.

But soon he was on the open road to Sleedon. His troubled

mood of the previous evening was gone; he felt unusually free. Bound up in his work, Page had few recreations. Neither golf nor tennis interested him; in fact, he was not cut out for games, being inclined now, although only forty-nine, to some sort of heart condition, which, despite Dr Bard's head-shaking, he dismissed as more annoying than serious. Henry, in fact, was a quiet sort of chap, born with a retiring disposition and disciplined in his youth by parents who believed strictness to be the basis of a good upbringing. Even when he became mayor, public functions were always an ordeal and Alice frequently had reason to reproach him for what she called his 'lack of go.' He liked his garden, and grew rather fine pelargoniums in his little greenhouse; poking around for bits of the old Stafford china he collected was another mild diversion; and he took immense pleasure in arranging the autumn orchestral concerts he had introduced to Hedleston and which were now an annual feature of the town. But above all, he did enjoy getting down to the sea occasionally, especially at Sleedon, which, although so near to Hedleston, remained the most unspoiled fishing village on all the north-east coast. He had known it as a boy, and now his son lived there. But beyond the attachment thus created, the charm of the village was spiritualized for him by the fact that here survived a part of the real old England.

This was Henry's passion, his religion, if you like, his obsession: the England that was, and must one day be again. With quiet sincerity he loved his country, the texture of its earth, the very salt of the sea that washed it. He was not blind to the deterioration which, since the war, had changed the structure of the national life. Yet this could only be, must only be, a temporary aftermath of that Homeric struggle. England would rise again. Her history proved that she had survived even more devastating disasters, when the country lay spent and bloodless, when the outlook seemed clouded beyond hope. Somehow, because she was herself, she had generated fresh life, renewed the cycle of her great tradition and, refusing steadfastly to sink into obscurity, had emerged exultant in the end.

13

Now the low outline of Sleedon lay before him. The spray was smoking against the breakwater of the harbour as he drove along the front, past the moored smacks and the drying nets, round the whitewashed coastguard station and up the cliff to David's cottage.

As he came over the sandy crest he saw Cora waiting at the gate. Bareheaded, blue-black hair flying about windblown cheeks, her dark red dress moulded upon her long limbs, she seemed to radiate that warmth and tenderness which had been the restoration of his son. She pressed his hand in both of hers, and even before she said it, he knew she was glad to see him.

'How is he?' he asked.

'A proper good week. He's upstairs now . . . at the writing.' As they went in she glanced up at the attic window, from which there came the muted sounds of a Bartók concerto. 'I'll call him.'

But Page was chary of disturbing David. His book, on pre-Islamic poetry, a subject that had interested him since he was at Balliol, was a stiff proposition. In the past six months he had taught himself three Arabic dialects and was now translating *Kital al-Aghami*, the *Book of Songs*. Better not risk breaking his concentration. Cora saw this hesitation. She smiled.

'Dinner won't be no more than half an hour, anyway.'

The daffodils pleased her beyond Henry's expectation. When she had admired and arranged them, in too tight a bunch, she led him into the garden, which lay at the back of the house, protected from the prevailing breeze by a dry stone wall, and showed what she had done in the past week. A new vegetable plot had been prepared and neatly laid out in the somewhat stony enclosure.

'And who did the digging?'

'Me of course.' She laughed happily.

'Isn't it too much for you? With the house, and the cooking . . . and David.'

'Oh no . . . no. I'm strong, I am. And I'm right fond of the

14

garden.' She looked at him shyly, with real feeling. 'You see, I didn't never have the chance before.'

When she left to go into the kitchen Henry paced up and down the narrow ash path, reflecting, without unkindness, on that 'I didn't never.' Well, what of it? He'd rather have a good-hearted young woman than a perfect grammarian, especially when that woman was Cora. Soon she was calling him from the back door.

In the front room the table was laid with a freshly laundered cloth; the cutlery, carvers, and china – in fact, all the little things he had given them – were noticeably displayed; and a promising roast chicken lay crisp and golden on the dish. Cora, in all she did, showed a cheerful competence, an air of responsive willingness that plainly expressed her eagerness to please.

As they waited, the long-playing record upstairs was switched off and a moment later David came in – a trifle aloof, as usual, yet Page saw at once that he was in one of his good moods. He looked well, too, and in spite of his usual queer rig-out – turtle-necked sweater, buff corduroys, and worn suède shoes – one couldn't help thinking what a handsome chap he was – extremely tall, like Cora, though thin, still much too thin, with soft blond hair, a fair skin, and fine even teeth.

'Work going well?' Henry asked him, while Cora carved the chicken.

'Pretty fair.' He accepted detachedly the tempting arrangement of wing, Brussels sprouts, and mashed potatoes which she handed him, studied it for a few moments, then negligently took up a fork.

'A new biography of Edward Fitzgerald came into the office.'

David raised his eyebrows.

'I thought you might like to look at it,' Page murmured, in self-defence.

David glanced quizzically at his father.

'Don't tell me you admire the Calif of East Anglia . . . the man who wrote that priceless couplet:

15

'The ball no question makes of ayes and noes.
But here and there as strikes the player goes.'

Page half smiled. He did not mind David patronizing him: it was no more than an attitude to which, as a classical scholar who barely missed a first at Oxford, he was surely entitled. Henry's own education, cut short by a sudden recall to the office on account of his father's illness, had been amplified by extensive reading, yet he had spent no more than two years at Edinburgh University, where Robert Page, who had been there as a student, insisted on sending him.

'Khayyám isn't too bad,' he argued mildly. 'Ruskin liked it.'

David made a grimace, and brought out a string of Arabic.

'That's my opinion of old Omar.'

'What does it mean?' Cora asked.

'I'm afraid I don't know you well enough to tell you,' David said, and went into fits of laughter so extravagant that Henry gave him a quick doubtful glance. Yet, recollecting those days when his son sat, head down and hands pressed rigidly between his knees, staring at the floor, fixed in a frightful depression, it was a relief to hear him laugh. The nights had been worse, endlessly without sleep, pervaded by fears of an unknown enemy. His military service had not been abnormally severe – he had fought in Crete, suffered an attack of dysentery in the retreat – yet the strain had produced an extreme sensibility which had persisted during his years at Oxford and ended, some eighteen months ago, in a serious nervous breakdown. Obsessive neurosis with a trace of paranoia, Bard called it, but Henry could not agree when the doctor insisted that he had noted pronounced neurotic tendencies in David as a boy – an outrageous opinion that almost broke their long friendship.

But it made little difference now. Observing David's elevated spirit, Page felt that this marriage, so extraordinary yet so fortunate, had saved him. A chance meeting on the front at Scarborough, where he had gone for vocational therapy, then, from weaving baskets with a blank face, he was home, still shaken, but restored, with a new confidence in the future. Doubly strange, since never before had he displayed any serious interest in women, least of all in one whose untutored mind was the antithesis of his own. Yet perhaps it was the very fact of Cora's lack of education that had made the approach possible. Sunk in the depths of the abyss, he had stretched out instinctively towards the simplest creature within reach. How lucky that the hand he had grasped was Cora's.

After dinner, while she cleared the table, Page and his son sat talking by the window. Usually David was uncommunicative about his work, but today his reserve had gone; he was gay and open. The translation of one of his essays, 'The Land of Night,' written during the war, had just appeared in the *Mercure de France,* and he produced a personal letter of congratulation which he had received from the editor. This recognition of his talent, a necessary stimulus for him, was also a secret encouragement to Page, who hoped that David might soon join him in making a finer thing of the *Northern Light*.

It was their custom to take a walk together, but this afternoon David excused himself and went upstairs to work – he was eager to make full use of a book which he had on loan from the London Library and which was due to be returned the following day. Cora, however, already had her coat on, so she and Henry started off for the harbour.

At first they did not talk. She had a gift of silent companionship which made him feel that he had known her for years. When they crossed the sandy cove, their feet crackling the dry, banked seaweed, and turned on to the breakwater, she took his arm, giving herself to the strong sea breeze with a kind of joyful abandon.

'You should have a warmer coat.' He had noticed that hers was of worn serge.

'I'm not a bit cold.' Then: 'Don't you love it out here?'

'Yes,' he said. It was a tonic to be with her.

At the end of the deserted pier they stood in the shelter of the lifeboat station watching the circling and swooping of the gulls. The wide sea was before them; the wind came salt and keen from the waves. He had the strange sensation that he could remain there for ever. At last he broke the silence.

'You've done a lot for David.'

'He has for me,' she said quickly. Then, after a pause, she looked at him, then looked away. 'I wasn't that happy neither when we run across one another.'

Somehow, in this bare statement Henry felt that she had honoured him with a confidence from the heart. Her reticence, an absence of that prattling communicativeness which he detested in women, had from the first endeared her to him. Yet he had noticed in her a humble longing for affection, a desire to attach herself to the family into which she had married, that suggested past hardships. Later this had been confirmed when she told him something of her life, how she had lost both parents some years before, had lived with an aunt in London, supported herself in a succession of underpaid posts. No note of self-pity had escaped her. But now it was as if, through her present happiness, there came the echo, faint yet unmistakable, of sadness.

'You were pretty much alone?'

'Yes,' she answered. 'That was about it.'

As a heavier gust came, Henry put a supporting arm about her shoulders.

'I don't want you to feel that way ever again. You belong to us now. And we'll never let you feel lonely. My wife was speaking of that only yesterday . . . wondering if it wasn't dull out here sometimes for David and you. You should come into Hedleston occasionally, both of you, to a dance.'

'I don't fancy the dancing much, I don't,' she said, then added, as though her remark might have sounded strange, 'David don't either . . . he's not that sort.'

'The theatre then, or a concert?'

She turned to him.

'You know I like it here. The quiet is the very thing I like. At night, in bed' – she coloured suddenly, as if she'd said something wrong, but went on – 'when the wind blows round

18

the house and you hear the waves, it's like being in a castle, if you know what I mean. I wouldn't change Sleedon, not now I wouldn't, not for any place else, anywhere.'

It was time for them to leave. When they got back to Henry's car he heard a record going in the attic; it sounded like Bruckner, the Fourth Symphony, in E-flat major, not his taste, but sure sign that David was seeking inspiration, so he decided he had better not go up. Unobtrusively, he slipped the envelope he left at the end of every month into Cora's outside pocket. It was always a slightly embarrassing moment, although he tried to be dexterous, like a conjurer getting rid of a playing card, usually adding some fatuous remark by way of patter – these young people were proud, but they must live. This time he said:

'That's for some seeds for your garden.'

But Cora did not smile. Her face, with its high cheek-bones and fine-veined, faintly hollowed cheeks, wore an odd expression. The wind had moistened her dark hazel eyes and swept a black tress across her brow.

'You're so good to us, you are, especially to me. You've made me feel . . . you make me . . .' She could not continue. Suddenly, she came near to him and quickly, awkwardly, pressed her soft lips against his cold cheek.

As Henry drove back in the grey dusk to Hedleston, slowly – there was no inducement to hurry – the thought of that impulsive caress warmed him all the way home.

### III

MONDAY WAS ALWAYS a busy day – news accumulates over the week-end – and Page was at the office early. Instead of going directly upstairs he went into the copy room. This opened on to the cobbled yard, a large, old-fashioned, but well-lit room where most of the news staff worked. The premises were not large – in fact Henry had to rent the adjoining building for his printing presses – and they were old-fashioned, but they had been exactly so for many years; they suited him, and he liked them. Peter Fenwick, the assistant sub-editor, was standing with Frank, the copy-taster, by the Associated Press machine.

'What's in from Egypt?' Henry asked, when they had said good morning.

'The Canal's still blocked,' Fenwick answered. 'The Americans can't get permission to raise the cement barges. King Saud had a talk with Eisenhower. He's to get jet planes and more Cadillacs. Nasser's still throwing his weight about . . . the Israelis won't budge. We're getting short of oil. The Edens have reached Panama . . .'

Page listened in silence, every word reopening the wounds, still raw, left by that humiliating debacle.

'What's the home news?'

'There's a gruesome story in from Belfast. Double murder and suicide . . . wife, lover, and husband, all with their throats cut.'

The details, which Henry ran through, were frankly horrible.

'Spike it,' he said.

'A paragraph on the back page?' Fenwick suggested.

'No, not a line.'

The rest of the news, which he read over quickly, was not inspiring. The Middle East situation looked worse: more trouble was undoubtedly brewing in Cyprus.

'Anything else?' he asked.

Frank, whose job it was to 'taste' the copy from the machines and pick out anything affecting the north-eastern area, said:

'How about this?'

The shet he gave Henry was a teletype of Saturday's late Parliamentary proceedings. He had marked two lines in blue pencil.

In reply to a question by Mr Burney Cadmus, North Eastern Boroughs, Mr Philip Lester replied for the Government that, so far as he was aware, there was neither substance nor shadow in the rumours circulating on what the Hon. Member had been pleased to term Project N.R.U.

'Project N.R.U.?' Henry looked questioningly from one to the other.

'Never heard of it,' Fenwick said.

'N.R.U.' Frank wrinkled his brow. 'Could it be the National Railroads Union?'

'Not a chance,' Fenwick answered. 'It's probably a false run. That Cadmus is always flying off the handle.'

Henry gave him back the sheet.

'Still, put a follow-up man on it. Young Lewis, if you can spare him.'

He went up the winding stone staircase to his office. Miss Moffatt, his secretary, who also dealt with the subscriptions, was sorting the mail. Elderly, of neutral appearance, rather like a retired school teacher, with a colourless complexion and greying hair, wearing, summer and winter, a clerical grey skirt and grey knitted cardigan, Moffatt was practically indispensable, doing all sorts of odd and important jobs without the slightest fuss. Brought into the office some thirty years ago by Robert Page, she had never quite accepted the son as his father's successor. This morning her manner was decidedly 'off'. Henry sensed at once that she had something on her mind. She gave him time to go through his letters, meanwhile unknotting a piece of twine from a parcel and rolling it into a neat, tight ball – she had a mania for petty economies, regarding string, half sheets of paper, and odd unused stamps as something in the bank – then, as he prepared to dictate, she said:

'He's been on the phone again.'

'Who?'

'Somerville.'

Henry looked at her in surprise. 'What did he want?'

'To speak to you. When I said you weren't in, and he

obviously knew you wouldn't be – the call came in at seven-thirty from Surrey – he left a message.'

'Yes?'

She took her memo notebook and read from the shorthand.

'Kindly convey my personal regards to Mr Page. Tell him that two of my executives will be in his neighbourhood next week. Say that I shall be most happy if he is good enough to permit them to call upon him.'

'There was a pause. In order to collect himself, Henry said:

'Go over that again.'

She did so, and at the second reading it sounded even more extravagantly urbane. The perplexity which had troubled him on Saturday returned with renewed force. He felt vaguely worried.

'What do you make of it?'

Tightening her lips, Moffatt made a sharp gesture, angry and disdainful, with her head.

'He wants to buy the *Light*.'

'He did. He was under the impression it was for sale. I told him he was mistaken.'

'He is not the kind who makes mistakes.'

'Well . . .' Henry said, at last, 'even if you're right it makes no odds. He may want to buy. But I certainly don't want to sell.'

'Is it as simple as that?'

'Obviously.' Because Page was upset he felt himself getting annoyed. 'If the paper isn't on the market how *can* it be bought?'

'Do you know Vernon Somerville?'

'Yes . . . at least I met him once.'

'Then you no more know him than I know the man in the moon. At least you know what he publishes. Have you seen this morning's *Gazette*?'

All the London dailies came into the office; they were arranged on the long, brass-bound, mahogany table by the window. She took the *Gazette* and placed it in front of him. This morning, spread over the front page, was a luridly retouched flashlight of three blood-splashed corpses, two men and a pitifully half-naked woman, sprawled on the floor of a tenement room, while above, in inch-high type, screamed the headline THE PRICE OF PASSION.

'Isn't it pretty?' Moffatt said, in an indescribable tone. 'It would look nice on our front page.'

Although Moffatt was easily put out and alarmingly ready to take offence, Henry didn't know what had come over her. He had to stop that nonsense. He gave her back the paper.

'Take dictation,' he said sharply.

When he had dealt with the correspondence she went next door to her machine and he passed along the corridor to the pillared Adam room where, every morning at ten, he held conference with his staff to plan the next day's news coverage and features. Malcolm Maitland, his chief assistant editor, was already there, talking with Hartley Slade, who managed the art department; and as he entered, Poole, the sports editor, came in behind him with Horace Balmer, the advertising manager.

As they sat down at the long polished table, Henry had a sudden impulse to mention the Somerville affair, but feeling this to be weakness on his part, he refrained. They began to discuss the format of the paper, going through Maitland's news schedule item by item, deciding what should be passed and what discarded.

The policy of the *Northern Light* had long been summarized in the phrase which, in modest pica type, could be found at the head of page one: 'All the news that's fit to read.' Set inflexibly against sensationalism, the paper had built up, over five generations, a reputation for integrity, fair-mindedness, and sound news presentation. It had become more or less a tradition in the district. Today, inevitably, the main news interest centred in the Middle East. Page and his staff went into this at length, worked through the national and county issues, came down finally to that subject of perennial interest – the weather. Heavy floods had occurred overnight in Lincolnshire and a reporter was sent out on this assignment with the chief photographer. There were, of course, local events to be reported, and various staff dispositions were made on these. Bob Lewis had already gone out on the N.R.U. assignment. Within an hour, after they had all spoken freely, an agreement was reached and it was possible to give some definite shape to the paper.

While the others went off, Malcolm Maitland walked along the corridor with Henry. Exceptional in ability and character, a staunch, hard-headed Northumbrian, Maitland was a man whose opinion Page profoundly respected. Son of a working 'shot-firer' in the small colliery village of Bedlington, he had been born in a typical miner's row. Entirely by his own efforts, he had educated himself at Durham University, where he had won two scholarships and, in his final year, the Whittingham Prize in Political Economy. At first he took up teaching in Tynecastle, where, in his spare time, enthusiastic for social reform, he started a night school for the local shipyard lads. Twice, later on, he stood for Parliament in the Liberal interest at North Durham, but was beaten narrowly on both occasions. Then, compelled by economic necessity, having lost a few of the illusions of his early days, but not his sense of humour, he abandoned a political career and took to journalism. Ruddy, ill-favoured, and walking with a limp – the result of an accident on the coal tip when a boy – he made no appeal to the eye, but rather to the mind and heart. He lived alone, a natural bachelor, in an apartment in Wooton and managed, as he put it, to 'do for himself' pretty well. Like a good northern apple he was hard, but sound all through. Even in his hobby, a life-long passion for trotting ponies, fostered no doubt by a lasting affection for the pit ponies of his youth – he actually boarded out a couple of old-timers at Mossburn Farm – the down-to-earth wholeness of the man was revealed. He was closer to Page than anyone else in the office.

'There're so many problems.' They were discussing a topic for the leading article, and Henry spoke irritably, depressed and more than usually on edge. 'So many things to be said and so little time to say them.'

Maitland nodded. 'It seems we're deeper in the hole than ever.'

'If only we could get rid of our cursed apathy. People don't seem to care any more so long as they get free physic and the football pools. Look at West Germany, how they've pulled themselves up by their bootlaces. When I saw that country lying in rubble in '43 I swore they were done for . . . that they'd never recover. But they have . . . magnificently . . , now they're on top of the world.'

'Don't forget they had one advantage. They lost the war.'

'That's not the answer, Malcolm. They've done it themselves by guts and sheer hard work, while we've been drifting, a ship without a rudder.'

'Ay, we're in a bit of a mess, all right. But we've been in worse ones.'

'If only we had someone to take charge . . . a real statesman . . . Disraeli, for example . . .'

Maitland paused outside Page's door, gave him a side-long glance, touched with understanding humour.

'You've got your leader there. And your headline – 'If Disraeli Were Alive Today.'''

As he left he glanced at his watch and said dryly:

'Don't forget our man of God has an appointment at eleven.'

It was almost that now, and before Page could get down to the advertising department for his routine conference, Gilmore, the rector of St Mark's, came in. He shook hands, a brisk, well-shaved Christian, exuding an aura of good-fellowship.

'Good of you to see me, Henry. You're a busy man, like myself.'

He had come about the St Mark's steeple, which in January had begun to slant. Death-watch beetle was the trouble and, since the old spire was beautiful and a landmark, Henry had opened a fund in the *Light* for its restoration.

'I've had the final estimate,' the rector went on, rustling his papers. 'Much more, I'm afraid, than we anticipated. Fourteen thousand pounds.'

'That's a large sum of money.'

'Indeed it is, my friend. Especially since contributions to your fund are less than five thousand.'

Henry did not care for that, at all. The paper's effort was purely voluntary, and although he was no Croesus, he had started off the fund with a hundred guineas of his own. However, he merely said:

'These are hard times for our country; taxes are high, and this is not a charitable time of year. Wait until next Christmas and we may do better.'

'But, my dear Henry, the need is urgent.'

He continued for some time in this strain, while Page's exasperation grew. Didn't he realize that all unnecessary projects and personal interests, all this eternal crying out for more, and still more, must be suppressed before the country came to ruin? Yet Page tried to bear with him, listened, discussed ways and means, promised him space on the middle page, but he was glad when the other finally got up. As Gilmore went out he slid a sheet of typescript, with a conscious air, on to Page's desk.

'Forgive me, if I leave you these few Easter verses, Henry. I trust on this occasion you may find them worthy of insertion.'

As the door closed behind the rector, from force of habit Page picked up the sheet. His eye was on the first deplorable line – 'A lily, fairest blossom of them all' – when the phone rang. Miss Moffatt screened his calls from the switchboard downstairs, and her voice came through.

'It's London again.'

'Not Somerville!' he exclaimed involuntarily, and was immediately ashamed of himself.

'No. It's from Mighill House. A Mr Jones.'

After an instant's pause he said:

'Put him through.'

'Mr Henry Page? How are you sir?' The voice had, a Welsh intonation. 'This is Trevor Jones, Sir Ithiel Mighill's confidential secretary. I haven't the pleasure of knowing you, sir, though I hope I may soon. Mr Page, Sir Ithiel would like you to meet him in London . . . or at his country house in Sussex. At your earliest convenience.'

Instinctively Henry guessed what was to come.

'I'm afraid I can't spare the time.'

'Sir Ithiel would be happy to send his personal plane to fetch you.'

'No, it's impossible.'

'I assure you, Mr Page, it would be to your advantage to come.'

'Why?'

'For obvious reasons.'

'I asked you why.'

'Sir Ithiel understands that the *Northern Light* is on the market. He particularly wishes you to do nothing until he has talked with you.'

Henry's throat tightened with sudden anger. He cut the connection abruptly. What on earth was it all about? Why should two of the most powerful press magnates in the country suddenly turn their eyes towards a small provincial paper? Although, in his concern, he probed every possibility, he could find no reasonable answer to either question.

With an effort of will he threw off the vague sense of alarm that was settling upon him and forced himself to begin the leading article. Suddenly the phone rang again. Henry almost started from his seat. But it was Dr Bard's receptionist reminding him of his noon appointment for his monthly check-over. Normally this interruption would have irked him; today he welcomed it; he wanted to get away from the office. Concentrating, he got his article into its first shape and rang for Moffatt.

She came in, bringing his letters, and when he had signed them he gave her the rough draft.

'I shall want to see this again when you've typed it.'

'Very well.'

From her tone, which was chilly, Henry saw that she had not forgiven his earlier brusqueness. While Moffatt did not actually indulge in huffs, she managed to punish his occasional transgressions in her own way.

27

'Do you wish your coffee?' she asked. 'It's past noon.'

'No, I'm going out. Back at two o'clock.'

'You'd better see this before you go.'

Impassively, she handed him a telegram.

FOLLOWING MESSAGE SOMERVILLE THIS MORNING BEG TO
ADVISE YOU I SHALL BE CALLING ON YOU NEXT TUESDAY.
ANTICIPATING THE PLEASURE OF OUR MEETING, SINCERELY,
HAROLD SMITH.

By this time Page was beyond surprise, but his fingers,
holding the buff slip, were tense.

'I wish to God we knew what was in their minds.'

Neither her expression nor her reply brought him any
comfort. She said briefly:

'We'll know soon enough.'

As he did not speak she went out.

Alone, Henry raised his eyes and found himself frowning
at the daguerreotype on the opposite wall of the *Light's*
founder, his great-great-grandfather, old Daniel Page, seated,
black garbed, in a stiff pose, one hand inserted beneath the
lapel of his frockcoat, the other, forefinger extended, supporting his brow. In his disturbed fancy he seemed to discern an
added gravity in that serious commanding face. Hurriedly,
he took his hat and left the room.

IV

THE PLANE LANDED at the airport on time – twelve forty-five
by Smith's Y.M.C.A. presentation watch, which he always
kept accurate to the second.

'Take both the bags,' he told the porter. 'There's a car
ordered for us. The name is Mr Harold Smith.'

The flight up had been agreeable and, expanding his chest in the keen air, he felt glad to be in Tynecastle again. A handsome black Daimler drew up with a uniformed chauffeur. They put the baggage in the boot, he tipped the porter ten shillings, noted the amount in his expense book, then got in with Leonard Nye.

'It's a long time since I was here,' he remarked, as they moved off. 'Fifteen years.'

Nye was lighting another cigarette: he was a chain smoker, a habit which, in Smith's opinion, never did any one any good. He answered, finally:

'They should have met you with the town band.'

Smith frowned slightly. Although Nye could lay on the charm when he wished, he had an unpleasant tongue, and was scarcely the colleague Smith would have chosen for this undertaking. But he tried not to take offence. A large, though flabby, man physically, he considered himself 'big' in every other way. 'My motto,' he would often say, 'is to look for the best in everyone and keep on good terms with my fellow men.' Besides, today he had every reason to be pleased with life. He made no comment as they drove along Harcourt Street, but actually they were not half a mile from the poor apartment where his mother, widowed when he was only seven, struggled and sacrificed to let him take his articles as a qualified chartered accountant. And now, within sight almost of that mean neighbourhood, he was returning – to the opportunity of his career.

When they had passed through the city he leaned forward and unhooked the speaking tube.

'What do you call yourself, my man?'

'Purvis, sir.'

'No, no. Your first name.' He made a practice of being on friendly terms with anyone who worked for him.

'Fred, sir.'

'Good. Well, Fred, don't take the direct road to Hedleston. Cut off at Bankwell and go by Utley Moor.'

'That's a long way round, sir. And the road's none too good.'

'Never mind, Fred. Take it.'

This was Smith's home ground. He'd never cared much for London, although he had done well there since he had come back from Australia in '49. If one owned a fine house in Curzon Street, like Mr Somerville, with an estate in the green belt by way of a change, there was something to be said for London life. But a suburb such as Muswell Hill, where he resided, was less agreeable, especially since Minnie had left him . . . but he wouldn't dwell on that now since, with God's help, the remedy was not far distant.

They were drawing near to Utley. Nye had his eyes half closed, his bare head – he never wore a hat – sunk down in his camel-hair coat. He had been on the town the night before and, except at lunch time, had slept all the way in the plane. Unobserved, Smith studied him, acknowledging his good figure and smart appearance – the light brown hair, marcelled, and with one bleached strand, the well-manicured hands, the severe dark suit which came from Poole's, worn with a fine fawn Shetland vest the plain grey tie and black pearl pin, the narrow-bracelet wrist watch, and the signet ring with the crest he'd fancied and calmly appropriated from *Burke's Peerage* – he was a dandy, all right, and good-looking enough, except for his rather full lips and greenish protuberant eyes under which a few fine lines made him seem older than his thirty-two years. From his manner, polished, confident, and easy, his air of elaborate indifference, his expensive tastes, his carelessness with money, and the air he could so well assume of not having a care in the world, one would never have suspected his irregular origin, which to Smith, with his evangelical morality, would have been almost insupportable. Yet you had to hand it to him. While he had neither depth nor genuine emotion, there was a sharpness about him, and a look of experience which, although he was difficult to get along with, made you feel that in an emergency he would not be a bad person to have on your side.

'Wake up, Leonard. We're on top of Utley.'

Smith wanted to stop the car but thought the driver might wonder at their interest in this remote spot. It was all very

30

well to be agreeable, yet you had to keep these fellows from knowing your business. However, they were moving slowly, jolting over the potholes, and the lie of the land was plainly visible, a big open sweep of bracken and heather, broken only by low stone walls, real North Country moorland.

'Well, there's the site,' he remarked in an undertone. 'Pretty as a picture postcard. It seems a shame what they'll do to it. Chimneys and prefabs all over the place.'

'Who cares? It's good for nothing else. And it's bloody cold up here. Tell Frederick to get a move on.'

'It's only one-fifteen. Page won't expect us until the afternoon. Before we see him we'll register at the hotel.'

'I suppose it's the usual provincial dump?'

'No, it's a Trust House. The Red Lion. First class.'

'It'd better be. I've a feeling this business is going to take longer than you think.'

'Don't worry,' Smith said. 'It should be easy now Mighill isn't competing.'

'I wonder why he dropped out so quick,' Nye said, with sudden thoughtfulness. 'It's out of character for old Ithiel.'

'His new Sunday illustrated is costing him too much; he can't match the figure we're prepared to spend.'

'That's too simple. Mighill and Vernon love each other like a mongoose and a rattlesnake. As for money, Vernon himself isn't too flush these days.'

'He's made us a handsome allocation.'

'You know why?'

'He wants the *Northern Light.*'

Nye looked at his companion as though he'd said something foolish.

'You mean he needs it.'

After that, there was a silence, while they began to descend the hill. Beneath them, in the valley, clear and shining in the rain-washed air, lay the slate roofs of Hedleston, offset by the green dome of the town hall and the delicate grey spire of St Mark's. A white plume of steam rose from an engine standing in the station.

'That's our town, then,' Smith commented. 'It's a fine one.

They have full employment, and two good clean industries – the Northern Machine Tool Company and Strickland's Boot Factory.'

Nye was not impressed. As they drove through the outskirts he kept throwing off sarcastic remarks, some of which Smith had to admit, were extremely amusing. Smith didn't speak till they drew near the Red Lion. Then he said:

'Look, Leonard, that early lunch they gave us on the plane, it was pretty light. How about another bite when we get in?'

Nye's expression became even more sardonic.

'What an eater you are, Smith. It's pathological. Because the world rejected you as a kid.'

'It doesn't reject me now.' Smith smiled, but he was hurt – like most self-made men he took pride in his obscure beginnings, which he exaggerated in conversation.

At the reception desk he told the clerk they wanted two good singles with a sitting room between.

'Shall you gentlemen be staying long?'

Nye looked him over.

'Suppose you wait and see, chum. Which way is the bar?'

As Nye strolled off, Smith went up to his room. It was clean and smelled of floor polish. There were fresh towels by the wash basin and the springs didn't sag when he pressed the bed. He unpacked, put his clothes neatly away, then placed a leather-framed photograph of his wife on the chest of drawers. This was an enlarged snapshot, taken some years before, of a pretty, commonplace young woman with an edifying expression and an anaemic air, dressed in her Sunday best and holding a Bible in her gloved hands. Smith gazed at it fondly, then, satisfied with his arrangements – he was a methodical person and liked to have everything in order – he rang the bell, ordered a double ham sandwich and a glass of milk. He wasn't too worried about Nye drinking; he could put away any amount and never show it. Leonard Nye was smart, and no mistake, perhaps too smart – Smith decided he must find an opportunity to make it clear that Mr Somerville had put *him* in charge of their joint enterprise.

He ate his snack in large appreciative bites, had a wash and a brush-up, then inspected himself in the mirror, going over in his mind the line he meant to take with Page. All the facts and figures were in his head – he had been working on them for the past three weeks – and he was optimistic. He knew the power of money. And even if an outright purchase failed, their alternative course of action had been planned at the head office in a series of conferences that covered every contingency. He wasn't 'one of your intellectuals' – Smith often proclaimed this a trifle smugly – but when it came to business he knew what he was about. Indeed, how otherwise would he have overcome the great misfortune that almost ruined his career?

After the death of his mother, seeking opportunity in the colonies, he had booked passage in the *Orestes* from Liverpool to Melbourne. On the voyage he fell in with a Mr Glendenning, an Australian business man, mainly in the dried-milk trade, but with many other interests – he owned several sheep stations, an evening newspaper called the *Melbourne Echo,* and a beach club at Bondi Beach outside Sydney. The night before they docked he asked Smith to go to Bondi and look into the position at the club.

The young accountant found it badly run down, the books in a dreadful state, and the manager so openly dishonest that his first gesture was to offer the newcomer a bribe. This was indignantly refused, and Smith set to work to straighten the place out, with such good results that Glendenning sold it eighteen months later at a handsome profit and, as a reward, moved his protégé into the office of the *Echo*. The urge to get on made Smith learn fast, and at the end of three years he was promoted to business manager of the Melbourne paper. It was at this time that he married the daughter of a lay preacher, Minnie Langley, whom he had previously met at a picnic of the Victoria Christian Association, in which he had now become a leading figure.

For the next nine years he worked successfully on the *Echo*: it was his suggestion that started a weekly coloured supplement which grossed an annual twenty thousand pounds' profit for the paper. He had begun to feel that his partnership could not be long delayed when, quite suddenly, Glendenning died, the paper was sold to the rival *Mercury* combine, and, within a period of weeks, Smith was left high and dry, without prospects or position, not even mentioned in the old man's will, a cruel blow which affected him 'in a certain way' – unable to recollect his lapse without a sense of deep humiliation, he never phrased it otherwise.

Some three months later he decided to return to England with his wife. Amongst the passengers on the boat was Vernon Somerville, who had just bought the *Gazette*. To the chastened Smith it seemed like fate, as if the frayed thread of his destiny might be repaired by another shipboard contact. Although Somerville kept much to himself, one evening after dinner Smith managed to approach him on the promenade deck. At first he was impatient, almost rude, but as Smith went on with his little prepared speech he kept looking at him sideways with increasing curiosity; finally, with a peculiar smile, as though he had observed something which demanded further study, he handed him a card to see him in London.

Smith's start in the *Gazette* office was relatively unimportant, but by persistent application over the past seven years he had improved his position until he was second only to Clarence Greeley, Somerville's general business manager. As a result, he had this priceless opportunity to take over and manage the *Northern Light*. He did not mean to let it slip.

It was time for him to go downstairs. Standing erect, he closed his eyes and, with clasped hands, petitioned the Lord for success in his coming meeting with Henry Page. He found Nye in the bar finishing a pint of beer and talking with the barman.

'It's nearly three. Don't you want to freshen up?'

'What for?' Nye said. 'The natives can learn to love me as I am.' As they went out he added, 'I pumped something out of that yokel. Page has a social wife who seems an altogether foolish and pretentious person, a kid daughter who

34

likes to dance, also a dope of a son who won't work on the paper.'

'I'm sorry to hear that,' Smith said simply. 'I'd have gladly kept the young man on when we take over.'

Nye threw him a sour look.

'Oh, come off it,' he said

The car was waiting, Fred saluted, and a moment later drove off in good style. Smith meant to be calm, but as they went along Queen Street the perspiration began to break on the back of his neck and the palms of his hands. He was naturally a heavy sweater, and the nearer he drew to the interview ahead, the more vital it seemed. Nye, on the other hand, wore an air of complete indifference. In five minutes they were at the *Northern Light* building, and without being kept waiting – a courtesy which appeared to hold a happy augury – they were shown up to Page's office.

V

As THE TWO MEN entered, Henry dismissed Moffatt, who was filing the subscription returns, and asked them to be seated. Smith, unbuttoning his coat, his briefcase held between his knees, took a quick glance at Page and was at once favourable impressed by the appearance of the owner of the *Northern Light*. He saw a smallish, thoughtful-looking man with a quiet manner, just of an age when one begins to get a trifle thick in the waist and a little thin on the top. His eyes were dark brown, the colour of the suit he had on, with warmth in them and good-natured lines at the corners. Encouraged, Smith sat down, cleared his throat, began with a few pleasant remarks, then tactfully came to the point.

'Mr Page,' he said, 'may I say that we approach you in the most cordial and friendly spirit. You know, of course, the

35

reason of our being here. The Somerville group is sincerely interested in your publication.'

Henry seemed to reflect for a moment.

'What I cannot understand is why there should be this interest in the *Light*.'

Since Page was apparently ignorant of the proposed N.R.U. scheme, Smith felt it no part of his duty to enlighten him. He merely said, with perfect truth:

'We are anxious to expand. Also, we know the reputation of your paper, Mr Page.'

'You believe that to be good?'

'We do, sir.' This was an opportunity for a compliment. 'We consider the *Northern Light* absolutely first in its own class.'

'Then why should I sell it?'

'I will tell you, Mr Page.' Smith leaned forward, speaking slowly and impressively. 'So far, owing to exceptional circumstances, you have been able to stand off the competition of the big London dailies. But that state of affairs cannot last.'

'I disagree. We are more than holding our own. Our latest figures show an increase of four thousand over the corresponding period last year. Our circulation is eighty thousand, whereas I question if in this area you sell more than nine thousand of your *Gazette*. As for Mighill's *Globe*, fewer than seven thousand come in and a good many of them are returned.'

'Granted. We know you've done well, Mr Page; we're not belittling your achievement in holding the fort. But times are changing very fast. What with our immense technical advances, special train and air transport services and, above all, our fixed determination to expand, competition is going to be much fiercer. There are only half a dozen independent papers of your type left in the provinces, and I promise you, within two or three years they will all be absorbed.'

'They may be, but not the *Northern Light*.'

'Naturally you are confident, Mr Page. But while I won't go into ancient history, you surely haven't forgotten the year when in the Midlands alone five provincial papers were all wiped out.'

'And hundreds of workers, including more than a hundred journalists, were flung on the scrap heap.'

'Precisely, sir. Then take Hanbridge, for instance. Only three years ago it had a morning paper, two evening papers, and a weekly. Now they are all gone, except for one evening paper, and that isn't owned, as it used to be, by the local people.'

'Hanbridge is not Hedleston.'

'Mr Page, be patient, and you'll see I am really on your side. You remember the case of the *West Country Bulletin* last year.'

'Only too well. It was iniquitous.'

'Of course you recollect it was the Jonathan group, not us, who were responsible. But it was a very sad affair . . . a small paper trying to fight off a great wealthy London organization, people losing their livelihoods, the local share-holders being ruined, and all because a little common sense was not employed in the first place. Now, it seems to me that any reasonable man would hate to see that occur again.'

Henry looked straight at Smith, who thought that perhaps he had gone too far.

'Is that a threat?'

'My dear Mr Page,' Smith said quickly, 'nothing could be further from the truth. I am merely trying to point out how very favourable this present situation could be for your good self. Now, if I may have your attention.' He opened his briefcase and, taking out a sheaf of papers, ran through the figures he had compiled from various sources over the past three weeks on the value of the plant, machinery, goodwill, and miscellaneous assets. Then he said, 'We estimate that the entire property is worth seventy-five thousand pounds. Naturally, our first offer to you was purely tentative. I am now authorized to double the original amount and to make you a firm offer of one hundred thousand pounds for the *Northern Light*.'

Henry didn't answer immediately. He kept looking from

one to the other until Smith felt sure he was going to accept. Then he said, moderately:

'I've no quarrel with you, gentlemen. You are only doing your job. Still . . . you must realize what's happening to our press today. A few powerful groups, bent on extending their empire at all costs, are reaching out for every paper they want, with no higher objective than increasing circulation and outselling their rivals in the cut-throat competition that now exists.'

Smith was about to interrupt when Henry went on.

'We all of us know the power of the press . . . for good or evil. It's incalculable. It can make or break an individual, create or destroy a government; it may even, heaven help us, start a war. It's the application of this power, without restraint or responsibility, towards ends that are entirely unworthy, by certain papers with enormous national coverage, that is the curse of our country today and may well be its ruination tomorrow.'

While Page was talking, Nye had become increasingly restive. Aware that the financial presentation of the offer was Smith's affair and highly sceptical that Page would immediately accept it, he had so far deliberately said nothing, lounging in his chair with his coat collar turned up and a detached expression. But now he suddenly broke in.

'I suppose you exempt your own lily-white product from this ruination business.'

'I do,' Page answered calmly. 'In its own limited sphere it follows those great papers that have maintained their principles – papers that lead and educate the people, and try to create intelligent citizens. rather than a nation of gaping primitives reared on a mixture of sex, sensation, and scandalous gossip.'

'You don't seem to like sex.'

'Not when it's thrown at me, day after day, in a brassiere and bikini.'

'Come now,' Smith said hurriedly, trying to smooth things down. 'There's no need for argument, gentlemen.'

But Nye had begun to sit up.

'Let me inform you,' he said, with a sneer, 'since it may not have penetrated to your cha :e and sheltered nook, that some of our citizens like to see little floosies in bikinis; they like to dream of going to bed with them instead of with their fat old woman. Sex and money are the two main objectives of the human race. Why run away from it? You ought to know that nothing sells a paper like a damn good adultery. Let them have it. What do you think a working man wants with his forning cup of tea at six o'clock on a foggy morning? Not the smarmy, soapy sermon that you serve up, but the bit of snap and spice we give him in the *Gazette*.'

'Indeed. So you brace him up as you did last Monday with three blood-stained corpses.' Page had turned rather pale and the vein in his neck was beating fast, but, as he took up some clippings from his desk, he still was calm and restrained. 'You've honoured me by doing some research on my publication. I, on my side, have collected some excerpts from yours over the past four days. Here are just a few of the headlines: MONTMARTRE NUDES ENTICE LONELY TOURISTS. BLUSHING BRIDE EXPOSED AS BIGAMIST. SMART TEDDY BOYS TAKE TO PERFUME. STRIP TEASE ARTISTE TO ENTER CONVENT. WOMAN OF SIXTY GIVES BIRTH TO TWINS. ATTACKED NURSE FAILS TO EXPLAIN ABSENCE OF BRUISES. MALE SEX MANIAC RUNS AMOK. WHITE SLAVES OF THE HAREM. THE BLONDE SPY WHO SEDUCED A KING. SPINSTER CLAIMS DAUGHTER WAS VIRGIN BIRTH – I NEVER HAD A LOVER SAYS MISS TOMPKINS. MARRIED MAN CHANGES SEX AND BECOMES WOMAN. I won't go on with your pernicious drivel. I merely tell you outright, even if I were desperate to sell, I would never do so to the *Gazette*.'

'Now look, Mr Page.' Smith, on the edge of his chair, was really anxious; everything seemed to be, going wrong. 'Don't let's be hasty. Take a few days to think things over.'

'No, my decision is final.'

'Then,' Nye said, 'we'll have to see that you get a little

extra competition. And believe me, it will be hot and strong.'

'I'm afraid you are making a grave mistake, Mr Page.' Smith threw Nye a look in a belated attempt to shut him up. 'We are quite determined to establish ourselves here by fair and legitimate means. We offer to buy, make you a most generous price. You refuse. Therefore we are forced to start an opposition paper. It's a free country. You admit we have a perfect right to come in.'

'You have the right,' Henry said, more slowly than before, 'but you will never succeed. In the first place, our population is not large enough to support two papers. And in the second, the *Light* is so firmly established nothing will supplant it. Don't you realize that we go back to 1769, when the paper was founded by Daniel Page, the man who fought with Wilkes for the liberty of the press and the right to publish parliamentary reports . . . and that James Page, my great-grandfather, led the struggle to repeal the iniquitous newspaper tax – the tax on knowledge, he named it – and was prosecuted for it? No, no, you'll never do it. I advise you not to try.'

'You wait and see,' Nye said. 'If you want to bet I'll lay you two to one you're out of business in eighteen months.'

'I don't bet. And you can't frighten me. You'll never start a paper here from scratch.'

'You're a trifle wrong there, Mr Page, I regret to inform you,' Smith said. 'We have ways and means that I'm afraid you are not aware of. Do change your mind, I beg you.'

'No.' Henry shook his head.

There was a pause. Smith let out a long breath and stood up.

'Well, sir, it deeply grieves me that we've failed to reach an agreement and must come into conflict, for, if you will permit me to say so, even though our meeting has been short, I like and respect you. And I will promise you one thing – that we fight you fair and square, with everything open and above-board. May I offer you my hand on that, sir?'

Smith held out his hand, and when Page extended his, shook it firmly. Nye, of course, offered no such civility. He lit a cigarette, dropped the spent match in the corner waste-basket, and preceded Smith through the door.

As soon as they were in the car he let out a few polite oaths.

'I told you he wouldn't sell.'

'You didn't help,' Smith said sharply. 'You only put his back up.'

'He never would have in any case. He's an obstinate old fool who'll insist on holding on, partly from sentiment, partly from vanity. We'll have to break him. Mealy-mouthed hypocrite, with his service to the public. What an outfit! It belongs in the Stone Age. Not a lift in the entire dump. Did you spot the old girl in the background? Like the ghost of Hamlet's mother. And the bearded ancestors on the walls . . . and the foxed lithograph, "Opening of the Manchester Ship Canal, 1894," over the desk . . .'

Smith let him run on. He had his own thoughts. Naturally he was deeply disappointed – instead of a quick result they would have months of work and heavy responsibility – but he was not discouraged. There would be greater opportunity to prove his worth to Somerville.

Immediately they reached the hotel he went into the tele-phone booth and called the head office. He made his report to Mr Greeley, his own particular chief. After a long con-versation which confirmed the instructions he had already received, he rejoined Nye.

'We're to go ahead . . . exactly as planned. Don't worry, it may take a little longer, but we'll do the job together.'

'We!' Nye said. 'From now on we're just a couple of puppets. They'll pull the strings in London. And we'll stay here and stand the racket.'

'No, we're on our own now. Greeley just said so.'

'Have it your own way. But God help us both if we don't come through.'

Smith looked at his watch – past four o'clock – and although he felt like sitting down to a good North Country tea, this was not the time for delay.

'Let's get out to Mossburn right away. The sooner we take up our option there, the better.'

41

## VI

SHORTLY AFTER Smith and Nye had gone, Henry left the office and drove directly home. His wife and Dorothy were out – they had gone with Mrs Bard, Hannah informed him, to the new film at the Odeon – and, after a pretence of eating, he went upstairs to his study, a converted attic room looking out on the back garden, which housed his books and his bits and pieces of Staffordshire pottery. For the rest of the evening he sat there, turning over all that had taken place and striving, despite a certain heaviness of mind, to adjust himself to a situation that must radically change the settled pattern of his life, which presaged, at the very least, a future clouded by uncertainty. He tried to tell himself that the threat to establish an opposition paper was an empty one. But no, he knew they had meant every word. The senior, Smith, who acted as spokesman, a heavy, clumsy, ready-made figure, with a full-moon, serious face, struck him as a reasonable man, not particularly intelligent, though probably good at his job and, allowing for a certain sumgness of manner, fundamentally well meaning and honest – the sum was not altogether unfavourable. The other, unfortunately, seemed a more dangerous personality: smooth, yet sharp, with a barbed tongue and a veiled, probing eye, he had the look of a man who lived by his wits – Henry felt instinctively that of the two, he was the stronger and by far the cleverer, most likely the one to be feared.

The realization that he had actually formulated that word 'fear' struck Page suddenly as so absurd that he swung back sharply to a firmer and more balanced frame of mind in which the trouble seemed less, the outlook clearer. Solidly established, his paper had the support, yes, even the affection, of the town. How could it be supplanted by some upstart sheet sponsored by the least reputable of London tabloids? The *Light* had lived through other crises in the past. This also it would survive.

Next morning Henry reached the office in good spirits, prepared for any eventuality. He was not long left in doubt. Moffatt, when she had said good morning, proffered a handbill of the ordinary give-away type, heavily smudged, still damp from the press. She said: .

'They have bought the *Mossburn Chronicle.*'

It was a possibility he might have foreseen. In Mossburn, not more than twelve miles distant, Herbert Rickaby, the ageing proprietor of the *Chronicle* – a weekly devoted to local news in the agricultural area it served – had for some time been anxious to sell. While the opening was undoubtedly limited, it at least provided a base for immediate operation and expansion. Glancing through the leaflet, Henry saw that it was an announcement of the purchase, with the statement that in future the paper would be known as the *Daily Chronicle* and would be widely distributed in Hedleston and district. There followed an exaggerated forecast of the merits of the new publication.

Moffatt was watching his expression.

'They've half a dozen men from the labour exchange giving these away by the hundreds. And a row of sandwich boards parading outside the station.'

'Well,' Page said, 'at least we know where we are.'

His first thought was to get all his staff together and make some sort of address, but the idea, distastefully theatrical, was so foreign to his nature he dismissed it. Instead, he waited until ten o'clock and went along the corridor for his morning news conference in the usual way. The five department heads were already assembled and became so suddenly silent as he entered and took his seat that, although he felt far from gay, he had to smile.

'Well, gentlemen, it appears we are going to have some opposition in the town. I gather you've all seen this.' He held up the handbill.

'You can't miss them. All over the place,' Horace Balmer, the advertising manager, said. 'And on Halley Brothers' hoardings too. After the business we've given them. It's too bad.'

'Somerville's money is as good as anybody's,' Maitland said bluntly. 'And apparently he means to spend it.'

'I wonder how much they paid Rickaby?' Poole speculated, and as no one answered, he added, 'Little enough, I'll bet. The old boy was dying to get out.'

'But how they'll do anything with that plant!' Balmer shrugged, so that his stiff cuffs with the heavy links shot over his knuckles. 'Fenwick tells me it's a single-roller, stop-cylinder Wharfedale. The circulation was never more than six thousand.'

'They'll manage, don't you worry.' Maitland alone seemed to treat the matter with proper seriousness – the others, puzzled, curious, even a trifle jocular, were certainly far from being disturbed. He went on: 'And if you think they're going to keep on printing fat stock prices, farm weather reports, and the prospects for spuds and swedes, you're a long way off the mark.'

'I agree with Malcolm,' Henry said. 'We're in for a long, hard struggle. These people will have all the *Gazette's* special features, syndicated articles, exclusive foreign-service reports, all fed to them from the London office. In addition, they'll play up local events to the limit, try every trick they know to capture circulation. I believe they'll fail. I'll go so far as to say they must fail. But we have to be on our toes, more than ever, and all the time. For that reason, if anyone has any suggestions I'll be glad to hear them.'

Glancing round the table, he saw that Poole, the sports editor, sitting with his hands bunched in his pockets and his long legs stretched out, wanted to speak. He was a tall, lanky fellow with an orange handlebar moustache and a rather scornful manner, both of which he had brought out of the commandos, together with a mania for physical fitness which regularly made him rise at six in the morning to run five or six miles, stop watch in hand, before coming to work. At

44

times inclined to be difficult, he had a little of the ex-officer's sense of being ill used by the postwar world, one of those angry young men who get angry wtih everyone but themselves. Yet, for all his moody assertiveness, Henry liked him and knew that he could be absolutely relied upon. Now, in his challenging style, he saia:

'I think we ought to play tnem at their own game. Brighten up the paper a bit. Put more bite and punch into our news.'

'I would question that,' Henry said. 'At this time, above all, we must maintain the character of the *Light*. We stand or fall by what we are.'

There was a murmur of assent from the others.

'Still, you have to admit . . . well, I don't say this because it's my department, but the customers do like sport. And some days we don't give them more than a couple of columns. Let's have fuller reports on the Northern League games and the boxing at Tynecastle. And more racing news.'

'That won't sell advertising,' Balmer objected.

'*They'll* do it.'

'If we come down to their level,' Maitland said abruptly, 'we're done for.'

'All right, all right,' Poole said, in a put-out tone, adding under his breath, 'We could do with some gingering up.'

'Would a Saturday pictorial supplement be likely to prove appealing?'

This came from Lawrence Hadley, a small, plump, apologetic man of fifty, with a rosy, polished bald head, who ran the photographic department with such unobtrusiveness that no one seemed to notice him until he appeared with his tripod camera to 'take the groups' at the annual picnic.

Maitland gave a short laugh.

'If we all look at this from our own special angles we'll never get anywhere.'

'Only a suggestion,' Hadley murmured.

'Yes, Lawrence,' Page said soothingly. 'But for another time perhaps.'

A pause followed, then Maitland spoke again, pulling

thoughtfully at his lower lip, his flat, brick-red, porous face sunk down on his chest.

'The way I see it is this . . . and I know from experience that it is so. Someone in the *Gazette* outfit, probably Somerville himself for some reason of his own, had the brainwave . . . to grab the *Northern Light*. Now, nothing is left to chance in these big organizations . . . it's all gone into very thoroughly in terms of cold-blooded finance . . . plans are made, a time schedule drawn, men picked and – this is the all-important point – a specific sum of money allocated for the job. This amount is available to the last penny, but mark my words, once the limit is reached, not another farthing will be forthcoming, the whole scheme is disowned, washed out, lopped off like a dead branch – or whatever you like to call it – and the men who have bungled it are lopped off too. Now, this being so, we've only got to keep our heads, sit tight, and continue getting out the paper. They may hurt us a bit, but it's going to cost them money, scads of it. I won't guess how long it will take, but one of these days, maybe with luck in twelve months, or, say, eighteen, the cash will run out and our friends will fold their tents and silently depart.'

It did Page good to hear this calm and practical summary of the situation, particularly since it came from Maitland. He made a sign of agreement, then said:

'Just one thing more – our general attitude towards them. I feel we should ignore them.'

'That's the ticket,' Maitland nodded. 'Behave as if they didn't exist.'

'But hadn't we better put a man on to them?' Poole asked. 'We ought to know what they're doing. And they'll certainly be spotting us.'

Henry didn't care much for the idea; it held implications of spying; and, after all, Smith had given assurances that their conduct would be ethical.

'Let's leave it in the meantime.'

'We'll hear from them, all right,' Maitland said dryly, as the meeting broke up. 'Just wait for their first edition.

During the next few days, this was the event that everyone in the *Light* office kept looking for with an increasing sense of tension. Not until the paper appeared would they know exactly what they had against them. Reports and rumours were not wanting – Nye, who had taken over the campaign, was shooting them out, giving emphasis on the speed and efficiency with which his arrangements were being completed. Already a considerable staff had arrived from London – amongst them Tina Tingle, a woman reporter, known nationally for her femininist articles in the *Gazette* – and had immediately gone about seeking lodgings both in the town and in Mossburn. This was followed by a further publicity barrage, at first through the medium of posters on the hoardings, then on Saturday afternoon, March 16th, a parade of men went through the town carrying boards with the splash headings:

GREAT NEWS FOR HEDLESTON
THE DAILY CHRONICLE
HERE MONDAY NEXT

That weekend was not an easy one for Henry. It rained heavily and the gloomy, dripping skies were in key with his state of mind. Always a poor sleeper, it was doubtful if, altogether, he had more than half a dozen hours of rest. Monday morning came at last. As he drove to work, his eye was nervously alert for signs of unusual activity in the streets and, sure enough, opposite the Northern Savings Bank a pack of newsboys were picking up supplies from a new bright yellow *Chronicle* van. Mounting the steps to his office, he felt his heart pumping hard against his ribs. Moffatt, he knew, would have the paper – yes, it was there laid out on his desk beside the vase of flowers she brought from her cottage garden at the beginning of the week. He gave it a quick, almost surreptitious glance, then, arrested, caught his breath.

Half of the front page was given over to a striking futuristic picture of a plutonium separator, and beneath, in 72-point type on a red and white panel:

47

## NUCLEAR REACTOR PLANT FOR HEDLESTON
## UTLEY MOOR SITE OF NEW ATOMIC TOWN

A great new atomic centre is to be built together with a vast supporting housing scheme at Utley on the outskirts of Hedleston. The *Chronicle* in its first issue is proud to present to its readers this exclusive statement revealed by an official high on the Atomic Research Board. This carefully guarded secret, now divulged, must, apart from its national importance, prove of immense benefit to the welfare, prosperity and economic future of the community . . .

Henry broke off and looked helplessly at Moffatt. Yes, it was news of the first importance, one of the biggest things that had happened to Hedleston in the past half century, and not only had he missed it, they had got it.

The sequence of events was now clear as day. From the very outset, foreknowledge of this scheme with its immense potential for development of the district and not, as he had been led to believe, a special regard for his paper had been the determining factor in Somerville's approach. Aware, in advance, of the prosperity and increase of population that must inevitably ensue, Somerville had not been deterred by his refusal to sell – he would come in at all costs. Although the information leaked to him was undoubtedly secret, he had not hesitated to use it and had turned it to account, with perfect timing, to launch his drive against the *Northern Light*.

Henry thought of his own main news offering this morning: a full report of the Spring Agricultural Show at Wooton, an event of annual significance, no doubt, yet how must it compare with this other! And for the first time, as he stood transfixed by these painful reflections, a consciousness of the power, unseen and resourceful, behind this calculated strategy bore down on him like a weight.

Someone knocked at the door.

'Come in.'

Young Lewis entered, with a dejected and contrite air.

'I'm sorry, sir, for not getting on to this N.R.U. thing,' he began. 'If only I'd guessed the U. stood for Utley . . .'

Page seldom lost his temper. He liked Bob Lewis, a promising, hard-working youngster who had attended the grammar school with Dorothy and, in fact, occasionally called at the house to ask her to go out with him. But, at this moment, the sight of him, in his callow inexperience, which seemed to typify the utter provincial inadequacy of the *Light's* resources, made Page flare up. He gave Lewis a thorough dressing down and sent him away.

Controlling himself, he turned to Moffatt, who, seated as though ready to take dictation, was in reality watching him, assessing him yet again in terms of his father, the man whom she had idolized, slaved for, who, of course, would never have found himself in this dilemma.

'It wasn't Bob's fault,' she said. 'He had no contacts on the Research Board.'

Page already regretted his action, but he ignored the remark.

'I want to know how many copies of this' – he couldn't bring himself to name the *Chronicle* – 'were sold. Ask Mr Maitland to send out a man.'

'There's no need. Fenwick sent up a memo fifteen minutes ago. Not a single copy's been sold.'

'What!'

'Ten thousand came in at six o'clock this morning. Another ten thousand expected at nine. All for free distribution. They wanted readers and they have them.'

A silence fell upon the room.

'Well,' Henry said firmly, 'a bad beginning is a good ending. Let's get to work.'

As he moved to his desk, he heard old Tom Gourlay – the blind newsvendor who, since Robert Page's time, had made his pitch outside the building – calling the *Light*. At that moment, it seemed a thin and solitary cry.

# VII

THE BLOW DELIVERED in that first edition of the *Chronicle* proved less damaging than Page had feared. The people of the town, even if they did not object to the manner of its presentation, were resentful of the news itself. Apart from some commercial interests, no one wanted an atomic pile on Hedleston's doorstep, nor a sprawling new suburb which must certainly deface the natural beauties of Utley Moor. And when, a few days later, the Parliamentary Under-Secretary announced that work would not begin on the project until the following January, the much vaunted sensation seemed to have fallen flat.

Even so, the pressure on the *Light* had begun, and it was continued with hectic intensity. Never had Henry imagined that so many shoddy devices could be put to use in the effort to sell a British newspaper. 'Giveaway' days with special numbers entitled the recipient to sets of cutlery, china, and other household articles; free plane rides – flips, they were called – to Whitley Bay and back; competitions with cinema tickets for prizes; a bathing-beauty contest, still in being, to discover and crown Miss Hedleston of 1956; there was no end to the blatancy of the campaign or the ingenuity of Nye, who directed it.

The paper itself was in full cry, saturated with the *Gazette's* sensationalism and supplemented by the inimitable contributions of that female reporter whose striking pseudonym, Tina Tingle, disguised the fact, dryly revealed to Henry by Maitland, that she had been baptized Elsie Kidger. This lady was, indeed, a remarkable figure in the staid streets of the northern borough. What met the eye were a green Tyrolean hat set upon a cropped head, mustard-coloured tweeds tight on a mannish figure, and a virile carriage which, with heavy-tongued brogues, vaguely suggested a one-time champion of the links. Every day she produced a feature article which, since her subjects ranged from the pains of childbirth to the pangs of the menopause, was presumably intended for her own sex, although Henry gathered that it made choice reading for the youths who frequented Antonelli's billiard saloon. In addition, with indomitable energy she conducted a question-and-answer agony column of nauseating intimacy entitled 'Tina Tingle's Tribune,' wherein the queries fell automatically into one of two categories: the first anticipating the bliss of the married state, the second bemoaning its miseries.

In the face of this, it was difficult to maintain calm and to hold a fixed policy of detachment. Henry's only consolation was the thought that, without question, Nye and his colleague were spending money like water. Yet he, on his side, was losing circulation, not, so far, to any desperate extent, but steadily, every week some hundreds less, and the growing worry at the back of his mind was how far the loss would go.

This morning, after a news conference that had not been noteworthy for its cheerfulness, he sat gloomily skimming the pages of the *Chronicle* which Moffatt never failed to place on his desk. Miss Tingle, he noted with aversion, was in superb form. In answer to the panting inquiry which began, 'Dear Tina, my boy friend, with whom I am going steady, sees nothing wrong with intimacies before marriage . . .' she gravely replied, 'My dear Gladys, your boy friend only wants to use your body for his own sexual satisfaction. Just take him aside and say to him quietly, "Thou shalt not commit adultery." Your girl friends who do "that sort of thing" and laugh at you for being morally strong and healthy will probably develop guilt neuroses. You will have the laugh of them in the end.' And again, responding to the plaint, 'Dear Miss Tingle, for twenty years my husband has been bawling at me as the result of his fiendish bad temper . . .' her tone was equally uplifting: 'My dear, your husband is emotionally sick but despite your tragic difficulties stick lovingly to him and you will know the joy and satisfaction of duty done. You never know what deep meaning may be found in situations that appear hopeless. Ear plugs might help. And cultivate a hobby. Singing, or the piano.'

Abruptly, Henry turned to the news items, where the invention of a mechanical brassière was chronicled under the caption: GIRLS, HAVE YOU TRIED THE PNEUAMTIC BRA – IT'S BOUND TO INFLATE YOUR EGO. Below, he noted, without much enthusiasm, that a man in Bradford, in thirty years of marriage, had kissed his wife 52,000 times, and that a Mexican woman had given birth to an infant with two heads, when there came a tap on the door and Horace Balmer entered the room. From his expression Henry deduced that he had something unpleasant to communicate and, as Henry's mood was already not good, perhaps he viewed him more critically than usual. Balmer was one of those sonorous men who at first sight impress, a notable mixer and Rotarian who 'belonged' to most things in Hedleston, from the Masons to the Loyal Order of Noble Dalesmen. Inclined to corpulence and double-breasted suits of a blue lighter than normal, he had an oddly consequential kind of walk, gliding along on his heels with one shoulder raised, and balancing himself it seemed, by sweeping movements of the opposite arm, from which his hand, the little finger weighted with a heavy signet, depended like a white fin. No one could grip a hand more effusively or utter gusty commonplaces with a greater flourish.

'I'm in trouble, Henry,' he began, with his usual camaraderie. 'I can't sell our advertising at the price.'

As Page remained silent he went on.

'They are undercutting our rates at every turn. I believe in some cases simply giving space away.'

'That's rather stupid, surely.'

'I'm afraid I don't agree. In my opinion they're a very smart lot. They go around saying they'll soon be the only paper in town, offering long-term contracts at favourable rates. We lost Henderson and Byles last week. Some of our oldest accounts are beginning to look shaky. When I went into Wellsby's this morning, and you know how important they are to us, I got the order but Halliday gave me a queer sort of look. I'm afraid there's only one thing to do.'

'What's that?'

'We must come down a bit ourselves.'

'No.'

'But why?'

'It's unethical. And it doesn't make sense. If we cut, they'll cut further. We've given our advertisers solid value for a hundred and fifty years. We have our standards. I won't lower them by engaging in a cut-throat price war.'

Balmer's expression had become pained.

'I think you're making a mistake. But of course it's your responsibility. I'm only warning you. I happened to run into their Mr Smith the other day – he's a fellow Rotarian, you know – and I assure you he's got a real business head on him.

'I'm glad to know that, Horace. But you're a good business man yourself. Now you go and do your best at our standard rates.'

Their Mr Smith . . . and fellow Rotarian, Henry thought, when Balmer had departed – the chummy phrases had ominous overtones. Once or twice he had passed Smith in the High Street near the office the *Chronicle* had rented in the Prudential Building, and the other had saluted him with a mixture of primness and deference that seemed to indicate a desire for amity. But it was another matter for Smith to become friendly with his staff. The interview with Balmer was, in fact, the beginning of a bad day for Henry in which nothing seemed to go right. Moffatt was very trying, sales were down another couple of hundred, and his confounded heart kept troubling him with sudden changes of rhythm, bumping along heavily at one time, then dashing off like a sprinter in the hundred-yard race. He didn't care to rely too heavily on the nitroglycerine pills Dr Bard had given him and he managed to do without one. But towards five o'clock he decided to call it quits and try to find some peace at home.

Unfortunately, the domestic climate during these recent

months had changed. Henry, not long after his marriage, realizing that he had made a mistake and must live with it, that Alice was unsuited to him both in mind and body, had set out philosophically, in his own phrase, 'to make the best of things.' If Alice did not come up to his dreams, what in life did? And through the years he had managed, by the exercise of tact and self-restraint, by tolerating Alice's whims, her inconsequential giddiness, and occasional outbursts of hysteria, to preserve an amicable relationship with her and to maintain a fairly equable home life. Now, however, in his wife's manner and, indeed, in Dorothy's – for, in Hannah's phrase. Dorrie *took after* her mother – there could be sensed an air of hostility expressed by a chilliness of tone when they addressed him and by occasional meaningful glances interchanged between themselves. Thus, when he entered the house this evening it was surprising to be greeted with a note of animation. They were in the sitting room, having tea, and as he appeared Alice actually smiled.

'Come and have a cup, Henry. It's nice you're back early. We've such capital news.'

'Good,' Henry said, 'I can do with it.'

Accepting his cup, he sat down and stirred it.

'Well, what do you think, but you'll never guess, never.' Alice drew a long breath. 'Dorrie has won twenty guineas.'

'Wasn't I lucky!' Dorothy exclaimed. 'And bright.'

Henry was tired; his brain was not working properly; he wondered if by some wild freak of chance this was some prize she had won at the art school.

'Well done,' he said absently. Then he knew it couldn't possibly be that. He looked up at Dorothy. 'What for?'

'It was like this. I was walking back from the station as usual. When I came to our road I noticed a couple of chaps at the corner, strangers, you know, talking together as if they'd lost their way. Sure enough, as I came up the one with a little black bag said to me, "Excuse me, miss, is this Hanley Drive?" "Yes, it is," I said, then I noticed a red, white, and blue ribbon in his buttonhole and like a flash I said, "And you're the Treasure Man!" He gave me such a nice smile. "Sure," he said, "and you're a very clever young lady to spot me." '

'Wasn't that exciting, Henry?' While he sat, stunned, Alice, unable to resist being a party to the narration, took it away from Dorothy. 'What's more, the man said to her, "Since nobody's spotted me for four days, you don't get five guineas, you get twenty." And he opened his little bag and counted out twenty-one brand-new Treasury notes into Dorrie's hand.'

'It was a thrill, all right,' Dorothy broke in. 'Then we got talking. The other chap was even nicer than the first. Really good-looking . . . sort of cool and casual, with a kind of American accent. They took my picture, too. Why, what's the matter . . . ?'

'How could you get the money . . . ?' Henry's voice came unnatural and stiff. 'To win it you must be carrying a copy of the *Chronicle*.'

'Well, I was.'

'Do you mean to tell me you actually bought their paper?'

Alice's expression changed slightly, and a faint colour crept into her face.

'Now, Henry,' she said. 'Don't get on your high horse. I like to know what's going on.'

'So Dorothy buys the paper for you?'

'Why not?' Her flush had now deepened, but she defended herself, calling up her most ladylike manner. 'I enjoy their society news. Goodness knows I get little enough from you. And Tina Tingle is amusing. So where's the harm?'

'Harm!' Although he knew that frustrated social ambition led her to the gossip columns, Henry could barely speak. 'These people are out to destroy us and you calmly support their paper. I never heard of such disloyalty. While you' – he turned to Dorothy – 'gushing about your luck like a little idiot . . . don't you realize they were waiting for you? The whole thing was a plant. Such a nice talk! I shudder to think what they got out of you. But we shall know for certain tomorrow. If only it wouldn't give them more damaging copy I'd make you send their wretched money back.'

As he got up and, choked with bitterness, moved towards the door, Dorothy began to cry.

'You're very unkind. You spoil everything.'

For once, Alice, who looked subdued and put out, did not support her.

'I don't understand,' she said, as though reasoning with herself, 'how . . . if they're so much against you . . . I mean, why should they give Dorothy twenty guineas?'

Useless to take the matter further; already Henry blamed himself for giving way, thinking with bitterness that this miserable conflict, though not of his seeking, must envenom and demoralize everyone it touched. He knew what to expect of the recent incident and next morning his fears were amply realized.

On the middle page of the *Chronicle* a full-length photograph of his daughter carried the caption DOROTHY PAGE WINS OUR JUMBO JACKPOT. She was smiling, ostentatiously displaying a copy of the paper and accepting, with her other hand, a fan of Treasury notes. Bracing himself, he read what followed:

Seventeen-year-old Dorothy Page, charming, vivacious and pretty brunette (why did you not enter our beauty contest, naughty girl, you might have hit that jackpot, too?), yesterday successfully spotted our Mystery Treasure Man and romped home with the bacon to the tune of twenty golden guineas. Our heartiest congrats, Dorothy!

Miss Page, known to her intimates as Dorrie and daughter, incidentally, of Mr H. Page, Editor of our friendly rival the *Northern Light*, had some interesting comments for our reporter. Both she and her mother – we thank you, Mrs Page – are regular and devoted readers of the *Chronicle*, which, they both feel, brings much-needed new blood to Hedleston and district. One of the younger set, Dorrie, art-school student and no slouch on the dance floor, enjoys a good movie, Jackie Dibbs' records and, pardon us again, the *Chronicle*. Like so many others, impatient with slow-motion living, she has no time for that dull spirit of old-fogeyism which for years has been stifling all that is go-ahead and progressive in the town. 'After all,' Dorothy smiled, 'we're in the atomic, not the stone, age. We ought to live a little faster than in the days of ye old stage coach. I'm all for rock an' roll. I believe the *Chronicle* helps.' Well spoken, Dorrie! We value your words, coming as they do from the daughter of Henry Page. We hope our readers will agree that they are high praise indeed.

When Henry went into the conference room a sense of oppression was in the air. Maitland, without raising his head, gave him a quick glance from beneath his brows. Poole, fidgeting with his moustache, had his eyes fixed studiously on the ceiling, while Hadley seemed trying to appear as though he were not there at all. Balmer alone, sitting erect, looked vaguely justified. Page felt grateful to Maitland when he broke the general constraint.

'Well, Henry, it's unfortunate. But there's no good crying over spilled milk. They did a very neat job on poor Dorothy.'

'She was partly to blame.'

'Yes, but naturally she didn't guess what it was all about.'

'At least they didn't slander us, merely suggested we were out of date.'

Surly, Balmer put in his word.

'In my view that's more damaging than abuse.'

It's this fellow Nye,' Poole said. 'He's master-minding the whole issue. I saw him playing billiards at the Lion the other night. He's a smooth devil.'

'We'll just have to laugh it off,' Maitland said.

'How can we laugh it off,' Poole fumed, 'if we're supposed to ignore their existence? When I think that I sweated my guts out in North Africa while that spiv was living cushy in New York, pretending to work for the Information Services, I could knock his block off.'

'Hear, hear!' Maitland smiled. 'Anyone second that?'

'Not me,' Balmer said sourly. 'If they're clever enough to

57

think up these things, we ought to think of something better. Violence is no good.'

Henry felt he must end the discussion before they started disagreeing amongst themselves.

'It's natural to want to hit back,' he said, 'and I've no doubt these attacks against us will hurt us for a while. But I'm convinced that a policy of restraint will pay dividends in the end. The town will respect us for it. And that's the one thing that will enable us to survive against all the jibes, cheap sneers, all the mud they can throw at us – the respect of the people.'

'The people!' Poole exploded, throwing back his head.

'Don't write them off,' Maitland said quietly. 'I believe they'll stand by us in a pinch. And I agree with Henry, we must just all of us put all we've got into the paper and wait things out.'

'I hope to God you're right,' Poole said. 'But if we go on losing circulation we may find we've waited too long.'

A rather grim silence followed; then, without further argument, they got down to business.

Yet all day the rankling conviction remained with Henry that he had been not only scored against, but made to look ridiculous in the eyes of all who knew him. Because of this, when he left the office at six o'clock, he made a point of stopping in at the Northern Counties Club. Lately, he had fallen into the habit of avoiding unnecessary personal contacts. Averse to discussing his worries, he wanted neither encouragement nor condolences – but now, in the interests of the paper, he felt the necessity of publicly displaying an attitude of indifference to this recent incident.

The Northern Counties, known in Hedleston simply as the Club, was an ancient and honourable institution, with a faintly Liberal flavour, the recognized meeting place of the royal borough's leading citizens. Built of cut grey stone, with a flat roof, the central portico supported by a pair of massive caryatids, its outward look was that of a mausoleum; indeed, acting there as air-raid warden during the war, Henry had often felt, as the bombs came crashing down, that it might end by justifying its appearance. Within, however, there were light, warmth, and the comforting aroma of good tobacco. Nodding to Duncan, the porter, Henry paused from habit at the bulletin board, and there, among the assortment of dog-eared notices, his eye, quite unprepared, was caught and held by the name Harold Smith. Yes, it was the manager of the *Chronicle*, proposed for membership by Herbert Rickaby, seconded by, of all people, the rector of St Mark's. For a moment Henry stood immobile completely taken aback. That Smith should secure so early this acceptance by the more responsible members of the community was another, and an unforeseen, blow. However, with an effort he pulled himself together and, resolved to make no comment on the matter, walked towards the main lounge. Not many members were about when he entered, although he sensed that his appearance had caused a slight stir. Then, between the Pompeian pillars of imitation marble that supported the ornate Victorian ceiling, he saw Sir Archibald Wellsby and Dr Bard standing together by the fire. He went towards them.

'Well!' Wellsby saluted him with a hearty back slap. 'Here's the proud papa, himself.'

Short, heavy, bald, and ruddy, with a small, good-natured, and humorously lewd red eye, Archibald Wellsby, or, as he preferred to be called, Sir Archie, exuded a persistent sporty joviality belied by the keenness of a business acumen that had made a fortune for him in the boot trade, and which he confidentially believed would carry him still further.

'I hear you've got these *Chronicle* fellows really scared, Henry. Not three months in town and they're pouring guineas into your lap. How'd you do it, man?'

'Better ask Dorothy.' Henry smiled.

'She was pretty sharp to spot the fellow,' Bard intervened pleasantly.

'And gave a pretty good account of herself.' Wellsby chuckled. 'I wish some of my lot had as much gumption.'

Page knew, of course, that beneath the banter they were both well aware he had been hurt; their predictions of his eventual victory seemed too ready and profuse. With inherent

59

kindness Edward Bard, who was his oldest friend, changed the subject, but several times Henry caught Wellsby's narrowed glance upon him, weighing him up, assessing the damage to his prestige and his paper. He had always sensed that Wellsby entertained an amused contempt for him as a man who neither drank, smoked, fished, shot, nor told off-colour stores – all of which Wellsby did to excess with unsurpassable verve and gusto. Page simply wasn't his type. Still, as they talked, and later, when they were joined by a number of the other members – Major Seaton of the Civil Defence Unit, Harrington, manager of the Machine Company, lawyer Paton, and Frank Holden, the banker – Henry managed to put a good face on things, and when he left, half an hour later, he believed that the effort had been worth while. Dr Bard, leaving at the same time, came out with him. The two men stood for a moment on the pavement. Suddenly, and awkwardly, the doctor said:

'We're on your side, you know. The committee weren't too keen on letting in Smith. But' – Bard shrugged – 'he seems a sound-enough citizen. And he had good letters of introduction.' Then, quickly, in his normal manner: 'You're looking fairly well. See you don't overdo things. Don't go off the deep end.'

'I won't.'

'How is David?'

'Wonderful. Completely all right again.'

Bard looked away, tapping the pavement with the ferule of his umbrella. With his greying temples, his long, thoughtful face, fine nostrils, and pursed lips, he conveyed more than ever the suggestion of calm judgment and well-considered caution.

'Don't go off the deep end there either, Henry. Remember what I told you: there's always the danger of a recurrence.'

'But why?' Page said, put out by his insistence. 'He had his breakdown and got over it.'

'Yes, but the primary disability remains.'

'What disability?'

Edward Bard hesitated, looked at his friend, then looked

away. Plainly he had in mind the opinion he had hinted at before and over which they had almost fallen out. Now, however, Henry had no wish to debate the matter. He said briefly:

'You're a regular Jonah, Ed. If you saw the boy . . . he's really fit.'

'Well . . .' Bard paused. 'I'm glad to hear it.'

There was a silence, then they said goodnight and parted, the doctor going one way to his evening surgery in Victoria Street and Henry the other towards Hanley Drive.

## VIII

SUMMER, THAT YEAR, was wet and cold. Both at the office and at home Page's life was as cheerless as the weather. In his overworked and worried state the attitude of afflicted reasonableness which Alice was now adopting began to wear him down. The childish strain in her nature, resenting his failure to fall in with her wishes, had made her feel, quite genuinely, that she was a woman both misunderstood and misused. Towards the end of June, when he told her that a holiday would be impossible for him this year and suggested she take Dorothy to her favourite Torquay, she shook her head with a reproachful smile.

'No, dear. If we cannot go together, *properly*, I'd rather not go at all.'

Dorothy's resentment was more overt and she would bounce past Henry on the stairs with no more than a mumbled word. He had no wish to bathe in family sentiment, yet he felt acutely this lack of affection and support. And as the weeks went on, was it merely his fancy, or did his acquaintances in the town suddenly become embarrassed when he met them? During the first week of August an encounter with the

Reverend Gilmore in Victoria Street brought this to a head. The rector saw Henry too late to avoid him and, caught in an obvious desire to cross the street, covered this with an excess of cordiality.

'Ah, Henry, my friend, how are you?'

For some time Page had brooded on Gilmore's action in seconding Smith for the Club, and now he decided to speak out to him.

'I'm having a difficult time,' he said bluntly. 'So difficult that I'd be glad of your moral support.'

'In what way?' Gilmore asked cautiously, shaking the rain-drops from his umbrella.

'By taking my part against this *Chronicle* rag. I've helped you in the past . . . why don't you help me now?'

The rector, having dried the umbrella and inspected the sky to ensure that it had cleared, looked at Page sideways.

'Well, now, Henry, the Church doesn't mix in politics – you know we're not allowed to – and I should be in all sorts of trouble with the Bishop if I did. Besides, don't you think that you are a trifle prejudiced? Nowadays we should be somewhat more liberal in our views. I admit that some-times our *Chronicle* friends do go a little over the score, but these are modern times. Their Mr Smith is a thoroughly well-meaning fellow. He called on me just after his arrival and we had a most interesting talk on his Y.M.C.A. work in Australia. I see him at St Mark's regularly every Sunday. And did you know . . . they've sent me a most handsome contribution to the steeple fund?'

'I see,' Page said stiffly.

'Naturally we are all *with* you, Henry, But we must be fair. There is some balm in Gilead. Lately" – he glanced at Page shyly – 'they've printed quite a few of my little inspirational pieces. And with success, yes, with success. I have a letter from Mr Nye in which he actually uses the words "a smash hit".'

Henry went on to the office, raging inwardly. Only Mait-land seemed near to him, but Malcolm's taciturn, hard-headed staunchness, though he valued it, held nothing of sympathy.

A dismal autumn dragged into winter. Rain, hail, and in February a heavy fall of snow that for weeks after covered the streets with dirty slush did little to maintain the morale of the staff of the *Northern Light*. Page had never worked so hard in his life, devising and planning, encouraging the others, striving for economies that would not show yet might cut costs, coming first to the office and leaving last, getting up in the middle of the night when he couldn't sleep to prepare and polish his editorials, straining every nerve to bring out each edition at the highest peak of perfection. And still the deadly and monotonous struggle went on. He had told Smith at the outset that there was no room for two papers in Hedleston. For months he had been losing money rapidly, and although he believed the *Chronicle's* losses to be much greater, his own had in the past five weeks accelerated at an alarming rate.

Page's first objective with the *Light*, indeed his whole family tradition, had always been that of public service, never the mere accumulation of wealth. He sold the paper at the basic price, used high-grade materials, and was generous with his staff, especially in the matter of pension settlements upon old employees. He himself drew a minimum salary of fifteen hundred pounds and, beyond the house in Hanley Drive, which was in his wife's name, he had no private fortune. Apart from goodwill, which he rated high, all the assets of the firm – following a patriotic decision of his father's after World War I – were invested in a War Loan, to the extent of one hundred thousand pounds. This he had always regarded as a suitable and satisfactory reserve.

But now, on this morning of March 1st, as Henry studied the *Light's* latest balance sheet, it was only too apparent how deeply he had drawn upon this fund. He thought things over a long time, then, with a suppressed sigh, taking advantage of a moment when Moffatt was out of her room, he picked up the telephone and made an appointment with Frank Holden ,manager of the Northern Boroughs Bank.

At eleven o'clock that same morning he was in Holden's office, a small cabinet behind the cashier's desk, darkly enclosed by mahogany panels and frosted glass, its hair carpet worn smooth by the feet of solid and thrifty Northumbrians. As he entered, the manager dismissed the clerk with whom he was conferring, shook hands cordially, and offered him a chair. Tall and spare, with horn-rimmed glasses and a close-cropped moustache, Holden had the keen and engaging air of a man anxious both to please and to get on. Twelve years younger than Henry, he came of an old Hedleston family and shared the same sort of background – indeed, his father, Robert Holden, had been Page's father's most intimate friend, and with him and Robert Harbottle, had formed a close companionship which caused them to be colloquially referred to as 'the three Bobs.'

Because of this, Henry had less embarrassment in broaching the subject on his mind, and after a few introductory remarks he said:

'Frank, I've come to see you about a loan.'

'Yes?' Holden said. 'As a matter of fact, I was hoping you'd drop in for a bit of a chat.'

There was a pause, then, as Page did not speak, the manager half smiled, as though to soften what he was about to say.

'You know, Mr Page, you've been drawing pretty heavily on us lately. I happened to glance through your account on Monday. It's . . . well, I suppose you know how much you're overdrawn.'

'Of course,' Henry nodded. 'I have let things run on a bit. But you've got my War Loan as security.'

'Yes, the War Loan.' Holden appeared to consider. 'What was that bought at . . . something like one hundred and four, wasn't it?'

'I believe that was the figure.'

'And now it's down to below sixty-five . . sixty-three and one half, to be exact. And I believe it will go lower. Why didn't you sell when I told you?'

'Because, as a good citizen, I considered it my duty to hold.'

Holden gave Page an odd glance.

'A good citizen looks after himself these days. Don't you realize that our failure to control inflation is impoverishing every holder of these government issues? Gilt-edged, indeed . . . trusting patriots like yourself are being ruined.'

As Henry was about to protest he went on.

'Anyhow, you've lost more than thirty-nine thousand pounds of your capital and if I'm any judge of the money market you may lose more. At the rate your debit balance is growing, in another seven or eight weeks your collateral won't cover it.'

'I'm perfectly aware of that,' Henry said. 'That's why I'm here to arrange a loan.'

'On what?'

'Why, naturally, on the *Northern Light* . . . buildings, plant, and goodwill.'

Holden took up the ebony ruler from his blotting pad and, after viewing it with apparent interest, began to turn it between his fingers. There was an appreciable silence, then, not looking at Henry, he said:

'I'm sorry, Mr Page, I'd like more than anything to help you. But it just can't be done.'

Henry was shocked. He had never for a moment entertained the thought of a refusal.

'But why?' he exclaimed, almost incoherently. 'You know me . . . the *Light* . . . there's our name . . . we have assets. You've had our account all those years . . . '

'I know, I know . . . it's hard to turn you down. But money is extremely tight these day. We're caught up in a credit squeeze that practically prohibits bank advances. The Government just doesn't want us to make any loans.'

'But this is a local, almost a personal, matter,' Henry protested. 'At least let us discuss it.'

'It would be pointless.' He looked at Henry apologetically. 'I haven't the authority to commit the bank. You would have to put it up to my directors.' He paused, inspecting the ruler again. 'Why don't you go along and see the chairman of the board?'

'Wellsby?'

'Yes. You know him pretty well. He'll be at the factory now. Shall I give him a ring and say you're coming?'

Henry was silent. He had the depressed feeling that, in the nicest possible way, Holden wanted to get rid of him. He got slowly to his feet, thinking: Wellsby . . . perhaps the last man before whom he would have wished to expose his necessity. Yet there was nothing else for it – he would need the loan and must have it.

'All right,' he said. 'I'll be obliged if you'd telephone him.'

Twenty minutes later he reached Wellsby's office in the tall administrative building recently erected on a neck of wasteland adjacent to the factory. This strip, long known in Hedleston as the Cowp, had been acquired through a particularly astute deal on the part of the boot manufacturer and, as the result of a street diversion from Victoria Square, had appreciated to many times its original value. As Henry entered, Wellsby was standing at the big plate-glass window which fronted Victoria Street, chuckling to himself and choking over his cigar.

'Come here, Page, and take a look at this.'

Outside, holding up the traffic and moving slowly round the square, was a long line of women pushing perambulators, go-carts, every variety of vehicle capable of containing an infant, the procession headed by a blaring sound truck with a double banner:

GRAND PERAMBULATOR PARADE
BONNIEST BABY COMPETITION
TODAY
IN THE TOWN HALL
READ THE DAILY CHRONICLE

'Not bad, eh?' He clapped Henry on the back. He was wearing plus fours and red and yellow chequered stockings, which magnified his enormous calves. He looked redder, shorter, and balder, also more jovial, than ever, glowing with that self-satisfaction which wealth acquired by business imparts to successful tradesmen. 'What d'you think of it?'

Page forced a smile.

'Enterprising, no doubt. Not particularly dignified.'

'Why, hang it all, man, what's wrong with it? It's a damn smart selling idea. Get hold of the mothers. They're only trying to push their product, the way I do mine. Look, there's that chap Nye. He's the brains behind all this. The other one – Smith – is a bit of a nonentity. But Nye really has something. My Charlie ran him up to Tynecastle in the Jag last weekend and came home full of him.'

'Did he?' said Page stiffly, finding it highly probable that Charlie Wellsby, the town's leading blood, should find Nye congenial.

'Certainly he did. They had a rare time together. So keep your eye on him,' Wellsby added facetiously. Turning from the window, he sank into his revolving chair and, with an effort, crossed his short legs. 'Well, what can I do for you? I'm in the market for some golf this afternoon, so let's come to the point.'

Henry came to the point, briefly and with all the persuasive force he could command. Yet while he spoke he sensed that Wellsby had already been advised of the purpose of his visit and, in fact, knew almost as much of his affairs as he did himself. Beneath that open geniality of manner his deep-set eyes were examining and alert. When Page finished he removed his cigar and slanted his gaze towards the glowing end.

'You're on a sticky wicket, Henry. You've listed your assets. But suppose you go under . . . what are they worth? Your offices are out of date; all that old Adam terrace ought to be pulled down, you couldn't raise a stiver on it. Your printing premises have some value, I admit, but that's the Harbottle property, you only rent it. So nothing much doing there. As for your goodwill, who would give a brass farthing for it if the *Chronicle* puts you out of business?'

'They won't.'

'So you say. But how have you made out so far? These fellows may not be very dignified, but they're on the ball. And their paper isn't altogether a rag. Doesn't compare with the *Light*, of course.' He inserted this hurriedly. 'But it gives . . . well . . . a different slant to the news.' A reminiscent smile twitched his lips. 'Yesterday there was a damn good report, juicy, of course, but amusing, on that libel case . . . you know, where that Italian count who'd been smuggling heroin and his lady-friend were caught naked in the bath.'

'Yes,' Page said bitterly. 'They thrive on that . . . fraud and fornication . . . and libel. Good God, man, journalism is an honourable profession. There have been great men in it and there still are . . . men of intelligence and principle, with a real sense of their vocation and their duty to the public. But this fellow Nye . . . Can't you see, to have this kind of paper running the town would be an abomination.'

'Come, come, now, Henry. That's putting it rather too strong. I'm only trying to show you what you're up against. We saw Somerville's yacht at Cannes last year, the missus and I, ocean-going, a tremendous affair. . . .' His voice dropped to a lower register, turned conciliatory. 'As a friend and neighbour I don't like to see you cut your own throat. Why don't you give up while there's time? Be wise. Get out while you can. If you wish I'll take a hand and see you still get your price.'

Henry saw that he meant to be helpful, that he spoke with the conviction that reason was on his side. But all the logic would not move him now. He was beyond it.

'No. My mind is made up.'

Wellsby removed his cigar, curling a loose, moist leaf with his forefinger, but looking at Page from time to time, reviewing his opinion of him and apparently being forced to revise it in a light which, if one could judge by his expression, was perhaps more favourable. Could it be that he was softening? Henry's anxiety, all the doubts, uncertainties, and humiliations he had recently experienced, became concentrated, grew suddenly to such a pitch that he was unable to speak. He waited, scarcely able to breathe. At last Wellsby said:

'I always took you for a clever man, Henry, though, if you'll forgive me, a bit of a milksop. Now I think you're a damn fool, but at least you have guts. Let me say, off the record, that I admire you.'

'Then let me have the loan. Twenty thousand pounds. From the beginning of next month.'

'No, no. I can't promise. I may talk it over with Holden and the others. We'll let you know.'

'When?'

'Later . . . later.'

Wellsby got up from his chair, made a vague gesture with his hand, indefinitely waving Henry away. The boot manufacturer had, in truth, been considering his own position in the matter. For some time now, feeling himself a very big fish in the backwaters of Hedleston, he had been moved by the urge to swim in wider oceans, or, to be more explicit, to stand for Parliament and become known to the nation as Sir Archibald Wellsby, M.P. Resolved to run at the next election, he was well aware of the need of the local paper's support. But would this be the *Light* or the *Chronicle*? Almost certainly the latter. Why then let sentiment interfere? A loan under such circumstances would be preposterous.

Though it was well concealed, something of this train of thought showed in Wellsby's face, and the hope which Henry had begun to entertain died coldly. He saw refusal in Wellsby's eyes, an impression confirmed by the excessive cordiality with which the other patted him on the shoulder, squeezed his elbow, inquired solicitously after Alice, and showed him to the door.

Useless to deny that this rebuff had set a heavy oppression on Page. At the same time, by some strange counterbalance of the spirit, his mood became more stubbornly set, his mind more determinedly active in seeking ways and means of carrying on the struggle. He would go on, on, on. Even if the bank would not advance on the *Light* offices, the Hedleston Building Society must surely prove more ᴀmenable and offer something on the freehold. But, as this would take time, he must first of all ask Alice to raise a mortgage on the house. It was something he shrank from, but he would do it. The more opposition he met, the more his resolution strengthened, the more there persisted in him the extraordinary faith that he would win.

God knows he had need of it. He had not been back in his room five minutes before Maitland came in.

'It appears,' he said, 'we'll be one short for the conference from today. Balmer has gone.'

'Gone?'

'Left . . . quit . . . skedaddled . . . whichever you prefer. Here is his resignation.'

Henry stared blankly at the envelope Maitland threw on the desk. Yet he should not have been surprised. Balmer had been increasingly difficult lately; he had not been getting on well with him.

'But . . . he must give a month's notice.'

'Not likely . . . when he's walking straight into another job.'

'Not . . . with the *Chronicle*?'

'That's about it.' Maitland paused. 'I suppose he hadn't the gall to tell you, so he's written you a nice, polite letter of regret. I've seen it coming. You know he's been chumming with their Mr Smith . . . Balmer'll go wherever there's more money. And there is more, apparently.'

As Page remained silent he went on.

'I'm afraid there's another spot of bad news, Henry. Two of the compositors, Perkins and Dodds, have gone over as well.'

This, at least, was something Page could not fully grasp.

'What's the meaning of it? Are they so sure we're going under?'

'No . . . I hardly think so . . . although they know we're up against it. It's probably the money . . . and the offer of long-term contracts . . . backed by the *Gazette*. I suppose they feel they can't lose.'

Henry bit his lip hard, trying to keep a grip on himself. If there was one thing he had counted on, it was the loyalty of his work people. Even at the best of times the *Light* was not overstaffed and good men were difficult to find.

'We'll need to get on to the exchanges straight away,' he said at last.

Maitland, who had been standing by, rubbing his chin reflectively, moved towards the door.

'I'll send out an S.O.S. to Tynecastle.'

'Try Liverpool and Manchester, too.'

He nodded. 'We'll worry through. See you later.'

All that day they struggled for replacements and by good fortune secured a typesetter from Liverpool with the promise of another from Tynecastle at the beginning of next week. It cheered Henry when young Lewis came in to see him, offering to work overtime, saying he'd do anything to help. And Poole, despite his uncertain temper and sultry humours, could, Henry reflected, certainly be depended on for something extra – he had declared a vendetta against Nye, and went about with a scowl, looking for a chance to corner him. Hadley, too, though he wore the worried look of a man with three children to support, was thoroughly reliable, and could be sent out to call on the local advertisers. As for the layout work, he himself would have to take care of that for the next few weeks. These readjustments eased the situation, but they were still too thinly spread, and in the end, thinking it over, Henry decided the time had come to call on his son. He had no other choice. David must leave Sleedon, temporarily at least, and fill the breach.

IX

At FIVE O'CLOCK Henry cut short his work and set off for Sleedon. The events of the morning had given him a bad headache which had persisted all afternoon, but now the refreshing cool of the sea marshes brought him some relief. As he drove up the familiar cliff road the first stirrings of the evening breeze had begun to ruffle the soft grasses of the dunes. Since he had given no notice of his visit Cora was not at the gate to meet him. The cottage had, indeed, an air of unusual quiet. Then he saw her, seated at the window, bent over some work. At the sound of his approach she raised her head, and her expression, absorbed and strangely pensive, brightened with pleased surprise. She started up and the next instant was at the door. Now, more than ever, it did Henry good to see her. For the first time in many days he felt a lifting of his spirits.

'I thought I'd run down for an hour. Am I a nuisance?'

'Never.' She took both his hands. 'It's a treat to see you. I was just setting down to a proper dull evening.'

'I can't believe it. You're never dull.'

'Well, I was. But not now I'm not. Come in.'

'Where's David?' Henry asked, beginning to take off his overcoat.

He expected her to say that he was working. Instead she looked at him and hesitated.

'He's gone to Scarborough – left this morning, he did – to see Dr Evans.'

This news was so unexpected that Henry drew up in the narrow little hall.

'Is he not so well?' he asked after a moment.

'No. At least, he is pretty well. But he's been worrying a bit lately.'

'About what?'

'Himself. Just worrying and worrying.'

'That he won't stay well?' Henry asked. 'I mean, that he'll have a relapse?'

'That's part of it.' She spoke slowly, and with difficulty, yet as though it eased her to unburden herself. 'It came on quite gradual like, about two weeks ago. First he lost interest in his book. Then he began to tell me what a bad time he'd had before we met. I tried to get his mind off it; I knew it wasn't good for him. But he went on – "if ever I got that way again, Cora" – that sort of thing. Then last Monday he came down from the attic. "Who were you talking to?" he asked me. I told him no one. "But I heard someone, I'm sure I did," he says. "You weren't talking to yourself?" I said

72

of course not and tried to make a joke of it. But he wasn't satisfied; he started to search every corner of the house, all the cupboards and everything, trying to find out if somebody was there. Of course there wasn't . . . no one at all. Then he looked at me sort of dazed. "Cora," he said, "I'm hearing things." I told him it was just a mistake. But that afternoon he said he must see the doctor. He wouldn't let me tell you. He wouldn't even let me go with him. I wanted to . . . but he wouldn't. He must do things himself, he said, and not depend on other people, or he'll never get over it.'

There was a pause during which Henry tried to adjust himself to this reversal of his hopes. He had come for help, only to find that he must give it. Then he saw that her eyes were bright with tears and at once suspected that something had gone wrong between David and her, something more than she had revealed in that brief and halting explanation. Abruptly he took her arm.

'Come on. We'll have a walk. A breath of air will do us good.'

They took their usual walk along the pier, and although scarcely a word passed between them it helped them both. Out by the lighthouse the breeze had fallen, the twilight air was luminous and tranquil. A faint mist masked the horizon, so that the sea, undulant, yet smooth as glass, reached to infinity. Through the stillness, there came faintly the sweet, haunting echo of a conch, sounding out of the mist from an unseen fishing coble. More than ever, as he stood in silence with Cora, Henry felt that they were near to one another. As they came back to the cottage she gave him a direct look in which there was both affection and gratitude.

'It's not fair on you, it isn't,' she said. 'You have enough troubles of your own.

'I can stand them.' He stopped at the door and made a show of looking at his watch. 'Well . . . I suppose I'll be off now.'

'No, you shan't, or I'll never forgive myself.' She spoke firmly. 'You shall come in and have a bite to eat.'

She would take no refusal – indeed, Henry's protestations were far from emphatic. He did not wish to leave so early and her offer of food made him realize his need of it. Inside the hall, she shut the door with decision, as though to exclude all possibility of his departure.

'You take a seat in the room while I make things ready.'

'No, I'll sit in the kitchen where I can watch you.'

This was a pleasure which relieved in part the depression occasioned by the bad news of his son. Her movements, competent and graceful, were infinitely soothing to the eye. The tension under which he had been labouring for weeks was relaxed by some mysterious force emanating from her. And suddenly, out of all reason, he heard himself say:

'Cora . . . you make me feel young again.'

'Good gracious.' She smiled back at him. 'You're not old. Nothing like it. I never think of you that way . . . no . . . never.'

The meal she prepared was simple – repeatedly, with expressions of regret, she blamed herself for 'having nothing in the house' – and consisted of bacon and eggs with tea and hot buttered toast, followed by a dish of stewed rhubarb from the garden. Often, as a boy, passing the summer at Sleedon, and after a day spent fishing from the pier end, just such a supper had been put before him. And with more than a trace of that youthful appetite, sustained by a flood of memories, he sat down to it.

He made Cora share with him, having long ago recognized in her the capacity to give all and take nothing, realizing, too, that, but for his visit, she would certainly have eaten nothing but that stale-looking bun and the glass of milk which, as they entered the kitchen, she removed from the table. In an effort to cheer her, he kept the conversation away from these anxieties which weighed on both of them. He had made up his mind to telephone Dr Evans in the morning, and until then the matter must rest. As for his own problems, this hour of escape, stolen, it seemed, from another world, was too precious to waste in brooding upon them. He did not pause to ask himself how such a respite could come about. It was enough to unload the burden he had been carrying for months and to forget that he must shoulder it again whenever he left this house.

As they were talking, a book, Carlyle's *Sartor Resartus*, half open beside the window seat Cora usually occupied, caught his eye. She saw him looking at it and coloured a trifle guiltily.

'I haven't done my chapter today,' she said. 'David would be cross. It's silly, but I just can't get myself to read.'

He gazed at her in surprise. Had David actually imposed this task upon her in the effort to improve her mind? Apparently so, for she continued to explain sadly:

'It just doesn't seem to concern me. I only enjoy doing things. I'll never get educated.'

Pity melted his heart.

'You have lots of good sense, Cora, which is more important. And that book would bore anyone.'

She did not answer, but when they had finished she rose and put a light to the driftwood in the fireplace.

'It turns cold these March evenings,' she said. 'I love a fire. It's cosy. The smell of it, too. When I think on all the little rooms I been in . . . with only a rusty gas ring. David don't care for it, though. At least he makes himself do without. It's all part of this new idea of his.'

'What idea?'

She was silent, her eyes lowered, for a long time, then, hesitantly, as if forcing herself to speak, she said:

'It's something that's come over him. Trying to, what he calls, abstain. I wish he wouldn't. Surely we're not meant to deny ourselves everything. If only he'd give way a little and take life sort of natural . . . it's not good for any of us to go against nature . . . not for him, nor for me neither.' She broke off, giving Henry a quick, troubled look, as though she'd said too much. He saw, of course, what she had unconsciously implied and it caused him a strange, sharp pang. Hitherto he had thought only of this marriage in terms of its benefit to his son. But now he thought of Cora, and suddenly he said:

'Are you happy, Cora?'

'Yes,' she answered, slowly. 'At least if David is. I do my best for him. But sometimes he doesn't act as if he really wanted me . . .'

'It's just his way. I'm sure he cares for you.'

'I hope so,' she said.

Again there was a pause, then with a nervous gesture, as if throwing off her thoughts, she bent and stirred the fire.

'That wood could stand more drying. I gather it at high tide along the beach. It's such a saving . . . and I enjoy it.'

'You like to be in the open.'

She nodded.

'Sometimes I walk miles and miles along the shore . . . not a single soul in sight. You'd be su'prised the things I find.'

'What, for instance?'

'You'd never guess.'

'Old sea boots?' He ventured a feeble joke, anxious to brighten her mood.

'No . . . this week a proper little crate of eggs.'

'Nonsense, Cora.'

'It's true. . . . It must have been swept off a ship's deck.'

'Weren't they all bad?'

Her face lightened. She almost smiled, but for a trace of sadness, her slow, rare smile.

'You had two for your tea tonight. Lucky I had them for you. It's the tide. It runs in so strong. Everything gets washed up on that North Shore . . . everything.'

All that she said was simple, open, and, like all her movements, unconsidered, perfectly natural. The flames, leaping from the hearth, made tongues of light amongst the shadows and set a warmth upon her face.

A silence fell. For years now Page had lived without real affection in his home. Dorothy, in her adolescent egoism, her bounce and bumptiousness, her hard, brittle outlook, cared little for him. With all the flippant heartlessness of the new generation, she ignored him, or at best was prepared to tolerate him – so long as he continued unprotestingly to subsidize her attendance at the art school where she, and others of her kind, wasted their time in pretence of slinging

76

abstract smudges on a square of millboard. One could not even say that she would grow out of it.

With Alice, too, the pattern seemed set, unalterable, unutterably stale. Page had always despised the man who professed himself misunderstood and unappreciated by his wife. Conscious of his own shortcomings, he had done his best to keep his relationship with Alice on an even and amiable footing. Yet now, for some reason, in a moment of illumination, he realized how starved and sterile his marriage had been, compelling him to live for years in an absolutely false situation. How early his youthful illusion of love had died when, on a brief and dismal honeymoon in the West Highlands, during a fortnight of steady drizzle, Alice had behaved like an affronted prude, mainly concerned, through circumstances and the weather, as to whether she should wire home for thicker underwear. The marriage act had long become for her, if not an ordeal, at least what she would have called 'a great nuisance.' Yet while her desire for him diminished, her possessiveness had increased. How often had he been subject to those alternating moods of self-pity and childish pique, the giddy ideas, short-lived enthusiasms, and terrifying lack of logic, the passionate preoccupation with trifles and total absence of interest in his work, the bursts of unreasonable temper that strained her nerves and his.

How different, he thought, was this big, quiet girl, so placid, but with such capacity for feeling, seated there, gazing into the fire, her eyes troubled, yet her hands at peace. She offered affection freely, seemd to ask it for herself. In her responsive stillness there was sympathy and understanding. Under the bitter pressure of his struggle for survival there had lately come upon Henry an almost painful desire to be understood. He recognized it as a softness, a weakness in his character, yet he could not repress it – a longing for tenderness, given and received. In Cora one could find just such a compensation, something rare and precious, something he had deeply missed.

At last, Page felt that he must be off. She came with him to the car in silence. Under a cold indigo sky, bright with

77

stars, the surf was pounding on the beach. They listened to the surge and sound of it, followed by the slow drag of the shingle. Streaks of moonlight made the Eldon Hills blue. Her breath came faintly vaporous, her breasts rose and fell. Suddenly she murmured:

'Must you really go?'

'It's getting on,' he said.

'It's not that late . . . I shall be more down than ever when you've left.'

A sudden agitation seemed all at once to have come upon her. She shivered. Her hand, still holding his, was soft and cold.

'Are you all right?' Henry asked her. 'Your fingers are like ice.'

She let out a choked, uncertain little laugh.

'Sign of a warm heart, they say. What a night! It's a shame to be in. Couldn't we go along the beach for a bit?'

'But we've had our walk, my dear.'

'Yes . . . it's so nice and bright, though.' Her voice was unsteady. 'There's a little hut at the end . . . with nets in it. I could show you. It's away from everybody . . . quite dry . . . we could sit and watch the waves.'

She looked at him hurriedly, nervously, with a strange, restless questioning in her gaze. When he shook his head her eyes fell.

'It really is late, Cora dear . . . not far off ten. I'm afraid I have to get back. We'll go another day.'

'Will we?'

'Cheer up, now. Everything's going to be all right . . . for you and David . . . all of us.'

Had she heard him? She did not answer. She took his hand, which was still in hers, and pressed it against her side. Then she said:

'You're nice . . . you are.' And again: 'Come back soon . . . please.'

It went straight to his heart. He gently kissed her hair.

Standing motionless, she watched him as he started the car and moved off.

For perhaps five minutes Henry drove ahead through the liquid moonlight which turned the long, straight country road into a river of milk, then all at once he braked and drew up with a jerk that stopped the engine.

The thought of Cora, of her look, sad and lingering, as she stood alone by the gate, pierced him to the heart. Why had he left her? He had not done enough to help her. A wild impulse took hold of him to turn the car and go back to comfort her. But no, no, that was impossible, beyond the bounds of reason, an action that would be misunderstood, which must surely compromise her. His throat turned tight and dry as he fought against the need to be with her again, if only to exchange a single word. Then he sighed and, after a long and heavy pause, started up the engine, pushed the lever into gear, and continued on his way to Hedleston.

X

ALL THAT EVENING Mrs Page had been sitting in the library at Hanley Drive, unable to dispel the tedium of solitude. It was Hannah's night off, Dorothy had a cold and had gone to bed early, and Catharine Bard, the doctor's wife, whom she had asked round after supper for coffee and a game of two-handed bridge, had at the last minute been unable to come, offering the suspiciously feeble excuse that her aunt had unexpectedly arrived from Tynecastle.

Alice was a person who enjoyed company and never found it pleasant to be left alone. Under the circumstances her mood was not particularly propitious – she felt herself overlooked and disregarded – and in default of someone better, she kept wishing that Henry would come in. Where, she asked herself, was he? His movements had been most erratic lately. He was not at the office when she called up just after seven. Occasionally, on the servant's day out, he had his evening meal at the Club, but at eight o'clock, when she telephoned the porter, he was not there either. Only one possibility, or perhaps she should have said certainty, remained – Sleedon. He must be there again. Really, it was too bad, the way he neglected her to rush out to the cottage at every possible opportunity.

Alice straightened the cushion at her back and, as she had failed to get on with the crossword, picked up her needle-point for the third time. But the stitching tried her eyes – in any case she was already tired of the design and had decided to give it to Hannah to finish in her spare time. Trying to settle her mind, she set out a game of patience. But again it was no use, the disappointments of the evening had been too upsetting, and compelled by a growing sense of self-pity, she fell into one of her dreams, filled not, tonight, with yearnings for the future, but with extravagant recollections of the past. While she sat there with the cards still in her hand, memories crowded upon her as she dwelt longingly upon those days of her girlhood when life was bright and carefree.

How happy she had been then, at Banksholme, the little estate her father had bought in East Lothian when they moved from Morningside Terrace, so quiet and countrified, with views of the Forth and the Bass Rock, yet near to the amenities and attractions of the capital. Their circle of friends was wide and distinguished – her father, even before his promotion to the Court of Session, was one of the most popular K.C.s at the Edinburgh Bar – and although the death of her mother, when Alice was seventeen, cast a temporary shadow upon the family, Rose, her elder sister, had adapted herself capably to the duties of housekeeper and hostess. Ah, then the future was full . . . full of promise. Did she ever imagine that her life would turn out like this, or that her marriage, from which she had expected so much, would lapse into a humdrum provincial routine climaxed by neglect and – one could no longer doubt it – financial disaster?

Tears smarted in Alice's eyes as she re-enacted her first

meeting – so unpredictable, yet so fateful – with Henry. At the University – which she was attending, not to take a degree, but simply because an arts course was 'the recognized thing' for girls of her station in life – he wasn't in anything like her set, made up of all the nicest young people in her year. How gay they all were when, after the forenoon lecture, arm-in-arm and chattering like magpies, they would walk along Princes Street to lunch at MacVittie Guest's, always at the same round table kept for them at the window by the waitress from Perth with the curly black hair – what was her name again? – yes, Lizzie Dewar, that was it, a nice girl if there ever was one, and knew her place, too. And afterwards there was always something interesting and exciting; she would tear around, very much in the swim, arranging the next Union Dance or the Debating Society meeting with Queen Margaret College.

It was the debate that made her speak to Henry, then a shy, quiet, awkward youth whom nobody took much account of – although he had written one or two good pieces for the students' magazine. Because of this she asked him to suggest a subject for discussion, and to give her a few ideas for her introductory address . . . goodness knew she had never pretended to be clever at that sort of thing. He did this so willingly that somehow she had wanted to take an interest in him – she had found out that he was in lodgings and very much on his own. So she asked him out to Banksholme.

And then, of course, he was asked again and they were taking long walks together on the links at Gullane, not golfing, for he played no games at all, but just talking, often of the oddest things. Occasionally, when it showered, they would shelter in a bunker, sitting together, looking out across the Firth. He wasn't the demonstrative kind, which pleased her, for she could never bear to be pushed about . . . never. And afterwards they'd have a high tea with bannocks, shortbread, and black bun at a run-down little place he liked called the Neuk, on the North Berwick road, beside the old flour mill.

Then they'd go home and her father, back from the Court in Edinburgh, or his Highland circuit, if he'd been away longer, would smack Henry on the shoulder and joke with him: 'Young man, isn't it about time you told me your intentions were strictly dishonourable?' Then they'd have long discussions, political, or about books, her father drawing Henry out, and afterwards, when Henry had gone back to his digs in Belhaven Crescent, she'd catch her father's eye fixed on her, and he'd say, 'There something *in* that young man, Alice. If you've any sense at all, you'll hang on to him.'

And she *did* believe in Henry, although she couldn't but see that he wasn't at all her style. Yet she felt she could help him socially, and in every other way, to make a name for himself, and when, quite suddenly, old Mr Page became ill and he had to leave the University to go back to Hedleston to the paper, at the last minute, just before he left, they were engaged. But oh, little did she imagine that after more than twenty years of loyalty and devotion she would find herself passed by and put aside, by a husband who at times seemed almost unaware of her existence.

Alice was again on the verge of tears when she heard the front door open. She had barely time to compose herself, put away the cards and take up her work, before Henry came into the room.

'You're still up?' he said, as though surprised. 'Is Dorothy in?'

'She went to bed long ago.' Alice glanced meaningly at the clock on the mantelpiece, which showed a quarter past ten, adding, with imposed restraint, 'I was beginning to worry about you.'

'Didn't they tell you from the office?' He sat down with a tired air, shading his eyes against the light. 'I've been to Sleedon.'

'Indeed.' That one word seemed sufficient – she said nothing more.

'David wasn't there. He'd gone to see Dr Evans . . . I don't think it's too serious, though. I'll ring Scarborough in the morning. But Cora was rather down, poor girl, so I stayed with her for a bit.'

Alice took a few quick stitches, doing them all wrong.

Although she kept her head down she felt the blood run into her face. So that was how he'd spent the last five hours! She tried to keep her voice calm.

'Surely you were there rather a long time.'

'Yes, I suppose I was. We took a walk on the pier, then she insisted on making supper. She game me a wonderful spread, too. And afterwards we sat talking by the fire.'

The quiet, almost off-hand way he said it made Alice think he was trying to pull the wool over her eyes, and she burned inside. She'd suspected for some time that his feeling for Cora was growing out of all reason and proportion. From the first moment when she had appeared on the doorstep, with that soft, clinging look, that 'I want to be loved' appeal in her eye, he had always doted on her, taken her part, given her things, utterly spoiled her. But now he had really gone too far. That he had been with her, in the cottage, the two of them together all evening long, while she remained neglected at home was nothing short of scandalous. Alice made up her mind. She must speak, once and for all, and put a stop to it. But as she looked up she found his eyes fixed on her in a strange and almost humble manner. Before she could utter a word, he said:

'Alice, dear . . . there's something I have to talk to you about . . . a matter of business that's on my mind. It's late, but will you bear with me if I do so now?'

'What is it?' she asked instinctively, forgetting Cora for the moment.

'You know' – he hesitated – 'that when I bought the house, I put it in your name. I wanted you to have something. Now . . . I'm afraid I need your help. I've put it off as long as I could. I'd rather do anything than ask you . . . but you realize what I'm up against. I must have ready money. And if you sign this document I can raise a substantial sum on mortgage.'

Still looking at her, he took a paper from his inside pocket and smoothed it on his knee. For a full minute Alice was speechless. Then such a rush of indignation came over her she could scarcely stand it. She began to tremble all over.

'Aren't you ashamed of yourself?' she said. 'Even to mention such a thing . . .'

He had his head bent, supporting it with his hand.

'Yes . . . in a way, I suppose I am. I feel very badly about it.'

'And well you might. Whatever I've thought of you I never believed you would give a thing and then ask it back.'

'But surely, Alice' – leaning forward, he spoke in a patient way that exasperated her more than ever – 'you appreciate the position I'm in.'

'I should think I do! For months past, you've been bringing us to rack and ruin . . . after refusing a marvellous offer that would have taken us out of this dreary hole for good, on the most favourable terms. But no, you had to go on in your own stubborn, selfish way. Even now, when you're just about finished and bankrupt, you're not content. You want to take the very roof from over our heads and land us in the street.'

'No, Alice . . . '

'The house is the one shred of security that's left us. And you're trying to wheedle it out of me so that you can throw it away with the rest.'

He gave a long, difficult sigh.

'It's hard for you, Alice. But try to understand, I beg of you. How could any man let himself be coerced and bullied out of his rights? I couldn't submit to it then. And I can't give up now. Even if I am beaten, though I still feel I won't be, I must go on to the end.'

'To the end, indeed.' Her voice was breaking. 'And what about Dorothy and me?'

He looked away and did not answer. In a different tone, as though thinking aloud, he said:

'Even at the worst I can always provide for you.' Then, after a pause: 'I thought, as my wife, you would see it differently.'

'As your wife! Do you treat me as your wife, except when you want something from me? All evening long I've sat here

84

alone while you spent hours on end with that Cora creature in Sleedon.'

He straightened up, slowly at first, as if not quite sure of what she meant, then with a sudden lifting of his head:

'What on earth are you talking about?'

'Don't pretend you don't know. I've seen her looking at you with those big eyes of hers, pressing your hand when you've given her something, yes, mooning over you as though you were the most wonderful man in the world.'

He looked startled, but said quickly:

'That's nonsense, Alice. But why shouldn't she be fond of me . . . and I of her? She's our daughter-in-law.'

'Then you don't deny it?'

'I don't want to deny it. I am terribly fond of Cora.'

'In other words, you love her.'

'If you put it that way, yes. After all, she's one of the family.'

'What an excuse!' She could scarcely breathe, but she had to go on. 'A child could see through it. Can't you see you're deluding yourself . . . getting more and more involved with her every day?'

He looked at her pleadingly.

'Don't let us have a row, Alice. We have enough trouble on our hands.'

'A row, you call it, when I'm only standing up for my position and trying to save you from yourself. I know how a man gets at your age . . .'

'How can you say such a thing!' He flushed deeply. 'After the children, when you wanted your own room, I gave myself body and soul to the paper. I've never even looked at another woman. You know the moral climate we live in here, in this small town . . . what you suggest is unthinkable . . .'

'Not for Cora, it isn't.' Alice began to shake, the words came faster and faster. 'You may say I'm prejudiced, I've never liked her, but there's something about her . . . she's a common woman and I'm not sure if she's a good one. She's got too much sex . . . I can tell, for you know how I hate that sort of thing. She'd take any man if she wanted him. If

I'm not mistaken, she'd rather have you than David. And I don't doubt that in your heart you'd rather her than me.'

Henry's mouth opened in a shocked fashion, then shut again. It frightened Alice to see how badly she had hurt him. His face was so white, as if this was something he'd never even thought of before, but which now he'd never get out of his head, that suddenly she couldn't stand it any longer. She wanted to scream, knew she was going to have one of her 'turns,' and wanted to have it. Her eyelids began to quiver, and her cheek to twitch. She felt herself go stiff all over, and before she could get up, her heels were drumming on the floor.

Hurriedly, Henry crossed the room and bent over her.

'Don't, Alice, please . . . not so loud . . . you'll wake Dorothy.'

'Oh . . . Henry . . . Henry . . .'

'Be calm, Alice . . . you know how these attacks distress you.'

At the sight of his pale, worried face so close to her a change of feeling came over Alice, a reversal so characteristic and complete that she flung her arms round his neck.

'I don't care. I deserve it. I'm a jealous, thoughtless woman . . . but I had to . . . I had to speak . . . Forgive me, Henry. I'll do anything for you . . . work for you, starve for you . . . go through fire and water . . . anything. You know what I went through having the children. You know I suffered, Henry, I'm so small. Dr Bard could tell you. What does it say . . . into the shadow of death? It was for you, Henry. Ever since I saw you in Professor Scott's lecture room I knew you were the one. You remember the Neuk, don't you, Henry, and the bannocks, and the links at Gullane? I'll sign the paper. I want to. I want to. Give me it now . . . and a pen, quick . . . quick.'

'In the morning, Alice. You're too . . . too tired now.'

Her hair had come unloosed; another paroxysm seemed imminent, but fortunately, a moment before, Hannah had returned from her day's outing and now, without pausing to remove her things, she came into the room. Immediately, with the prudent and impassive resourcefulness that distinguished her, she brought the smelling salts and some aromatic vinegar, then, in silence and without the slightest fuss, she helped Henry to restore Alice to a state of calm.

'There now, Mrs Page,' she said finally. 'Just lie still awhile, then you can get up to your bed.'

'Thank you, Hannah. You're very good to me,' Alice murmured. 'You're all good to me.'

She smiled up at Henry. Everything was changed now; in the soft glow of reaction she wanted with all her heart to do what he wished, to obey him in everything. She rested on the couch for some minutes, then, while Hannah went to the kitchen and heated some milk, he assisted her upstairs. When the milk was brought she was in bed. She drank it gratefully, her hand still shaking a little, so that she almost spilled some on the newly cleaned eiderdown. Afterwards she swallowed the triple bromide Henry gave her. Then, after Hannah had gone, she said, very quietly, in a low voice, almost a whisper:

'The paper, Henry.'

He looked at her in that same queer way, then, without speaking, produced the paper and uncapped his fountain pen. Lying sideways on the pillows, Alice signed her name on the line where there was a pencilled cross.

'There, Henry. You see what I do for you. Goodnight, dear, and God bless you.'

When he switched off the light and left the room she closed her eyes. She felt peaceful and relieved, purified too, knowing that she had done her duty. She fell asleep immediately, thinking, of all things, of old Miss Taggart, who kept the Neuk Tea Rooms on the North Berwick road and who wore a cairngorm brooch in the shape of a thistle.

# XI

SOME WEEKS LATER, just after ten o'clock on June 21st, a date which was to become important, Leonard Nye entered the executive offices of the *Chronicle* in the new Prudential Building. In the morning Nye was never communicative – he did not answer the greeting that Peter, the youth who operated the switchboard, gave him. As he went along the corridor, Smith, who had heard him come in, called through his open doorway.

'Is that you, Leonard?' Then louder: 'I want to see you.'

Nye ignored the throbbing appeal. Smith's attempts at authority, infrequent though they had become, were best stifled at birth. If he wanted advice, or an ear into which to pour his increasing lamentations, Nye decided that he could come and find him.

He went to his own side of the office, a pleasant, airy room overlooking Victoria Gardens, which he had made comfortable with leather armchairs, a television set, and a couch. This last, ordered in a rare moment of optimism, had proved a somewhat unprofitable investment.

Nye's manner this morning, although apparently as casual as ever, revealed a certain inner tension which seemed heightened by anticipation. In fact, even as he peeled off his wash-leather gloves, he went straight to the desk and, standing there, flipped rapidly through his mail, as though expecting a communication of particular importance. One letter, in a buff envelope, marked 'Office of the Borough Surveyor' and stamped on the back with the borough arms, seemed to be the object of his search. He took it up quickly, ripped it open with his thumb. As he read it a look of satisfaction spread over his face.

'Good,' he said to himself. It was just as he'd expected; in fact, as he'd foreseen. After reading it again, more slowly, he put the letter carefully in his wallet, then lit a cigarette and, standing by the window, inhaling the smoke deeply, gave himself up to serious thought. After a few minutes he nodded, swung round, and settled himself at his desk to run through the rest of his mail, which apparently contained nothing of consequence. Finally, he turned to the newspapers, taking the *Light* first and leaving the *Chronicle* to the last – its format was now practically standard and, in any case, he knew exactly what had gone into it. He'd just got through an article by Henry on the season's musical programme in the park, which caused him to smile ironically, when the door swung open and Smith plunged in.

'Didn't you hear me?'

'When?' Nye said coolly. 'Did you call?'

Smith eyed the other suspiciously, took a chair – the hard one – then looked pointedly at his wrist watch.

'You're a bit late getting in, aren't you?'

'Well, you know I'm not an early riser. I haven't the temperament for it. Is there anything fresh?'

'Yes, there is.' He paused gloomily. 'A wire from Greeley. He's coming up again.'

'When?'

'Today. His train arrives Tynecastle Station at two-twenty. I'm to send the car. Of course I'll go to meet him. I'm worried, Leonard; I think it looks very bad.'

Greeley, the managing editor, Nye had to admit, was bad news at any time, a real hound dog for rooting out the worst features in a balance sheet, and murder on expense accounts. But there was more, much more, in this visit, his third in six weeks – Nye had expected it and he knew that it meant a definite showdown.

'Why doesn't he come by plane?' Smith grieved, poring over the telegram in his hand as though attempting to memorize it. 'The airport's a lot handier.'

'The M.E. never took a plane in his life. He's the cautious type, like you.'

'Cut it out, Nye. Can't you see how serious this is for both of us? Unless we can convince him. We're not that far off the end of our allocation. London was very queer yesterday. When they called Tingle back I knew it was a bad sign. And last week at head office Somerville really laid it on the line. When he had us both up in March it was bad enough. This time he gave me the works. We've got to deliver at all costs, or else. I'm desperately worried.'

Nye looked at the other with barely concealed contempt. For some months after their arrival in Hedleston, the joint rebuff they had received from Page had served to draw them together. But the two men were fundamentally opposite and Smith's dull personality, pedestrian methods, and uninspired outlook had by now thoroughly antagonized Nye. Actually it had taken him all his time to get along with his heavy-footed colleague without telling him what he thought of him and, in fact, what he knew of him. In sad truth, Smith's career had been slightly more tarnished than he made out and his manner of glossing this over, between humility and bombast, jarred the susceptibilities of a realist like Nye. He considered the man a clod, besides being a crashing bore, with his platitudinous honesty and plodding self-sufficiency, both supported by the delusion that he was the calm, successful type, while all the time he was sweating with anxiety, putting his foot in it, nerving himself to do better, longing to win friends and influence people.

'It doesn't seem to bother you much.' Smith broke the silence.

'For God's sake, stop whining,' Nye exploded. 'Don't you realize yet that I'm in dead earnest? I mean to beat the living daylight out of Page. The minute I laid eyes on that noble upholder of morality and the British constitution I made up my mind to put him out of business, period. But I don't go howling this from the housetops; it's just not my style'

A pause followed, then Smith speculated unhappily, his mind still on Greeley.

'I wonder if he'll stop the night this time. Or go down sleeper?'

'He won't stay.'

'We might have to entertain him. Why are you so sure?'

'Because I know,' Leonard sneered. 'Don't bother to arrange a floor show.'

Smith gazed at Nye doubtfully but said nothing, and presently he heaved himself to his feet and made for the door.

When he had gone Nye pushed the papers aside and settled down to further serious reflection. Although he had trained himself to remain casual and relaxed under all circumstances, this did not prevent him, when the occasion arose, from concentrating his thoughts with a kind of sardonic intensity. From the outset he had fully understood that all the drive and initiative must come from him – Smith might adequately control the financial side, but beyond that, he would contribute nothing. Nye's promotion and publicity, viewed in retrospect, had been first-rate. He had launched the *Chronicle* with a bang and, working strenuously, both editorially and as a feature writer, had, in his own phrase, stirred things up in this half-dead town. But for some months now there had been clear indications that something more was needed if the *Chronicle* was to come out on top. While Smith kept plugging along, hoping to wear Page down, Nye had realized that, on their side, this war of attrition could not go on for ever. All the evidence from head office – confirmed now by this sudden visit from Greeley – showed plainly that Somerville would not, or could not, stand it. Nye had it, in fact, from the inside that financially Vernon was having a difficult time. Something immediate and decisive had become essential, a line of strategy quite different from the ordinary, laboured routine, a brilliant stroke that would knock out Page once and for all.

So, as long ago as last March, after the first recall by Somerville, Nye had put his wits to work. It had not been easy. But he was rather good at that sort of thing, and at the end of the previous month he had come on something, quite unexpected, that gave him an idea. Followed up with tact and skill, this had developed into what he could now dispassionately regard as a certainty. Going over the details, one by one, as he sat there, he did not see how it could fail. He hadn't meant to spring his plan quite so soon – it would have been amusing to keep Smith in the dark a little longer – but now, with Greeley bearing down upon them, it was time to bring the rabbit out of the hat.

About an hour later Smith set out for Tynecastle, driven by Fred. Once he was well out of the way, Nye went to lunch, telling Peter where he could be reached. In this provincial town he found the refinements of life, to say the least, scanty. He couldn't, for example, get a decent haircut and he had to go to Tynecastle for a manicure. However, the table at the Red Lion wasn't at all bad – and they had a surprisingly good cellar.

Although Leonard had regard for his figure and always watched his calories, today he was in the mood to do himself rather well. When working for Jotham in Paris in '49 he had developed a fair gastronomic sense, and used to lunch quite often at Maxim's and Lapérouse. And, of course, in New York a few flattering paragraphs, judiciously spaced, had enabled him usually to dine free at the more select restaurants and night spots. Today, he ordered a few potted Morecambe shrimps, followed by a rare *filet mignon* and a green salad, then some ripe blue Cheshire cheese. With the steak he proposed to drink a bottle of Pouilly '47, a glass of Dow's port with the cheese, and a brandy with his coffee.

The fact that he had placed a mine under Page and was about to explode it gave zest to his excellent meal. There was in the elegant Nye an active ill-will, a fount of indefatigable vindictiveness which derived, if not from prenatal sources, at least from his origin and upbringing. Leonard, in fact, had arrived in the world without being invited, the accidental product of one of those liaisons, presumably based on higher thought, which from time to time occur in the literary world. His father, Augustus Newall, a large, heavy, cheesy man with yellow teeth and a tendency to soft, wide-brimmed black hats, had been frenetically acclaimed in the

92

early twenties for a volume of advanced poetry. *The Black Stallion*, which, in terms of the stud book, might well have been by Baudelaire out of Gertrude Stein. His mother, Charlotte Nye, an emancipated, youngish woman, some years out of Girton, violently intellectual, with a firm belief in her own talent and a highbrow contempt for bourgeois convention, was impelled to compose, carefully, a letter of adulation to the new luminary, which succeeded in its object and brought the two together.

It was a meeting of twin souls. First she sat at the feet of the master, then she warmed them in bed. They set up house together. But Charlotte had a temper, nor was she sufficiently good-looking to hold exclusively the amorous Augustus, who, in his brief and pampered heyday, frequently and with calm avidity possessed his female admirers on the nearest couch – indeed, occasionally on the drawing-room carpet. After some eighteen months the unhappy mischance of Leonard's conception broke up the meeting of minds, which, begun on a plane of aesthetic rapture, descended now to violent recriminations and ended, shortly after Leonard's birth, in the mutual hatred of two disillusioned egoists.

At first Leonard went with his mother, who, turning on the rebound to the stage, began to secure small parts in provincial repertory. Always an incubus, the child was dragged unwillingly around the country until judged old enough to be returned to his father, who, the well of poetry having run dry, was now turned critic, reviewing the work of his contemporaries with professional savagery. Thereafter the boy was shuttled between one parent and the other, greeted with concealed chagrin and despatched with obvious relief, until his father, deciding to live abroad, finally boarded him out with a hitherto unacknowledged aunt who maintained an obscure tobacconist's establishment in the Fulham Road.

This good woman did not treat her charge badly; in fact, even when Augustus's lean remittances became more and more infrequent she continued to feed him. Yet already the formative influences of his curriculum of rejection, acting on a temperament well fitted to receive it, had sharpened and

93

embittered young Nye. He saw that he owed nothing to anyone, and, as he grew older, there hardened in him an excusable, if cynical, determination to trust no one, never to regard the feelings of others, and henceforth to live only for himself. When, at the age of twenty-one, he turned instinctively to journalism, these were the qualities allied to his inherited brains and a natural gift for the stinging expression of his thoughts, which had laid the foundations of his success.

After his meal Leonard felt quite inspired, ready for what the afternoon might bring. As it was not yet two o'clock and Smith would not be back until three, he drifted to the billiard room and practised a few difficult cushion cannons. Joe, the marker, offered him a game, but Nye didn't want to get involved – he told Joe they'd play that evening. Then, at half past two, he went to the phone booth and, carefully shutting the door, called Hedleston 7034.

'Hello, hello.' He had to wait several minutes before the connection was established, then, in his smoothest and most honeyed tone, he resumed. 'Hello, is that you, Mrs Harbottle? How are you? Good. I'm very glad to hear it. But the rheumatism . . . of course . . . well, it is a troublesome thing. Now look, my dear Mrs Harbottle, this is to let you know that I'll almost certainly be over this afternoon, myself and two other gentlemen . . . yes, both very nice . . . to complete our little affair. Do you hear me? What? Good gracious no, it isn't a mean thing for you to do. On the contrary, you're more than justified. Now, Mrs Harbottle, we've been over all that before when you signed that little paper for me. You remember, don't you? You can't withdraw now; that would be a very serious matter; we'd have to bring in our lawyers. And besides, it's such a wonderful opportunity. What's that? Yes, naturally, old friends are best, but not when they let you down and impose on you. For years you've been practically swindled, and you'll never get another penny from them now. So that's settled, then . . . we'll be over. Good. No, don't trouble to make tea for us. I'll come for tea with you later in the week and have some of

your lovely griddle cakes . . . they's so delicious. Good . . .
excellent . . . till this afternoon, Mrs. Harbottle.'

When Nye came out of the sticky little booth where he'd
actually been grimacing in his effort to get things over to the
'old trout', as he called her – who was not only close-fisted
and difficult, but deaf as a post – he needed another brandy
to slacken his facial muscles. He had it, then got back to the
office.

Not a minute too soon. He had barely re-established himself at his desk when Greeley and Smith arrived.

The managing editor was a man of past fifty, exceedingly
tall and excessively thin, with a long, hollow, chilly face. He
always struck Nye as having recently been resurrected from
the tomb, cadaverous, yet persistently exhaling decorum and
propriety, as though prepared by a reputable undertaker. His
pursuits, even, were necroscopic: on his vacations he visited
ruins, explored catacombs, and had last summer taken to
digging for shards in the caves of southern Italy. Although
the day was warm he had on a coat, which he now wriggled
out of, first placing one wool-lined glove methodically in
each outside pocket. He was wearing the usual dark suit and
stiff-winged Gladstone collar, above which his bony larynx
protruded noticeably, as though impacted in his gullet, moving
up and down every time he swallowed. But despite the oddity
of his appearance and some eccentricity of manner, he had
a penetrating legal mind, having been a barrister of considerable standing before his seduction to trade by Somerville.

'You didn't find time to accompany Mr Smith.' His glance,
severe, held a hint of reproof.

'Someone has to hold the fort,' Nye explained.

The conference began with an examination of accounts
and the past month's sales returns. Nye sat and watched
while the two experts went over the figures. As Greeley's
skeletal fingers flicked through the piled papers, his expression lengthened, gradually took on the appearance of a
prosecuting attorney. Finally he removed his horn-rimmed
glasses and leaned back.

'This is more than discouraging. Worse than I anticipated.'

'We've tightened up our production unit,' Smith mumbled, 'and cut the overhead. If only they'd get started on the Utley project. You know we counted on that for a big influx of new readers. But they keep postponing it. . . . Heaven knows, I'm not responsible.'

'Never mind Utley. You are actually *losing* circulation you had already gained. Which means that Page is getting it back.'

Immediately Smith broke into a long apologetic explanation, prepared beforehand, stressing all that they had done, the difficulties they had encountered, and promising improved results in the immediate future. Greeley let him labour on to the end, partly because he was favourably disposed towards Smith but also because he wanted to hear and weigh all the evidence. Then, with lateral movements of his jaws, as though chewing each word before ejecting it, he said:

'Of the amount allocated for this unfortunate project, there remains a balance of less than ten thousand pounds. Pegging revenue and expenditure at their present levels, I estimate that your probable loss will absorb this in less than six weeks. What, may I inquire, will you do then?'

'We hope, naturally . . . we're so near our objective . . . well . . . we would anticipate a further appropriation.'

Emphatically, Greeley shook his head.

'It's a great pity for you, Smith, I know you're hardworking and conscientious, but I am afraid I cannot advise Mr Somerville to supplement the original budget. In my view the entire enterprise will have to be written off, unless something totally unexpected turns up.' Looking across, he caught Nye staring, and added, in the disapproving tone he usually adopted towards him, 'Perhaps Mr Nye has a suggestion to make.'

'Well,' Nye said, 'in point of fact, I have.'

He took time out to light a cigarette. He wasn't going to be put down by Greeley, who might have eaten his dinners in the Inner Temple and sat on the Royal Commission, but who, to his mind, was nothing but a cheese-paring sod who had tried to cut his expense account when he was in America and whom, actually, he had once seen change a shilling at the Paddington Station bookstall so that he could tip his porter sixpence. Still, at the present moment he had no wish to antagonize him. His manner was tactful and reasonable as he said:

'It seems to me that you're both taking a unilateral view of the situation. You're so concerned with our figures, costs, and percentages you can't see beyond them. It's been a hard job starting the *Chronicle* – this fellow Page was stronger than we expected – and in spite of a lot of first-rate promotion over which, incidentally, I've absolutely slaved, we've lost a packet and haven't quite swept the board. That's what you're looking at. Now, Mr Greeley, while at head office you've been wringing your hands and watching us, I've been keeping my eye on the other side. And what I couldn't see I made it my business to find out. I can tell you that Page has been losing capital just as steadily as we have, and for the past two months he's been trying desperately to raise more ready money. Five weeks ago he went to the bank and asked for a loan. He didn't get it. He went to the chairman of the board and still didn't get it. What next? He began to strain his credit. As the bills kept piling up he mortgaged his house, put up his life insurance, sold his collection of china, borrowed a few hundred from his assistant editor, even asked some of his old employees to take a twenty per cent salary cut. Now, all this doesn't mean that he can't carry on a bit longer and make things painful for us. But it does show that he's in a very bad way, ready for that one final punch that will finish him off.'

Greeley had been listening attentively enough, but now he moved impatiently, though with a certain inquisitiveness.

'Even if there is something in what you say, this stalemate might still drag on indefinitely. And where, if I may borrow your sporting phrase, would this final punch come from?'

Nye leaned forward, speaking slowly and logically. Much as he disliked the managing editor, he wanted to convince him; it was essential to carry him along.

'The *Light* building, such as it is, is owned by Page. He does not own the printing hall. This belonged to a Mr Harbottle, a close friend of Page's father, and is now owned by Harbottle's widow. For years the hall has been let to the *Light* for a more or less nominal rent on an annual, long-standing, amicable agreement – I have a photostatic copy of the lease here.'

Greeley was definitely attentive now, but suspicious – Nye was treading on his line of country. As for Smith, he was listening, mouth slightly open, as though hypnotized.

'I discovered all this more than a month ago, and I may tell you it took quite a bit of ferreting out. What did I do about it? Nothing. I didn't want to start working on Mrs Harbottle too soon. But around the beginning of June, through that fellow Balmer, who came over to us, I got to know the old lady. I took pains to be nice to her, had tea with her, casually brought up the subject of the lease, showed her how she was being put upon by the low rental and, after considerable effort, brought her to the point where she is prepared to sell the hall . . . to us. Now, can you imagine what it would mean to Page, who's already in tremendous difficulties, if suddenly, without any warning, he finds he can't print his paper?'

'What nonsense are you talking?' Greeley said. 'Show me your copy of the lease.'

Nye produced it and waited while Greeley looked it over. It wasn't long before he removed his glasses and gave a snort of contempt.

'This is a perfectly valid annual lease. Renewal doesn't fall due for another four months. And even admitting that rent restriction does not apply to business premises, the freeholder is obligated to give a quarter's notice. Seven full months altogether. Your idea is worthless.'

'Wait a bit,' Nye said. 'There's a little matter of the Factory Act of 1901.'

Greeley looked surprised, as Nye hoped he would, and finally said:

'Well?'

'I told you the hall was an old building. And I mean old. I've gone into this thoroughly and you may take what I'm saying now as gospel. On three separate counts that printing hall contravenes the statutory provisions of the Factory Act. One, the windows do not amount to ten per cent of the floor space. Two, there are not two separate exits to the building – inadequate escape in case of fire. Three, the inside walls and passages have not been lime-washed within the past fourteen months. Now,' Nye went on quickly before Greeley could intervene, 'having bought the hall, we, the owners, are immediately responsible to effect the alterations to comply with the Act. We go to the Borough Engineer, whom I've already threatened to expose for laxity in letting this thing run on, and get the premises immediately condemned. He must do it, and he will. It's the law. Until we carry out the improvements – at our leisure – the hall is closed down. The *Light's* off the streets, just like that, and Page is faced with the impossible job of finding new premises, moving his presses – in a word, he's out of business.'

There was a silence, then Smith let out a long, gasping breath.

'That's it,' he said. 'You've got it this time. And all dead legal.'

Greeley was looking at Nye questioningly. Impressed, in spite of himself, he didn't want to show it.

'He could find other premises . . . move his machines.'

'Without a bean . . . and in debt all round?'

'No, no,' Smith urged eagerly. 'He'd never get back in circulation. Never.'

'It is not a very ethical procedure.'

'It's perfectly legal. And more,' Nye added innocently. 'We'll be the ones complying with the Act.'

Greeley shook his head disapprovingly, but continued stroking his chin, still thinking it over, thinking too of those high-pressure instructions given him by Somerville before his departure.

'Can you supply a rough estimate for the alterations?'

'Around fifteen hundred pounds, perhaps even less. Then the hall will be as good as new . . . ready for us to move into.'

Another pause. Greeley was looking very searchingly at Nye.

'What price does this person ask for the property?'

Nye met his eye. He was ready for him.

'Naturally I secured an independent valuation. The figure was placed at just under four thousand pounds. Mrs Harbottle has agreed to accept three thousand five hundred pounds. And she's prepared to sign a bill of sale this afternoon.'

Again, Greeley, stretching his neck, went through the motions of careful cogitation. He had been one of the earliest sponsors of the scheme to buy the *Northern Light*. To see it fail was against his interest. With a cautious clearing of his throat, he said:

'I can't say I altogether approve. Although, if the position is as you state, there would seem to be no legal objections, it's an irregular proposal.' His face contorted suddenly into a death's-head smile. He rose to his feet. 'I don't in any way associate myself with any subsequent action you may take, but in the circumstances I think we ought to go and look into it.'

He put on the coat and gloves, in methodical slow motion, and led the way out. As they followed, Smith surreptitiously seized Nye's hand and pressed it with clammy intensity.

'You've saved us, Len,' he whispered hoarsely. 'By God, you've a head on you.'

Nye, with a withering glance, withdrew his hand sharply.

# XII

ON THE MORNING of July 1st Page came to the office earlier than usual. The day was fine and promised to be hot – recently the weather had turned sultry, bursts of torrid sunshine alternating with brief warm showers. His first action, rapid and involuntary, was to look at the returns. Then he drew a sharp breath of satisfaction. Again sales showed a definite increase, only nine hundred copies, to be sure, nevertheless a continuation of that positive upturn which had sustained and encouraged him during the past month. He felt, with a surge of anxious hope, that there could be no doubt about it – the trend was unmistakable. If only he could hold out a little longer he was saved.

Yet no one knew better than he how hard it was to keep going. These last four weeks had been a nightmare. How had he come through them? Even with the most rigid economy, by stretching his credit to the limit, using every means to stave off mounting demands for payment, existing from hand to mouth, on promises, postponements, and the goodwill of his staff, relying more and more on Maitland's dogged support, he was almost at the end of his tether. What a situation, he thought, with a sudden painful tightening of his nerves – this balance of hope and uncertainty was almost insupportable.

Moffatt had not yet appeared; he could hear her taking off her hat and coat in the next room. Without waiting, Henry collected the unopened mail from her desk, pushed aside the obvious bills, slit the first solid envelope, which bore a Manchester postmark. Then he winced, as though he had been stung. The letter was from the Northern Mills Pulp and Paper Company, which, for the past twenty years, had supplied the *Light's* newsprint. It expressed regret that his order of 25th June could not be executed.

While he sat staring fixedly at the letter, Moffatt came in. As a matter of routine it was she who saw to this business of supplies, every month, after receiving from Fenwick a note of the amount required, sending an order which was delivered the following week. Not looking up, Henry said:

'Get on to Mr Spencer at the Northern Mills.'

'I tried him late yesterday when our order didn't come through . . . they say he's not available.'

'Not available? Is he on holiday?'

'I doubt it.'

Her tone made Henry raise his head sharply.

'Get me the number.'

In a few minutes he was through to Manchester. Spencer could not, apparently, be found, and he was obliged to speak with the head clerk, who, while disclaiming all responsibility, insisted in the face of every argument that the delivery could not be made.

Henry put down the receiver, thoroughly alarmed. Paper . . . he must have paper . . . without it he could not print a word. Moffatt was still there, tapping a pencil on her shorthand pad, her gaze consciously averted, awaiting his next move with pained resignation. The strain had told on her; she looked thinner, dried up, more forbidding than ever. While she drove herself on with unflagging energy and heroic devotion, her temper had worn threadbare and her attitude towards Page had become so critical as to verge at times on open hostility.

'You realize it's their money they want,' she said, in a detached manner, as though reminding him of an elementary fact.

'When did we pay them?'

'Not since the end of April. They've written several times. It's a large amount.'

'How much?'

'I gave you the exact figure last week.'

'I know you did. But I cant' carry everything in my head.'

'It's nineteen hundred and sixty-five pounds, ten shillings. Shall I get the invoice from the file.'

'Never mind.'

He didn't have to look at his passbook to learn that the *Light's* balance at the bank was precisely seven hundred and nine pounds and fivepence. On top of this the printer's wages were a week overdue, and some of the delivery staff hadn't been paid for a fortnight. Both Poole and Lewis had volunteered to go without salary until further notice and Maitland, besides advancing two hundred pounds, had not drawn his cheque for the past four months.

'Find out from Fenwick how much paper we have on hand.'

She came back almost at once.

'Just enough for eight days. Not more. We're practically out.'

'Impossible. Why wasn't I told?'

'You said to cut costs to the bone . . . to run on a three weeks' margin. That's why we've so little left.'

It was true; he had been forced into this situation through sheer lack of ready money. Henry bit his lip hard to suppress a groan, then sat racking his brain for the best thing to do. Although rationing of newsprint had been removed and the pool system substituted, the situation was still difficult. Even if he had the cash it would take weeks to establish connection with another firm. He must go to Spencer himself.'

'Look up the next train for Manchester.'

'You can't go. The chapel leader's coming this morning to see you about the men's back wages.'

'Put him off somehow . . . at least till next week.'

'He may bring out the men.'

'Not if you tell him I'll see him on Monday.'

'And what's going to happen on Monday?' She threw the question at him.

With a great effort Henry saved himself from shouting at her.

'Please hand me the timetable.'

The morning express had gone and, since there was nothing

103

fast until the evening, he was obliged to take a local. At half past one, after a journey of exasperating slowness, he got into Manchester and went direct to the mills in Rose Street.

Here he was known to most of the staff and usually passed directly into the manager's office. Today he was asked to wait in the samples room. For fifteen minutes he sat there before the door opened and Spencer came in.

'I hoped you'd not come, Henry.'

'What's all this about . . . ?'

'Let's try and keep calm. Sit down.'

He took a chair at the table beside Page. A heavily-built man, nearing the retirement age, deliberate in his movements, plain and slow-spoken, he seemed at an unusual loss for words. His expression lay between concern and embarrassment.

'I shirked seeing you. That's why I told them not to let you up.'

'Why not?'

He brushed a non-existent dust from the table.

'It's a hard thing for a man like me to tell a man like you, Henry. Must I say it?'

'I know I'm a bit behind.' Page coloured. 'But surely my name is good. Many a time you've let me have six months' credit.'

'Things are different now.'

'I don't see why. You know you'll get your money.'

'Do we?'

Henry felt the hot blood of humiliation mounting higher on his forehead.

'I admit we've had some temporary difficulties, but we're on the upgrade again. You must give us a little latitude. We're one of your oldest customers.'

'We're aware of that. We don't like the situation any more than you. But in these hard times business is business. And rules are rules. Under the pool, we can't continue to supply over a bad debt. These are my orders from the board, and I can't overrule them. There's no use arguing, Henry, it's absolutely final.'

Henry stared at him in silence, trying to master his emotion, to marshal and direct his thoughts. But for the moment it was beyond him. At last he said:

'I must have paper. Enough to tide me over till I can settle your account. Where am I to get it?'

Spencer shrugged. 'Where indeed? Though you know I'd like to help you.' He reflected for a moment, then said, without conviction, 'There's a couple of places in the city you might try. Jobbers they are, actually. I'll give you a note of them.'

Taking a stub of pencil from his waistcoat pocket, he wrote out two names and addresses.

'Sorry the way things have turned out,' he said. 'I hope there's no hard feelings between us.'

He stood up, offered his hand, and, after a brief goodbye, Page went out to the street.

And now there began for Henry an afternoon such as, in his wildest imaginings, he could never have foreseen. The interview with Spencer had brought him to a state of nervous excitement which increased as the day went on. All his other worries became insignificant in the face of the hard fact that unless something were done, the *Light* would be out of circulation within ten days. Burning in his mind was the need to find, here and now, a sufficiency of newsprint to carry him over this last emegency. Other arrangements might be made later on. But these, in his unsettled state, seemed distant and illusory. What mattered most was immediate certainty.

He went to the first address Spencer had given him – it was a long way off at the east end of the city – and found there a quite reputable firm of jobbers. Unfortunately, they had cleared their stock at the beginning of the previous week and could give no promise of delivery. He therefore set out for the second address, and after much difficulty came upon a large dilapidated warehouse in Hassocks Lane. One look at the premises and its proprietor was enough – both smelled strongly of the black market. But the man had paper, and in this extremity nothing else mattered. After interminable haggling and a visit to the dealer's bank, where Henry telephoned Holden to send out a certified cheque for six hundred and fifty pounds, he procured twelve tons of newsprint with delivery guaranteed in two days' time.

It was almost three o'clock when the affair was completed, and as he could not find a taxi he had to hurry to the station to catch the three-ten express. He boarded the train just as it had begun to move from the platform and, completely out of breath, found a corner seat in one of the compartments.

He felt exhausted and degraded, but at least he had accomplished his objective. He took off his hat, wiped his brow, and tried to relax. For some minutes all went well, then he began to feel most unlike himself. His breathing had returned to normal, but he suddenly felt giddy, and inside his left arm, extending to the tips of his fourth and little fingers, a strange pain started to plague him. It had the stabbing quality and nagging intensity of toothache. At first he fancied he had wrenched his shoulder and that this neuralgia was the result, but as his giddiness increased, accompanied by an attack of palpitation, he realized that in the course of this hectic afternoon he had overtaxed his heart. Instinctively he felt for his nitroglycerine pills, only to discover that in his haste that morning he had come away without them. There was nothing for it but to lie back, close his eyes, and, since he was conscious of the curious glances of his fellow passengers, try not to make a fool of himself.

Somehow he got through the journey. At Hedleston Station, once he was out of the train, the fresh air revived him. He took a taxi to the office. He must reassure them about the paper and he felt that when he had swallowed a couple of pills he would be all right. At the *Light* building he climbed the stairs cautiously and opened the door of his room. Moffatt was there, filing some papers in a desultory manner.

'Ask Mr Maitland ‚ come and see me.' As she did not move, he added, 'I've straightened out the paper shortage.'

She turned slowly, her expression so extraordinary it drew him up short.

'You might have saved yourself the trouble.'

'What do you mean?'

'If you'd gone through all your mail this morning you'd have seen this.' She came sombrely, accusingly, to the desk and pushed across a letter, went on, before he even looked at it, in that same flat, extinguished tone. 'They've bought the printing hall and had it condemned. We can't use it for at least three months; light, water, and power are all cut off. They've posted an officer outside. We're done for.'

It took a long time for this to penetrate the mist of Henry's fatigue. When it did, all at once, his giddiness returned. Nothing in the room moved, but he, in some strange manner, seemed to spin and collapse, like a top that has finally run down.

## XIII

WHEN PAGE CAME to he found himself on the floor with his collar undone and, for some obscure reason of Moffatt's, a damp cloth slopping on his forehead. Both windows were open and Maitland was there, beside him on one knee, fanning him with a copy of the *Light*.

'You're all right now,' Malcolm said. 'Just take it easy.'

'Oh, Lord,' Henry muttered. 'How did I make such an ass of myself?'

An immediate anger at his own weakness was deepened when he discovered that Moffatt had telephoned for Dr Bard.

'You shouldn't have done that,' he said, sitting up and beginning defensively to straighten his tie and restore some order to his appearance.

Moffatt, on the point of replying, closed her lips grimly.

The doctor arrived just as Maitland helped Henry to a chair.

Bard came in quietly, nodded to Maitland and Moffatt, then, still without speaking, drew up a chair and put two fingers on Page's wrist, observing him with that detached air of academic inquiry which made him seem less a doctor than a professor of advanced mathematics.

'It was the heat,' Henry said, embarrassed by the doctor's silence.

'Yes, it's been rather warm today.'

'I was in Manchester and overtaxed myself a little . . . that's all.' He could not bring himself to reveal the cause of his collapse.

'Just so.'

Bard continued to listen, merely glancing up occasionally at Maitland, who stood, with an expression of concern, in the background.

'I'll take you home then,' he said finally. 'And we'll stop at my place on the way.'

In the car Henry made no attempt to talk, for now he was fully occupied by his thoughts. His brief unconsciousness had damped the shock of the sudden and unexpected blow delivered by the *Chronicle*. His brain was working clearly and logically and already he had decided what he had to do. Under the threat of persecution, his gentle nature had become compact, capable of infinite resistance, inflexible. As he made up his mind, his temples throbbed with the force of his determination.

When they arrived at the consulting room, Bard made him stretch out on the couch. Although he disdained a bedside manner and recoiled from the bustling clichés of the popular physician, Bard had the best practice in Hedleston and he made a particular point of keeping himself up to date. He took Page's blood pressure, then, while Henry watched with restrained impatience and an eye on the clock, wheeled over a trolley of electrical apparatus with a vertical recording drum.

'Not that again,' Henry said. 'Why don't you just use your stethoscope and be done with it?'

'We'll try this, if you don't mind, just for old times' sake.'

Henry had to submit while Bard pressed small lead discs on his left wrist and on various points of his chest, meanwhile running the current through the machine, to which the discs were wired. Finally the doctor drew off a number of tracings and took a long look at them by the window.

'Henry,' he said, coming over and seating himself on the edge of the couch, 'do you remember what I told you when you were an air-raid warden?'

'In a way . . . yes.'

'You wouldn't listen to me then. But you must now. I want you to knock off and rest for at least six weeks.'

'Later, perhaps.'

'I insist.'

'Ed, I appreciate all you do for me, but I simply can't promise anything just now.'

A pause followed, then Bard said seriously:

'Listen to me, Henry. You've got the kind of heart that needs a lot of care. If you look after it you'll probably outlive me. If you don't . . .' He made a slight but expressive movement.

'I do try to be careful.'

'You may think so, but you're mistaken. On the surface you seem calm enough, but underneath you're strained and overwrought. For months now you've been living under the worst kind of tension. It's little short of suicide for you.' He lowered his voice and went on as if appealing for agreement. 'A sensible man knows when he's had enough. I'm your doctor and your best friend and I tell you you're not physically capable of carrying on this fight. Under these circumstances it's no defeat to give in. Remember old Socrates: 'There is no failure in unavoidable surrender . . . to know when to give up the struggle . . . there also is a kind of triumph.''

'Are you offering me the easy way out?'

'In your own interests . . . yes.'

'No, Ed,' Henry said. 'I'm afraid I have to go on.'

Again there was silence, broken only by the sounds of traffic from the street outside.

'Very well, if you want to kill yourself, go ahead.' Bard moved unemotionally from the couch, broke a glass ampule and began to fill a small hypodermic syringe. 'Meantime, I'm going to give you a mild hypnotic. Then you'll go straight home to bed.'

When he had done, Henry got up and began to put on his things. Bard's pessimistic prediction had not greatly disturbed him, there were too many other things on his mind; more-over he had always thought Ed a man who carried caution to extremes. But he could not let him feel that he would ignore his advice completely.

'I will go slow,' he said, 'in a week or so.' Then in an odd tone he added, 'Perhaps even sooner.'

'You'd better.' Bard raised his eyebrows. 'You're a poor patient but not a bad sort of chap at bottom. Come and see me tomorrow; I'm going to start you on dicumerol injec-tions. And here – he handed Page a box of cotton-covered capsules – 'if you feel queer again crack one of these and inhale it.'

He telephoned the cab rank, saw Henry into the taxi, and directed the man to Hanley Drive. Page let the cab start off along Victoria Street in the direction of his home, but when they reached the traffic lights at the corner of Park Street he told the driver to turn right and go back to the *Light* building. He felt completely recovered from his attack, better, in fact, than he had been for weeks. His head was clear, the pain had gone, he was no longer breathless, and, perhaps because of the injection Bard had given him, he was suffused by an extraordinary sense of calm which seemed to clarify and strengthen his vision. Apparently the fortune of the *Light* could go no lower, it was on the verge of collapse – creditors swarming, funds attached, payroll delayed, news-print delivered only for hard cash, word from the union leader to 'sell out or pay up,' and now . . . the printing hall shut down. But Henry was not going home just yet, not by

110

any means. He looked at his watch – not quite five o'clock. There still was ample time.

He paid off the cab, took the stairs quietly and without difficulty. He found Maitland at his desk, absently drawing patterns on the blotting pad, sunk in gloomy meditation. At the sight of Henry he started up.

'What now?' His eyes expressed his surprise and concern. 'What are you back for?'

'To get the paper out.'

Malcolm's ruddy, homely face turned pale. He thought Page had taken leave of his senses. Scraping back his chair, he came forward.

'Come now, Henry. You've had a rough day. You ought to be in bed.'

'Later,' Henry said.

Maitland's look of dismay deepened. He said, with open alarm:

'Look here, man. You know the machines are inoperable. We can't print a line.'

'That makes no odds. Good God, don't look at me like that! Don't you realize the *Light's* never missed a single edition, not for a hundred and eighty-eight years? Not even when James Page had to issue holograph bulletins during the Napoleonic Wars? So long as I'm alive and have two brass farthings to rub together I'll get it out somehow.'

'Somehow?' Maitland echoed. 'I don't follow.'

'We'll produce a token edition by duplication. The text can be typed on a stencil and run off on our office duplicating machine.'

Maitland's face had lightened perceptibly; apparently he no longer thought Henry mad, but he looked at him doubtfully.

'You'll only get eight hundred copies off your stencil at the very outside, and the last couple of hundred will probably be blurred.'

'We'll use more stencils. We'll cut our size to the minimum. With six typists working all night we'll put out a single-sheet edition of five thousand copies. Let's stop talking and

111

make a start. Get Moffatt to phone Miss Renshaw's Bureau for all the typists and machines she can give us. We'll pay overtime and a half. Bring me everything from the A.P. machine. And tell Fenwick, Poole, and young Lewis I want to see them in my office at once.'

Fifteen minutes later Page took off his jacket and, filled with a calm intoxication, a sort of lucid frenzy, settled into his chair, with Fenwick, Poole, and Bob Lewis grouped about his desk, ready to dictate their concentrated copy. Moffatt, dispossessed of her usual chair, had brought in her typing stool. Maitland was seated beside Henry, savagely massaging his lower lip, a gleam of anticipation in his eye.

'We'll let the whole town know what the blighters have done to us.'

'No, not a word, Malcolm. This edition will speak for itself, and the entire country will hear it.' A wild, fierce exultation boiled up in Henry – perhaps he was at that moment a trifle mad. 'It'll speak so loud it may shut up the *Chronicle* for good. Yes, by God, they think they're smart, but mark my words, they may have over-reached themselves at last.' He turned to Moffatt, who was looking at him as though she'd seen a ghost. 'We'll have a block-letter heading – 'THE NORTHERN LIGHT' – and below: "All the news that we can print." '

XIV

NEXT MORNING, following her usual after-breakfast conference in the kitchen, Mrs Page set out to walk to the town. Despite Hannah's repeated urgings 'not to pity herself,' Alice was in low spirits, less from her conviction that she was being brought to destitution, than from the sorrowful suspicion that social ostracism had finally overtaken her.

The week before, Lady Wellsby had given a large party and neither she nor Henry had been invited. It had been a bitter pill for Alice to swallow, she had always prided herself on being particularly *close* to Eleanor Wellsby, and it seemed ominously to presage an equal deterioration in her relations with Catharine Bard, and her other friends. Furthermore, she had begun to suspect that the tradesmen were less respectful than before. Mr Scade, the butcher, had been quite disagreeable last Saturday when, having forgotten to order the joint, she asked him to deliver at short notice. Alice was therefore disinclined to venture upon the busy streets, yet she had felt the need to cheer herself, and now she was on her way to her little dressmaker, Miss Jennie Robinson, who was altering her grey moiré, the one she had bought in Jenner's when she was in Edinburgh visiting her sister last spring and, as she explained to Hannah, she had 'never liked the ruched sleeves'.

Her progress along Park Road was agreeably uneventful, but as she approached the centre of the town her eye was caught and held by a most unusual spectacle. At the news-stand in Victoria Square a large crowd of the townspeople had collected, talking excitedly amongst themselves and pressing round the stand, to buy some sort of bulletin.

Alice's curiosity was aroused. She joined the queue and after some difficulty secured a copy of what appeared to be no more than a single sheet of slightly smudged typing. Then she saw the heading: THE NORTHERN LIGHT. At first she could not understand; she thought this must be an advertisement of some sort; then, through her confusion, there came a stab of realization. This was the actual paper! A shiver of consternation went over her. She took a few indecisive steps forward, like a startled hen, wavered, then halted, saying to herself, 'I can't face it'. Abandoning the visit to Miss Robinson's, she turned and started back for Hanley Drive, avoiding the main thoroughfares, exclaiming over and over again, 'This is the end.'

Meanwhile, the commotion round the news-stand showed no signs of abating and, from his office window, which afforded an angled view of the square, Archibald Wellsby stood observing the unusual scene with an absorbed and contemplative eye. No one, he flattered himself, was more capable of judging the temper of the town, yet the reaction provoked by the appearance of the stencilled *Light* had astounded him. During his regular morning round of the factory, just completed, it had been, in every department, the subject of indignant comment. Halliday, his manager, who accompanied him, had condemned the *Chronicle's* sequestration of the printing hall as iniquitous – it was shameful that an old Hedleston institution should be forced to the wall by outsiders. Jim Davies, his six-foot head foreman, captain and international half-back for the Rugby League Fifteen, a real personality and general favourite, to whom even Wellsby genially deferred, had summed up the general feeling when he said bluntly:

'It's a proper dirty trick, Sir Archie. Just when Page was getting the better of them. Something ought to be done about it, but I don't suppose anything will.'

These remarks, especially that suggestive and stimulating phrase, 'just getting the better of them,' were circulating through the convolutions of Wellsby's mind as, still planted at the window, he thoughtfully lit his first cigar of the day. Personally, he was not particularly worked up over the event; nevertheless, there was an aspect of the situation which appealed to him strongly, as a shrewd and successful speculator. His vanity, which was considerable, assured him that he was the leading figure of the borough. When he presented the cups at the local sports, or gave away the prizes at the grammar school, the three hearty cheers always asked for Sir Archie made sweet music in his ears, as did the laughter and applause which greeted him when, cigar in hand and beaker of port at elbow, he delivered one of his famous speeches at the annual banquet of the Loyal Order of Noble Dalesmen. Often when coming away from such an event, snugly ensconced beneath the fur-lined rug in the back of his Daimler, he would say jovially to his wife, who had, perhaps, been the least appreciative of his audience, 'Ellie, you're married to the most popular man in Hedleston.'

And now, narrowing his gaze, as though to bring everything into perspective, he began definitely to perceive what an opportunity was presented him to rise even higher in the general esteem while furthering his essential motive of 'doing himself a bit of good on the side'. A loan of ten, fifteen, yes, even twenty thousand pounds, off his own bat, would mean little enough to him and it would almost certainly save the day for Page and the *Northern Light*. The news of it would go through the town like wildfire. By Jove, they'd think the world of him, stepping into the breach, standing four-square for justice and fair play, upholding the rights and dignity of Hedleston. Besides, Sir Archie cogitated wisely, it would prove a thoroughly profitable investment when he came to stand for Parliament. Although not a man to be bound beforehand, Page would certainly back him to the hilt at the next election. Henry was, above all, reliable, which was more than could be said of this chap Nye, who seemed just a trifle too smart to be trusted. A man of swift decision, Wellsby puffed hard at his cigar for a few seconds – sign of intense mental concentration – then pressed the buzzer for his secretary.

'Put me through to the *Northern Light*.' As he stood waiting, a thought crossed his mind. 'No . . . let me speak to Lady Wellsby.'

By this time Mrs Page had reached home and, through one of those extraordinary mutations which so notably distinguished her, the abject mood in which she had begun her circuitous return was gone. Self-justification had effected the transition. She went into the library and sat down, sustained by a growing sense of vindication, resolved at all costs to be calm, level-headed, and composed. Henry had brought his upon her – from the very beginning she had warned him; he had ignored her warning; *this* was the result. Permitting herself the final indulgence of a tragic little smile, she lapsed, as she occasionally did when talking to herself, into the simple doric of the North: 'Well, my fine lady, you'll never see your Hawaii now. And your braw reception for the Philharmonic, that's gone to the wa' as well.' Then she set herself to face the future with fortitude and enterprise. She would be loyal to Henry – she had always been a good wife to him in spite of everything – and if unable to restrain some words of reproach, she would temper them with condolences. Already, too, tangible sacrificial schemes were flitting through her head for the support and regeneration of the family. Naturally, her jewellery would be the first to go, not that she had much of it, for Henry's taste had never run in that direction, and in any case, unlike Eleanor Wellsby, she had never been a woman to bedizen herself. But at least, with her few bits and pieces, she would ensure that they all had bread.

And there was more, much more, that she could do: as her vision widened, exciting possibilities took shape before her. Might she not open a shop to sell her needlepoint, or perhaps a tea room, where in a quietly refined and ladylike manner she would every afternoon attract a superior clientele? After some consideration she decided to name the café the Lavender Lady, and she began in her imagination to design a fetching uniform for Dorothy and herself, in that shade, which had always suited her colouring. A brilliant idea came next when she remembered those wonderful home-made wheaten scones that Rose used to bake at Banks-holme and which must surely prove an irresistible attraction at the new establishment. She would write to Rose, dear Rose, for the recipe, this very day. . . . But this thought of her sister, and of her old home, swept Alice from the future to the past. Her dream life, which fed on fantasies, and into which she could be swept by a word, an odour, by the echo of a distant cry, the faint pealing of church bells, the tinkle of a piano on a still Sunday afternoon, now took possession, and in a flash her mind had lost itself in a maze of nostalgic recollection. Back, back she went to her childhood, scenting the rich aroma of baking in the big dark kitchen, seeing herself accept a scone warm from the oven, dripping with golden butter, and run out, laughing, to the swing behind the shrubbery. She heard the creak of the swing, the clip-clop of her father's pony as the trap came up the drive, the faint thin bleating of lambs upon the Cheviots, the shrill drawn-out cry of the village fishwife as, bowed beneath her creel, she passed along the lane: 'Fresh fillets . . . all fresh today . . . fresh frae the Firth . . .'

There was a knock on the door and Hannah entered.

'What about your lunch, Mrs Page?'

Abruptly, Alice came back to Hedleston, blinked for a moment, became again the saviour of the household, and said, very quietly:

'I'll just take some toasted cheese and a glass of milk.'

'Nothing more?'

'Nothing, thank you, Hannah.'

She *knows*, Alice told herself, when Hannah had gone, and she felt that her old Scottish maid would respect her, not only for her reserve, but for this first step towards retrenchment. Still, when the toasted cheese came in, nicely set out on a tray, it was a generous portion, and Alice enjoyed it. This was, in fact, one of her favourite dishes, and Hannah, perhaps because of the occasion, had made it particularly well. She finished every bit of it, then went upstairs to take her usual rest.

Somewhat to her surprise she fell asleep and it was past three o'clock when the ringing of the telephone roused her. She took up the receiver and immediately heard Lady Wellsby's voice.

'Alice, my dear, is that you? Eleanor Wellsby here. Alice, we want you and Henry to come to dinner next THURSDAY. Not a party, just a cosy little evening for the four of us. Is that all right?'

Startled, and not fully awake, Alice could not believe her ears. She managed to say:

'Yes . . . yes . . . I think we're free.'

'Good, then we look forward to having you. Only this morning Archie was saying how little we had seen of you lately . . .'

'Indeed, yes,' Alice could not resist saying. 'I must confess,

I was rather hurt not to receive cards for your party last week . . .'

'My dear, that was the dullest affair. Besides, we realized Henry was so worried, and I'm sure you were too, that you couldn't possibly have wished to come. But now, naturally we want you both. What a man that husband of yours is . . . he's really turned the town upside down! Till Thursday, then. Come early.'

A warm glow suffused Alice as she replaced the receiver. She was esteemed, in the depths of her adversity, and for herself. That Eleanor Wellsby, of all her friends, should at this fatal moment come to her support was the greatest compliment she had ever received.

She tidied her hair, studied herself in the mirror, and went downstairs, where Hannah brought her a strong cup of tea and some digestive biscuits.

'Is it the mutton for tonight, Mrs Page?'

Again Alice felt that bond of sympathy, but she restrained herself. She told Hannah to cook the joint as usual. After all, it was in the house, and who knew where their next meal would come from?

The afternoon was wearing on. Refreshed by her long rest and by the tea, Alice determined to be busy. Henry had not come in yet; she had heard nothing from him all day. While awaiting him she would write the letter to her sister, not only to request the recipe for the scones, but also to communicate the news of her misfortune. She sat down at her bureau, took a sheet of notepaper, and, after a reflective pause, bent on unbosoming herself to the full, began.

*My dear Rose,*
*The most dreadful thing has happened . . .*

The sound of a car outside interrupted her. Then, as she raised her head, she heard Henry's key in the front door. A few seconds later he appeared. By this time she had thought of many things to say to him, less in anger than in sorrow, but before she could speak he came directly to her, kissed

118

her, then took her hand. He was very pale and on each of his cheeks there was a small bright flush.

'Alice,' he said, straight away, as though he could not contain himself, 'my belief in decency, right thinking, and the essential goodness of people has been restored.'

Her eyes widened at this opening, so typical of Henry in his uplifted moments, yet so unexpected it astonished her. But he completely took her breath away as he went on.

'This morning the bank – Wellsby, if you like, for it really comes out of his pocket – made me the loan. Far more generous than I expected. And on what security? On the name of the *Northern Light*.'

'I don't understand,' she faltered, disturbed by his elation. 'I saw the miserable little sheet.'

'That is precisely what did it, my dear.' He spoke less excitably now, trying to keep command of himself, but she had never seen him so moved. 'Our effort to keep the paper going has finally brought things home to the people. All morning we've been swamped by telegrams and phone calls. There's a wonderful editorial in tonight's *Tynecastle Echo*. . . . Tomorrow there'll be another in the *Manchester Courier*.' He smiled, shakily, the first time for many weeks. 'Even the clergy are getting behind us, at the eleventh hour. Gilmore rang me to say his sermon will be on us on Sunday . . . the text, "Let there be light" . . .'

'But, Henry,' she protested, unconvinced, 'how will you carry on?'

'Token editions till next Monday . . . and that should do us some more good.' He smiled again. 'Tom Gourlay tells me people are paying him as much as half-a-crown for them at collector's items – he's making a fortune. On Monday we start printing again in earnest. Major Seaton has loaned us the Armoury Building for as long as we need it; the machines are going in tomorrow. Poole and Lewis, all of them, even Hadley, are taking their coats off and getting down to it.'

'But, Henry, you can't go on printing in the Armoury?'

'Of course not. It's only a temporary measure till we find

something permanent. In fact, if I'm not mistaken, we'll be back in our own premises before the year is out. Don't you see how this has backfired on the *Chronicle* lot? They've bought the printing hall and I still have the lease. They're compelled by law to make the statutory alterations within three months. At the end of that time, if I'm any judge, they'll be out of business, and glad to dispose of it. I tell you, Alice, I've never felt so happy. I've settled our outstanding account with the Northern Mills. I've paid the staff, and all my bills. Thank God, I'm clear and out of trouble, and if you're a patient lass it won't be too long before you have the house back in your own name.'

'So you actually think . . . ?' she said, still distrustful, unwilling almost to believe in this turnabout, after she had reconciled herself so agreeably to disaster.

'Let's say that I'm most hopeful, Alice . . . and deeply thankful too. And now' – he put his hand to his forehead in a tired manner – 'I have to get back to the Armoury. I'm meeting Seaton there at six o'clock. But I had to stop in and give you the good news.'

'If it's really so good, Henry' – she looked at him questioningly – 'I mean, for instance, will you be able to have the Philharmonic this year.'

'Of course. I'm going ahead with the concerts. It's the best kind of publicity, and besides, we enjoy them.'

'Then . . . I'll actually be able to give my reception as usual?'

He laughed happily and touched her cheek.

'Yes, my dear, have it by all means. You know I like you to be pleased. And there's talk of getting up a testimonial dinner for me. You might enjoy that, too.'

When he had gone Alice sat a long time in silent communion with herself. Then with a shake of her head, as though acknowledging that certain things were beyond her comprehension, she slowly tore up the letter she had begun and, taking another sheet, started afresh.

*My dear Rose,*
    *The most extraordinary thing has happened . . .*

# PART TWO

## I

IT WAS RAINING as Leonard racked his cue and stared out the window of the billiard room at the dripping, half-dead street. Joe, the marker, stood with him, fingering a cube of green chalk.

'It's very wet,' he said. 'We could have another hundred up, Mr Nye.'

But he'd had enough – he wasn't in the mood and the table was so completely on the skew the balls had worn a track into one of the top pockets. Outside, in the grey afternoon, some workmen were squatting under a tarpaulin shelter, drinking tea, before a brazier of coke. They seemed always to be drinking tea, which one of their number was deputed to keep boiling in an outsize billy-can. The hole in the pavement they had made two weeks ago was still there, surrounded by uprooted cobblestones and flanked by hurricane lamps.

The sight of this stoic inertia, which ordinarily would have amused Nye, seemed for some reason to put an extra chip on his shoulder. He and Smith were in the same sort of mess, all right, but their tea was running out, and fast.

Well, he thought, the hell with it. He got his raincoat and umbrella from the cloak room, left the hotel, and started for the office – there was nothing else to do. For the past month getting out the *Chronicle* had become a perfunctory routine – they were down to mere twenty-six thousand copies, while the *Light* was selling a clear seventy thousand, almost back

121

to normal. It was perfectly evident to Nye that they would never reduce the lead Page had gained on them. Most of the staff had gone back to London, but Smith was still here with him, making a show of running the paper in the illusory hope that someone might be induced to buy it. They had tried to sell it back to Rickaby, but he wasn't having any part of it. The bright idea at head office was to salvage something of the loss, but there hadn't even been a nibble and there wouldn't be, if Nye was any judge. Smith still kept up a show of activity, which became progressively more pointless and feverish, but he was all washed up and he knew it. At the rate sales were slipping, Somerville wouldn't hold on much longer, and every day now Nye expected they would both get the hook.

Nye kept telling himself that for him it made not much difference, that he was just a little different from the average newspaper man, jumping to the boss's word, lamentably underpaid, and seldom given the chance to improve himself. In Fleet Street his ability to deliver the goods was generally recognized, and while he might cut a few corners, what was the odds so long as he got there before the other fellow? He knew that he had brains, talent, personality — he did things easily and well. Without any fuss he'd picked up French and German and spoke them fluently. He was well up in modern art and could knock off an article on Picasso, Buffet, or Mondrian with the best of them. He had some idea of music, too, and although he had never had a lesson in his life, he could sit down at the piano and play anything by ear. His tennis game was better than average and at billiards he could string together a break of a hundred any day of the week. When he chose to exert himself, there were few men or women he failed to please; as the saying went, he had a way with him. When he was Jotham's foreign correspondent in Europe he had done a smashing job on the international set at Antibes and Deauville — all due to his ability to get into places like the Eden Roc and the Normandy, and be perfectly at ease there, when the average fellow might well have been thrown out on his ear.

It was then that he first developed his amazing capacity to distort an interview and, while using the exact words of his victims, succeed in creating damaging impressions which never failed to titillate his readers. How the feeble letters of protest, always tucked away in a remote corner of the paper, entertained him! It amused him also to produce an occasional diatribe against some popular book of the moment when by detaching phrases from the context he misrepresented the author's purpose and made him appear a scoundrel or a fool. Later on, for Somerville, this talent had flourished in his weekly articles from New York during austerity, when his biassed comments on American prosperity had done much to foster the bitterness prevalent in Britain at that time. He could almost certainly get another American assignment, probably from Mighill, and be well out of this bloody English winter. Or with luck he might talk himself into covering the film festival at Cannes . . . that was an idea to which he might give some thought; he had all sorts of contacts on the Riviera, where, he reflected with some pride, he had interviewed all the leading personalities from the Gabor sisters to the Aga Khan. Yes, he had been around, he knew what he was doing, and could always pick up a first-class billet.

Nevertheless, despite this effort to inflate his ego, it was gall and wormwood to his pride, a constant and corroding source of bitterness, to have failed here, above all to be beaten by a man like Page. From their first meeting Nye's hostility towards the owner of the *Light* had steadily increased until now it had risen almost to an obsession. Of course, he told himself savagely, if only Smith hadn't been so damned ladylike in his tactics they'd have won hands down. It was true that his idea on the printing hall had backfired – the very thought of it still made him squirm – but at least it had been on the right lines. Half measures were no good when you were in a fight. It must be all or nothing, and Smith had never gone all the way. Still, Smith was the one who would really take it on the chin. He had imagined it would be so easy, had banked so completely on success, especially to reinstate himself with his wife, that it was laughable to see how his morale had crumbled. In these last weeks the important look had vanished, and although he still kept sweating around looking for some way out, anyone with half an eye could see that he was pooped.

By this time Nye was in the Cornmarket. In front of the Old Town Håll a poster had been set up announcing the concert – the first of the Philharmonic group – that Page had organized for the St Mark's Steeple Fund, and which was due to be held on Sunday, September 15th. Though Nye told himself that the names Page had raked in were mediocre, second-class highbrow talent, that didn't help him much. He swung away from the poster, then, as he crossed the square, he saw Page come down the steps of the *Light* building. Lately Nye had tried to keep out of his way, for the sight of him was more than he could stand. A young woman was with him. She was a looker, all right, tall, with curves, not too much, just right. Even at that distance you could tell she had something. For a second Nye wondered who she might be, then Page's son – he'd seen him twice before, a tall, long-haired, poetic-looking bird – came after them and she smiled and took his arm. None of them saw Leonard – he didn't want them to – and keeping them in the corner of his eye, he half turned towards a shop window to light a cigarette. They got into Page's five-year-old Vauxhall – to Nye it all seemed part of an act to sport a small out-of-date car – and drove off.

Leonard went on to the office. As he expected, Smith was there, trying to seem busy, at his desk, but actually writing a letter to his Minnie – Nye knew it was to her from the way he slid it under the blotter as he came in. You couldn't help noticing how much weight Smith had lost; he looked as though the crows had been at him.

'Anything fresh?' Nye flung himself into a chair.

'Not a thing.'

It was pathetic. He still sounded hopeful, in a far-away fashion. It annoyed Nye, who wanted to rub him on the raw.

'What's the word from the Honourable Vernon?'

'Nothing.' Smith blew his nose several times – his catarrh was on again. 'At least, no news is good news. If only . . .'

'. . . something would turn up.' Nye finished it for him, imitating his tone.

Smith reddened.

'Your bright idea didn't help much. In fact, it practically wrecked us.'

'How was I to guess that Page would bring out that bloody stencil? You never know where you are with a prig like him. God' – Nye's temper boiled over – 'I'll never forget that first day when he opened up on us with his sermon on the sanctity of the press. If there's a type I can't stand it's the mealy-mouthed do-gooder, the uplifter who wants to create Utopia with his niggling little broadsheet. I think I know human nature. As for the newspaper trade. I know it inside out. It's a ruddy business, like any other, with two main objectives: money and power. To get there you need circulation. For circulation you must give the customers what they want. And what do they want . . . at least the bulk of them? They want the juicy bits – sex, scandal, and sensation. Old Jotham proved this to the hilt when he ran the *Sunday Enquirer* up to the seven million mark and kept it there on a straight programme of police-court reporting and key-hole news. So why make a fuss about it? People are only human. I'm the sort of fellow that sees no harm in a bit of fun, so for God's sake let's have it before the big bomb drops. The world's gone down the drain anyway, and all the Pages and uplifters that were ever born won't pull it out again.'

Smith, who had listened to this diatribe in silence, said:

'You may say what you like. I bear no grudge against Page. He's a fine man.'

'Yes,' Nye said bitterly. 'I just passed him. He did look fine . . . on top of the world.' He stubbed out his cigarette. 'The son was there. They had a skirt with them.'

'A young woman? Quite attractive?'

'That's the understatement of the week. She's a looker, all right, tall, with curves, not too much, just where you want them. Even at a distance I could tell she has something.'

'She's David's wife.'

'David,' Nye sneered. 'Brother, you sound like one of the family.'

Smith began disapprovingly to shuffle the papers on the desk. Now that he was in trouble, Nye thought derisively, the pious streak in him showed up. The other day when he had barged into his room he was kneeling by the bed trying to get a little help from Heaven . . . worse even than Holy Ithiel Mighill, who held a hymn fest every Sunday night at his country house in Surrey.

'Why haven't we ever seen her around?' Nye asked after a pause.

'Who?'

'That dame, of course.'

'They live very quietly . . . at Sleedon.'

'She didn't look the quiet type to me.'

'Oh, let's leave the Pages alone,' Smith said, very short. 'They're decent people.'

'It's nothing personal. I just hate their entrails, all of them, on principle.'

'You're a great hater.

'I have gall. I admit it. And now I'm going to have a beer.'

Leonard got up and left Smith, walked down the street to the Victoria Bar, where he had a Scotch and a chaser of Bass. He supposed it was natural in a town like Hedleston, where there was nothing on view but a few drabs hanging around the station after dark, but somehow he couldn't get the thought of young Page's wife out of his head. She had impressed him and he wondered why he'd never seen her around. Probably young Page kept her pretty tight; he looked the jealous type, and soft on her, you could tell at a glance.

Nye was not susceptible to women. For one thing, he didn't trust them. And, as he delicately expressed it, he'd been there and back so often he was inclined to be blasé. So although it did cross his mind that this one would be good in the bed, there was more to it than that – she interested him in quite a different way. She seemed not to belong to the Pages at all, but to be on his side of the fence. It was as though some subconscious affinity existed between them, something hidden and altogether unexpected.

How could he explain this vague, peculiar feeling? He kept asking himself that question and failing to find the answer. The closest he could get to it, though it wasn't at all near, was by recollecting a comparable sensation. One night, long enough ago, when he was a green young reporter starting in Fleet Street, he went out to dinner with some pals. They had too many drinks and when he left them to go to his digs a tart picked him up in Piccadilly. They went into Hyde Park – it was pitch dark, he scarcely even saw her face. Ten years later, as he jumped on a bus at Victoria Station, a woman got off. For perhaps two seconds on the step of that bus their eyes met in a sudden impact of mutual recognition, and he knew, less from the evidence of vision than from a sort of inner shock, that here was the unknown with whom that particular intimacy had occurred.

Although when put to it, Leonard could turn out a tasty double column on Freud, psychology was slightly off his beat, and, of course, he fully realized he'd never even exchanged a word with young Page's wife, still less laid a finger on her. But while he couldn't explain it, she gave him the same sort of reaction he had previously experienced – that in some circumstances, not particularly creditable to him, he had been associated with her before. He told himself it must be pure imagination. He might merely have caught a glimpse of her when she came to do her shopping in Hedleston and this, registered at the back of his mind, might well have produced the illusion of previous association. And yet . . . he wasn't quite convinced. Uncertainty was beginning to get him down when Smith walked in. Nye watched him as he sat down, took off his hat and mopped the rain from behind his ears.

'Nothing came through,' he said, 'so I thought I'd join you. Peter's looking after the phone. It's chilly in the office.'

'Have a drink?'

'I think I might.' He moistened his lips nervously.

Nye waited. He'd been expecting this for some time. He knew Smith . . . through and through. He knew that although he passed for a strict Good Templar, when he was in real trouble he gave way. For him it was poison and afterwards he had the most ghastly remorse, but on three occasions, to Leonard's knowledge, he had gone out on a terrific splurge – not for fun, but because he couldn't help it. In Australia when he lost his job with the *Melbourne Echo* he went on a bender that lasted for three months. Two years ago, the summer his wife left him, he spent his whole vacation in a Brixton pub and wound up on the verge of DTs. So now Nye was curious.

'What are you having?' Smith asked.

'Scotch and a beer.'

'Well . . .' He gave a kind of sick smile. 'I'll just have my ginger ale.'

'Not yet, chum,' Leonard thought. 'But it's coming to you, all the same.'

There was a long silence. The rain beat on the window. The saloon was empty. In the public bar two men were arguing about next Saturday's football results, puzzling over tables of computations in Mighill's *Globe*, which neither could understand. Nye tried to turn his thoughts towards Cannes and the possibilities of the film festival, but they wouldn't go there.

'Look, Smith,' he said at last. 'It may surprise you, but I think we ought to go to this concert.'

'Concert?'

'Page's charity do. On Saturday.'

Smith stared at Nye, sunk in his chair, his overcoat draped around him.

'You're not serious.'

'I'm not sure whether I am or not. But I vote we go.'

'Why?'

'Just an idea.'

'You and your ideas.' He gave Nye a sulky look and

drank his ginger ale in a quick gulp. 'The last one was a beauty.'

Nye wasn't going to start another wrangle on that score. He waited, knowing Smith couldn't resist trying to find out what was on his mind.

'What is it?'

'I think,' Nye said, with mocking satire, 'it would do us good to mix socially with all these nice people. You're a man who enjoys high society. Besides, we don't want to crawl out of town. Let's put up one last good act in public and go out with a bang. Can you get tickets?'

Smith gazed at him doubtfully.

'I believe so.'

'Fine. Get seats near the front if you can.'

Before Smith could shape his next question, Leonard got up, paid for his drinks, and went out.

II

TWO DAYS LATER, in the afternoon, when Dorothy returned from Tynecastle and was going to the pantry, according to her habit, for a glass of milk and a biscuit, Mrs Page, bustling brightly about the house, intercepted her in the hall.

'There you are, Dorrie. I want you to take a little note out to David and Cora.'

'To Sleedon!' Dorothy protested, making it sound as if it were the North Pole.

'Yes, dear. Your father just called me from the office. We want them to come to lunch Sunday, before the concert.'

'But, Mother, I've had a hard day. And it means taking the bus. That old Sleedon rattletrap shakes you apart.'

'You can take your bicycle, dear. You've scarcely used it since you got it. It's a lovely afternoon.'

'The front tyre's flat.'

'Then blow it up. It'll do you good. You haven't been getting nearly enough exercise lately.'

The reason for this unexpected commission, like the unusual appearance of Henry with David and Cora in the streets of Hedleston, lay in the report which Dr Evans had sent Page from Scarborough. That cheerful psychiatrist, while maintaining his optimism, had suggested that it would be well for David to vary the essential quiet of his life at Sleedon by coming more frequently to town and 'mixing more with people'. This advice, which bore out the view she had previously expressed to her husband, gratified Mrs Page and put her in a responsive mood. With a smile she slipped the note in Dorothy's blazer pocket.

'There, dear!'

'Oh, well,' Dorothy said resignedly. 'If harm comes of this, Mother, I'll hold you responsible.'

Actually, Dorothy was quite pleased to go. She had nothing whatsoever to do; Bob Lewis had phoned her at the art school to say he was working late and couldn't take her to the movies, and the prospect of a visit to Cora brightened up what had promised to be a dull evening. Although she did not see much of her, she liked her sister-in-law, who could always be depended on to give her a good tea. She went to the coach house and wheeled out her bike, then, having persuaded Hannah to give her a hand with the pump – the rubber end of which tended to blow off at the psychological moment – she set out for Sleedon.

She had not gone very far, however – only to the corner of Draycot Avenue and Park Street – when she saw someone on the pavement signalling her to stop. Instinctively she braked, drew into the kerb, and jumped off. Only then did she recognize Leonard Nye.

'Well, Miss Dorrie, I'm glad I caught your eye. This is an unexpected pleasure.'

'Is it?' Dorothy said unwillingly.

She had no particular animus against Nye for his opposition to her father. That had been something quite detached from her own absorbing preoccupations, although it had been exciting, in a way, watching Henry, whom she thought of as not a bad old bird, mucking through trouble in his usual sentimental style, and there had, in fact, been one pleasurable moment when she thought they might all be out in the street, with their goods and chattels, or what was left of them, in the best traditions of Orphans of the Storm. No, the point was more personal. She had her own quarrel with Nye, and while he was smiling all over his face as though everything in the garden were lovely, she hadn't by any means forgotten what he'd written about her when she spotted his wretched Treasure Man. Admittedly it was some time ago, but it had got her teased to death at the art school – for weeks after, all the meatier bits in the article had been thrown at her. Since then she'd passed him in the street and he'd always taken off his hat to her, but until now they had never spoken to each other.

'I imagined you'd gone,' she said, in a voice that hoped he had.

'We shall be soon.' He took no offence. 'I thought I'd like to say goodbye before I left. Just to show there's no ill-feeling.'

'Isn't there?'

He kept on smiling, not very naturally, but as if he were keeping the look glued on his face.

'I hope not. Your papa has given us a bit of a doing. But, oh, well, in our job we have to learn to take the rough with the smooth.'

He brought out his cigarettes and offered her one and, not wishing to seem too juvenile, she took it. As he flashed his lighter – he was the type who carried one that always worked – he said:

'Are you off for a spin?'

'Yes.'

'That's a nice-looking machine. A Humber, isn't it? Have you had it long?' Then, as her face reddened slightly, he said quickly, 'Oh, I'm sorry . . . I didn't mean to be inquisitive.'

'I was allowed to buy it with part of the money I won from you. The rest my father made me give to charity.'

'Well,' he said considerately, 'at least you got some good out of it.'

Although he pretended not to notice, Dorothy was beginning to feel extremely uncomfortable, standing there, puffing amateurishly at the cigarette, in the public street. She often had a weed with the other girls when they were having coffee at the Espresso, but this was different – in fact, completely non-U – and if Henry ever heard of it she knew he'd go off the deep end, and with reason. She groped around for an excuse to leave, but before she could think of one he said:

'I was just on my way to the hotel for a cup of tea. I don't suppose you'd care to join me?'

'I'm sorry. I'm going to have tea with my sister-in-law at Sleedon.'

'Oh, yes.' He nodded quickly. 'I saw her in town the other day. She seemed nice.'

'She is.'

'It's extraordinary, though,' he meditated pleasantly. 'I've been two years in Hedleston and never run into her before. She must lead a very quiet life.'

'Yes, she does,' Dorothy said shortly. 'You probably know that my brother's been quite ill. And she realizes that the country is best for him.'

'I did hear something of that.' He nodded sympathetically. 'He's lucky to have such a good wife. Did they meet when he was in the Army? Was she a nurse?'

'Good gracious, no,' Dorothy burst out. She was on the point of correcting him rather contemptuously when, with a sudden brain wave, she realized that he was pumping her, exactly as he had done before. It was the same too-pleasant manner, the same indirect way of trying to worm things out of her. This, she thought, really is a bit thick, and seeing a chance to get her own back, instead of snubbing him off, she put on a soft look and laughed.

'What's the joke?' he asked.

'Oh, nothing. It's just that you're so wrong. How did you get those ideas in your head?'

'I must be mistaking her for someone else. Who is she, then?'

'Why,' Dorothy improvised, making it as different as she could, 'she's the daughter of an old Scottish friend of Mother's She and David have known each other since they were children.'

'Oh!' he said, looking rather put out.

'Her parents are both very close friends of ours. We all used to take holidays together. At St Andrews. They had a house quite near . . . Banksholme. . . . Of course, that was before she grew up and went away to teach.'

'To teach? Where?'

'At a girls' school in the north of Scotland . . . Aberdeen, to be exact.'

'I see.' He sounded more disappointed than ever. 'What was her name before she married?'

'Elizabeth Castleton,' Dorothy answered, not batting an eyelash. Where it came from she didn't know, probably out of a film she'd seen, but it sounded rather well. 'They're a very old West Lothian family, though not terribly well off. He uncle was a writer to the signet.'

'Castleton,' he repeated, as though trying to place the name, but failing, naturally enough, to do so. He tried it again a couple of times, frowning hard at the nearest lamppost, but without any luck. To Dorothy, pleased at having confounded him, it seemed a good moment to leave. She adjusted the pedals and took a preliminary hop.

'I'm afraid I must be off. Elizabeth is expecting me.'

'Oh, yes.' He came to himself, dropping his cigarette, but forgetting to pick up his charm. 'Nice to have seen you again. So long.'

'Goodbye, Dorothy said politely.

As she swung round the corner of the avenue she glanced back over her shoulder. He was still standing there, with a morose expression, looking more cast down than ever.

Soon she was out in the country, and as she sped along

133

she felt well satisfied with herself. She'd evened the score. For some dirty reason he'd wanted her to disclose Elizabeth's, or rather – she smiled – Cora's humble origin, and she was jolly glad she'd dished him. She sang for a bit, riding with no hands, improvising on the name Castleton, and keeping up a good pace; it wasn't long before she drew near to Sleedon. As she coasted down the hill into the village she caught sight of Cora walking on the pier. A minute later she had bumped her way out over the rough stones. Cora turned just as she reached the end of the breakwater.

'Dorothy! What a nice surprise! Oh, do be careful, dear. It's dangerous on the bike.'

'Not a bit of it,' Dorothy said, but she stopped making circles round Cora and got off – she could see that it made her nervous when she went near the edge. 'I brought a note from Mother.'

'For David?'

'No, for you. Why not? Don't look so startled.' Dorothy produced the letter and handed it over.

Cora took it doubtfully, with an air of misgiving, which was natural enough in view of Mrs Page's previous treatment of her. But when she'd opened and read it her expression changed. Her face shone with pleasure.

'Your mother is very kind, Dorothy. She's asked us to dinner – I mean to lunch – tomorrow.'

'So what? Our grub is nothing to write home about.'

'Oh, it's not that . . . I just appreciate the thought.' She folded the letter carefully, put it back in the envelope, as if it were something to be treasured, then straightened up. 'Let's go up to the cottage.'

'Don't you want to stay and look at the briny?' I know you like to. You're out here a lot.'

'Only when David's working.' She smiled. 'Now I'm going to give you your tea.'

They started off, wheeling the bike between them. The quality in her sister-in-law that attracted Dorothy could be summed up in her own phrase: Cora was decent. She was, Dorrie reflected, quite without pretence, never making out

134

that she was glad to see you when she wasn't, but really being glad, and meaning it. She never tried to be anything but herself, and she would take endless trouble for other people. The way she looked after David, cooking and washing and mending, making a wonderful job of the garden, besides putting up with all his highbrow airs and graces and treating his literary labours as though he were a combination of Shakespeare and Milton, struck Dorrie as the prize example of her decency. But there was something else about her that was hard to explain, a sort of warm softness, a sense of strain that showed through her quiet manner, that seemed to keep her on edge and make her sad. However, at present, she wasn't like that, but really in good spirits.

In the kitchen, while Dorothy set the table, Cora made tea and stacks of hot buttered toast and opened a tin of sardines. Then, in spite of Dorothy's telling her not to bother, she whipped up a batter and made a batch of those drop pancakes that simply melted in one's mouth.

'Cora,' Dorothy said, when her sister-in-law sat down at last with her own cup of tea, 'how come you're so wizard at these pancakes?'

'Well, Dorrie, if you promise to keep a secret, I'll tell you.' She spoke gaily, still lifted up by Mrs Page's invitation, and she looked unusually pretty sitting there, flushed from the stove, and with the air from the open window ruffling her thick hair. 'It's because one summer I did nothing else. I had that kind of job, you see. And I must have made hundreds of pancakes for hungry trippers. Yes, hundreds, I did.'

'Good gracious! I hope you ate some yourself.'

'No, I didn't . . . not much. The smell of the fat gets you down . . . when you're among it all day.'

It sounded so comic Dorothy burst out laughing.

'I wish I'd known that when I was talking to Nosy Parker Nye this afternoon. If I'd told him that Elizabeth Castleton made pancakes for a living I'd really have raised his hair on end.'

Cora, half smiling, did not understand in the least. Dorothy had to explain the joke, so between mouthfuls of tea and pancake she gave a full account of her meeting with Nye. She thought it would amuse Cora no end, but to her surprise she didn't seem to think it funny at all. In fact, all the pleasure went out of her face and she appeared quite disturbed, taking on her anxious look again.

'What could he want,' she asked, 'stopping you like that . . . in the street? He didn't have no right.'

'Oh, that's how they are . . . these reporters. Always trying to take people down a peg. You know what a sweet job he did on me.'

'Yes,' she said slowly, as if thinking things over. 'But that was different. I don't even know the man. And he certainly never knew me.'

'Well, he doesn't know you now.' Dorothy laughed. 'Believe me, Miss Castleton, I really led him down the garden path.'

'Did you? That was smart of you, Dorrie.' She shook her head, as though trying to brush something off and not quite succeeding, for after a pause she said, 'I thought they'd gone . . . all the *Chronicle* lot.'

'They will soon. He told me so himself. In fact, he actually said goodbye.'

'Did he?' She seemed reassured, and her expression lightened. 'We'll be well rid of them. Your father . . . all of us. From the very beginning they've been up to no good. Well . . . it's time for David's tea.' With a glance at the clock on the mantelpiece she rang a little bell on the table beside her, then smiled at Dorothy. 'That's our signal. He's so busy, dear, don't bother him with what we've been talking about.'

A few minutes later David appeared. Dorothy, who had not seen him for some time, was surprised to find him so much thinner, and his manner was more remote than ever, but he seemed pleased to see her. He took a cup of tea from Cora and, standing with one foot on the fender, began to sip it slowly, in the statuesque manner which he usually adopted in the presence of his sister.

'Try one of these pancakes,' Dorothy said. 'They're terribly good.'

'The Greeks,' David smiled, 'never proffered any good things to the Trojans without wishing part for themselves. Give the child another pancake, Cora.'

'No, really,' Dorothy protested, 'I was just thinking of you.'

'Yes, do have one, David,' Cora said. 'You ate so little lunch.' She put a pancake on a plate and offered it to him.

'Go on, David,' Dorothy urged.

'The comedy of a pancake.' He raised his brows amiably. 'To eat or not to eat . . . that is the question. Still . . . thank you my dear.'

In a polite manner he accepted the plate, but placed it on the mantelpiece behind him and, continuing to sip his tea, began to discuss the programme of the forthcoming concert which he criticized at length for failing to include Mahler and Hindemith.

It's always the same, Dorothy thought, watching her brother indignantly. Why must he be so up in the air? It made one feel like kicking him. She noticed, too, that when he finally went off to his room, the pancake remained untouched upon the mantelpiece. Without a word, Cora replaced it with the others, wrapped them in a napkin, and put them in the cupboard. Again she seemed to have something on her mind, but when Dorothy had helped her wash the tea things – a task which Dorrie never dreamed of performing at home – she had succeeded in throwing this off.

'Now,' she said cheerfully, 'we'll pick some flowers for your mother.'

They went into the garden, where Cora cut a great bunch of asters. She wrapped them in brown paper and tied them on to the carrier with string.

'I have enjoyed myself, Cora. Thanks for everything. See you at the concert.'

Dorothy would not for the world have allowed herself the faintest demonstration of emotion and, having thus briefly said goodbye, she coasted down the cliff road and pedalled off for home.

# III

ON SUNDAY AFTERNOON, at five minutes to three, Harold Smith, manager of the *Chronicle*, and his editor, Leonard Nye, left the Red Lion together.

'I don't see why we're doing this,' Smith worried, as they came down the steps of the hotel. 'I still think we oughtn't to go.'

'What!' Leonard said. 'When we're all dressed up!'

His humour was more than usually acid. For the past four days all sorts of confused notions had been hammering at him but never quite ringing the bell, yet in spite of his own uncertainty and Smith's last-minute protests, they were on their way to the concert.

Fred and the car were no longer with them, so they walked, and at the corner of Park Street joined the stream converging on the Town Hall. Presently they were inside. They had timed things well. Already the orchestra was tuning up; the auditorium was full; and in the reserved seats most of the local notables were assembled with their wives, in their best attire. The Wellsby family had turned out in force; Dr Bard was there with Mrs Bard and her aunt, beside Gilmore, the vicar of St Mark's, Paton, the lawyer, Major Seaton, and Harrington of the Machine Company, who was next to Mr and Mrs Frank Holden. Some had come because the proceeds were for a 'worthy cause,' others because they had been obliged to suffer the philanthropic nuisance of buying a tickets, others, again, because these Autumn Philharmonic Concerts were now a recognized social occasion in Hedleston. Yet many were there purely because Henry's quiet persistence year after year had raised the standard of taste in the borough and taught a fair proportion of its honest burghers to appreciate good music.

Nye, however, had no such opinion.

'What crap,' he said to Smith, after surveying the audience. 'They're all trying to look like grand opera was their lifelong passion. I'll give you ten to one they don't know Chopin from Chinese Chopsticks.'

He broke off sharply – at that moment, acknowledged by a murmur of applause, Page came in with his wife and daughter, followed by David and *her*. Nye watched them take their places in the centre of the first row, only a couple of rows ahead and directly in front. At least Smith had done well on the tickets: actually it turned out that he had got them as a favour from Page.

At the last minute Nye had, in fact, almost given way to Smith and backed down. In the past two days he had made some inquiries locally, in addition to his interview with Dorothy, and in his own words, he had got nowhere. He had felt it idiotic to be here, making a show of themselves when everybody knew they were licked, and Smith was obviously of the same opinion – staring at his programme, he looked as uncomfortable as any man could be. But whenever Nye set eyes on *her* again he knew he had done well to come. There was something . . . something about her . . that hit him again, and hard.

At first she was smiling; she seemed shy, talking in low tones with her husband, but apparently looking forward to the event. She had on a dark red dress, not new or fancy, but it did something for her – red was certainly her colour. She wore no lipstick and with her pale face, dark hair and eyes, she looked unusual, and damned attractive. She was turning round to talk to someone when suddenly she saw Leonard. Immediately, her expression changed, stiffened a little, and her smile died. Then she removed her eyes quickly, in a put-out manner. He had stared at her hard; it was natural she should look away; yet he could have sworn she was disconcerted at the sight of him.

The concert began. There was an overture, then a little

stout woman with a bust came on to sing, very beautifully, one of Schumann's *lieder*. Next, another performer, a man, appeared and began a violin solo. Distantly, Nye recognized it as Kreisler's *Schön' Rosmarin*, but he wasn't listening; he was thinking, thinking and studying young Page's wife, quite convinced now that Dorothy, the little rat, had deliberately misled him.

She must have sensed that he was watching her; as the concert went on, she grew more and more restless and uneasy. That didn't surprise him: naturally she would know him as one of the group who had been fighting Page. She wouldn't exactly be prepared to like him. Yet there was more to it than that. Once or twice he felt that she was on the point of turning round again, but she checked herself. At last, David began to notice that she was not attentive to the music. He bent towards her and whispered:

'Are you all right, dear?'

Nye couldn't hear her answer, but apparently she reassured her husband, who glanced at her once or twice, then back at the stage, where the orchestra was tuning up for the main item on the programme, Tschaikowsky's Sixth Symphony in B minor. For the next few minutes nothing happened, then, to discover if Nye was still watching her, very slowly and guardedly, so as not to attract the notice of the others, she turned her head. They stared straight into each other's eyes. Now Leonard was sure that she was scared – yes scared stiff. She went white and gave so perceptible a start that David swung round and saw Nye. He threw him an angry look, bent close to her, and took her arm.

'Is anything the matter?' Nye heard him say.

'No . . . nothing.'

'No one is annoying you?'

'No . . . it's very warm in here . . . I felt a little faint.'

'Would you like to go out for a bit?'

Nye saw that she wanted to leave but was afraid to admit it. She lowered her head, took a handkerchief from her bag and put it to her nose. He could smell the eau-de-cologne. It didn't seem to help. She whispered:

'Perhaps if I had a glass of water.'

'Yes, dear.' David was worried. He half rose from his seat but, finding himself blocked, leaned over to his sister at the end of the row. He had to speak louder; Nye heard him distinctly.

'Go out quickly,' he said, 'and get a glass of water for Cora.'

Cora! The name hit Nye like a bullet. By God, that was it! All afternoon he'd been getting nearer and nearer. And now he was there. Cora Bates . . . Blackpool . . . that summer three years ago.

He didn't wait to observe the restorative effects of the water. He reached under the seat for his hat.

'Let's go,' he said to Smith.

'What . . . already?' Smith was sunk down, with half-closed eyes, in a kind of doze. 'We can't move while they're playing.'

'Never mind. Let's get out of here.'

'But . . .'

'Can't you see it's important?'

He got up and, followed awkwardly by Smith, squeezed his way into the aisle, to the obvious annoyance of their neighbours. Cora, very pale, was acutely conscious of their departure, and Page himself gave them an indignant glance. Not that Nye cared . . . not now.

On the way back to the hotel Nye maintained a complete and almost brooding silence, refusing to answer Smith's persistent questions, but when they arrived he preceded him into the bar, ordered a drink, and began to speak.

At first Smith did not fully grasp the implications of what Nye told him. His mind was slower, grooved in altogether different channels. He looked amazed, incredulous, and somewhat at a loss, yet from Leonard's manner he realized that there was more in this than met the eye.

'I can't believe it,' he said at last, in a startled fashion.

'No?'

Nye wasn't going to argue; the certainty of his conviction

141

made it a waste of breath. The waiter brought his pint. He took a long pull. Beer had never tasted better.

'Are you sure?' Smith said again, all on edge.

'As sure as I'm sitting here. One thing about me, I never forget a face.'

'Then why didn't you recognize her at once?'

'I only saw her for a minute at Blackpool. It was three years ago. And I wasn't interested . . . not then.'

'But . . . only for a minute. You must be making a mistake.'

'Look,' Nye said, 'I'm a reporter. It's my job to remember. I'd just come back from Paris after that Lanson affair. Vernon suggested I go up and do a feature on the Wakes. Blackpool in August isn't exactly my line, but I thought it would give me a rest. It wasn't that bad. I knocked around a lot with a fellow called Haines, who was working for the Mighill group. He was the one on the case. I told you I wasn't interested. But I happened to be picking him up that afternoon . . . just got a glimpse of her. And it registered.'

'She looks the last person in the world . . .'

He was so hard to convince that for an instant he almost shook Leonard, who burst out angrily:

'Couldn't you see how worried she was at the concert? She's got something to hide.'

'I noticed nothing.'

'Then you're blind.'

'They're all such decent people.'

'There's a skeleton in every cupboard, Smith.'

'You think the Pages know?'

'I'm damned sure they don't. That's just where we're on velvet.'

At last Smith knew what was in Nye's mind.

'No, no,' he protested hurriedly. 'I can't see it that way. Even if you're right, we couldn't . . .' He stopped short. The perspiration which afflicted him in moments of stress broke out all over him. He wiped his big, sappy hands on the seams of his trousers. There was a brief silence, during which Nye watched him satirically, then hesitantly he temporized. 'It would be fatal if you were wrong. It . . . it would be criminal libel.'

'Relax, Smith,' Nye said easily. 'Have a drink. I know what you've been up against lately. You need a stiffener.'

'No, Len, I daren't touch it.' He swallowed hard. 'I need all my wits about me. For if you're right it might . . . in a way . . . alter our position.'

'For God's sake!' Nye gave a short, explosive laugh which caused the others in the bar to look at him. 'We were sunk. And now, with a bit of luck, we're home.'

'No, no . . . not so fast. I won't be rushed. First you must do one thing for me. Go out right away to see the girl, in Sleedon. If we can only get an admission, then we'd . . . we'd . . . well, we'd know where we were.'

'Don't worry, I'll see her,' Nye said. 'But first I'm going to get on to head office. I'll tell them nothing . . . they don't have to know a thing about this . . . I'll simply swear to them that if they give us another three weeks grace we'll hand them the *Light* on a platter.'

He finished his drink, got up and started out for the office.

IV

WHEN DAVID AND Cora arrived home that same evening David was still brooding on the strangeness of his wife's behaviour at the concert. Her attack of faintness was in itself unprecedented, and although the hall was stuffy, this explanation had for him the appearance of an excuse. During the performance, with that exaggerated sensibility which was his curse, he had felt Cora's distress was caused by the presence, immediately behind them, of the editor of the *Chronicle*. Now, Cora seemed unusually dull. As she prepared their simple supper he made no reference to the events of the afternoon, yet he hoped that she would do so. Her silence, an unnatural abstraction which indicated that her thoughts were elsewhere, confirmed his suspicion. Presently she said she had a headache and went upstairs. He attempted work for an hour, less for what he might accomplish than to give the aspirin tablets, which he had told her to swallow, the opportunity to take effect. But she was still restless and awake when he came to bed, and presently she put her arms round him and whispered, with a troubled intensity which, in the context of the afternoon's events, heightened his uneasiness:

'You still care for me, don't you, David?'

'You know I care for you.'

She pressed her body hard against his.

'You never show me that you do now.'

He saw that she wanted him to make love to her – he could feel her heart beating like an imprisoned bird – and he wanted her, too, but he would not yield. He said patiently:

'You know what I keep explaining to you, Cora. I have to try and strengthen my will in every way. Besides, by doing without, we get to love each other more.'

'But it isn't right. It's bad for both of us.'

'No, no, it only sublimates and preserves our love.'

'I don't understand . . . I need it . . . tonight especially.'

'Try, Cora, dear. . . . We should have more to offer each other than our bodies. We must raise our physical desire to a spiritual plane.'

'You don't really need me' – she spoke almost with bitterness – 'not any more, you don't.'

'But I do, that's the whole point. Remember when I wouldn't eat those pancakes you made the other day? Afterwards I wanted them more than ever.'

She kept silent for a long time, then gradually withdrew to her side of the bed. At last, in a different tone, she said:

'I've been thinking on what you said about getting a bit stale on your book . . . and wondering if you wouldn't like us to go away for a while. A change might be good for us.'

144

Surprise silenced him for a moment.

'I thought you liked Sleedon.'

'Oh, I do. But it might be nice to have a break.'

'Where would you want to go?'

'Anywhere. You've always said you'd take me to France some time. I'd like to go with you to some quiet little French village . . .'

While his anxiety increased, the strained note in her voice touched him, as did the simplicity, the lack of guile with which she had exposed herself. He saw now, with a sinking dismay, that the encounter with Nye had been serious enough to arose in her the instinct of flight.

He scarcely knew how he answered, except that he left the matter indefinite. She did not persist and, after a while, fell into a restless sleep. Listening to her breathing in the darkness, he began to seek for the cause of her distress and to torment himself by assuming it the worst. Obviously, before he met her, she had known Nye. But in what capacity? Had he been her employer, her associate, her friend? A stab of pain ran through his nerves. Of all the men he would have wished her not to know, this fellow was the prime example. From the first glance he had felt an instinctive antipathy towards him, not only because of his hostility towards the *Light*, but because of something in the man himself. Dwelling upon this, David was conscious of a tightness binding his forehead. He well knew the danger of such a train of thought and tried to close his mind to it, as he had been taught at the clinic. But peaceful, impersonal images would not focus on the screen of his sight, so there he lay, rigidly immobilized, harassed by doubt, suspicion, jealousy, and, above all, by fear for himself, that recurrent fear which drove him to extremes of self-denial in the hope of hardening himself against it, and which, alternating with brief periods of exaltation, made up the persistent cycle of his psychosis.

Just over two years ago he had suffered what was politely termed a nervous breakdown. It had begun as a general lassitude, a strange torpor of the mind, and was succeeded by a depression of frightful intensity. In this darkness of the spirit he became the prey of his fear, not only that he might go out of his senses, but that he had been marked as the victim of some dreadful calamity. As this developed, it shaped into a complex of persecution and, since he was still at home, he took to concealing his service revolver beneath his pillow, to be prepared for the materialization of his unknown enemy.

At first he had been treated by Dr Bard, then he was removed to a private institution on the cliffs at Scarborough. Here a total blank supervened, a period of which he recollected absolutely nothing. They must have put him to basket-making, which he accomplished in a state of stupor. He remembered his surprise when, six weeks later, as the opacity began to lift, he discovered that he had made with his own hands more than two dozen wicker trugs, all of a close and intricate design, something he could never have accomplished in his normal state.

The institution doctor, Evans, a plump, breathless little man, with a jolly, rather worldly air, told him, with a cheerful smile, that he was breaking through. 'You're out of the woods, my boy, and into the underbrush.' Yet if he had come that far, it seemed that he could go no further: he still slept badly, was still frightened, silently depressed, withdrawn from life.

At this point Evans, in an effort to restore his confidence, gave him permission to leave the institution ground for an hour every evening, advising him to stroll on the promenade and mingle with the people there. David had no wish to go, but, since he liked the doctor and had indeed acquired a sort of automatic obedience to him, he went – not to the crowded esplanade, from which he shrank instinctively, but to the comparative solitude of the old fishing harbour, where he sat watching the slow, slaty surge and recession of the sea.

One evening he heard someone address him – the first person unconnected with his illness who had spoken to him for three months. He raised his head and saw a girl, tall, rather poorly dressed, very pale, and ridiculously thin, staring down at him with big hazel-dark eyes. Something in her expression, a look of settled sadness, made him sense instinctively a hopelessness equal to, if not greater than, his own. He made some reply, trite enough, but such as it was, enough to induce her to sit down on the bench. The sense of her presence, the slight contact of her thin arm under the cheap cotton of her blouse sent a faint stir through him. He asked her nothing about herself. Nor had she any of that tactless curiosity that might have been expected from a chance acquaintance. They simply accepted each other without question, as might two lost souls meeting in some lonely corridor of the damned. They talked very little and only of the most banal things, but there was comfort in what was said. When it was time for him to leave he hesitated, tongue-tied, then something broke through: he asked her to meet him in the same place the following evening.

They met and continued to meet; soon they were together every evening, also on Wednesday afternoon when she had her weekly half holiday. He began to feel a lifting of the darkness and to see the world with altered vision. Under the unspoken endearment of her clasping fingers, his senses reawakened. Objects for so long curiously remote drew near, colour reappeared, he felt the sun again, the dew on the grass, the sweetness of summer rain. It was as though life had been restored.

Dr Evans kept watching his progress with a genial knowingness that was hard to bear. He had been told of these meetings with Cora: in the early days of David's freedom he had instructed an attendant to follow him, fearing that he might 'do something stupid' – a cheerful euphemism which he applied to suicide – that dark cloud that had long hung over young Page's mind. But David had no need of this indirect encourgement to amuse himself – indeed, he resented it. In his own strange way, he was in love with Cora. He had in regard to her no illusions, seeing her as she was, with all the limitations of upbringing, her lapses of grammar, simplicities, and undeveloped mind. And yet something within him found in these apparent drawbacks the

147

very qualities which put him at ease in her society, freed him of his complicated tensions and, above all, of those doubts, embarrassments, and personal misgivings which had previously afflicted him when he thought of other women. She restored his confidence with her tenderness, built him up again with her devotion, so that, still fearful of the future, he could say to himself, 'Here is someone who will help me.' A fortnight before he was due to return to Hedleston they were married at the Scarborough Registry Office.

All this flickered through David's mind with a new intensity as he lay awake, vainly trying to find in their beginnings some clue to Cora's present behaviour. Towards morning he had perhaps an hour of sleep. He awoke to find that Cora had gone downstairs. When he joined her they had their coffee and toast in the kitchen alcove, and, although to outward appearance she was as usual, he knew her brightness was unnatural. Their conversation somehow seemed forced, and neither made any reference to her remarks of the previous evening.

After breakfast he could not bring himself to sit at his desk. When he told Cora he would take a walk to the breakwater, he could have sworn she looked relieved. The more he thought of it, as he tramped down the cliff road, the more he became tormented by the certainty that for some reason she had wanted him out of the house. An impulse took hold of him to turn back and have the matter out with her. But no, he could not do it. She must speak first, must open her heart to him. And why . . . why did she not do so?

The circuit of the breakwater became a dragging penance. Consumed by a restive impatience to know what was happening at the cottage, he still would not allow himself to hurry. At the harbour end he stopped, according to custom, to exchange a word with Martha Dale, the old woman who kept the news stall opposite the store. At last he turned back, began to walk up the hill. Then at a bend of the road, almost at his own gate, with a sudden sickness of heart he drew up short, his worst suspicion confirmed.

# V

THAT SAME MONDAY morning Nye, having breakfasted, and
run through his mail, telephoned the Victoria Garage for a
drive-it-yourself car. Then, just after nine o'clock, he took
off for Sleedon. He had purposely waited overnight to give
Cora time for meditation, which he thought would help to
make her more amenable. Besides, there was no need for
undue haste; he had managed to convince the head office that
something of real importance was about to break and, as
he'd assured Smith over a second cup of coffee, the thing was
as good as in the bag.

It was a fine autumn day, the sun already burning off the
early mist and gilding the groves of beeches on the Eldon
hills. Above the dunes, sand martins were darting and
wheeling, with shrill, piping cries. Outside Sleedon Nye
stopped the car and parked it off the road by a deserted
barn – he saw the need for discretion, up to a point – then
he walked into the village. It seemed to him no more than
a ragged, run-down little dump that stank of fish and rotten
seaweed, with a few blistered old tubs drawn up on the beach.
There was a stone pier with a broken-roofed kiosk selling
papers, Kodak films, and confectionery, but no promenade
or bandstand, and only one shop; in fact, nothing to look at
but the sea. Not much like Blackpool, he told himself, not by
a long chalk.

The house was easy to find – it wasn't much either – surely
old Page, as the big-hearted philanthropist, might have done
better for his son. Leonard gave it the once-over, then went
up the garden path and rang the bell. He felt himself in top
form. He had plenty of bravado and, in his own phrase,
didn't give a damn for anybody – not once in the past ten

years had he had an assignment that made him bat an eyelash. As there was no answer he rang the bell again – it was of the homely pull-and-chance-it variety. Then he heard the sound of footsteps. The door opened. It was Cora.

'Good morning.' He gave her a bright smile. 'Mrs Page, I believe. I'm Leonard Nye, representing the *Daily Chronicle*. I wonder if you could spare me a few moments.'

At the sight of him her face did not greatly change. He could tell that she was frightened, but she had been expecting his visit and had braced herself to meet it.

'What do you want?'

He had his patter ready; it went with the smile.

'I understand your husband's writing a book. That's always a matter of public interest. I'd be glad of a few details.'

'My husband is out at present.'

'Then I'm sure you will oblige me, Mrs Page.' He whipped out his notebook, the eager-beaver touch. 'Now, what is the title of the proposed work?'

'You must ask my husband,' she said. 'Anyhow, we want none of your sort here,' and she pushed the door shut.

At least she would have shut it if Nye's shoe had not been in the jamb – he was too old a hand at the game to be caught napping. As if nothing had happened, he turned on the charm, affecting a playful air.

'At least, Mrs Page,' he said, 'tell me something about yourself. You are recently married, I believe?'

She did not answer.

'And before your marriage you were, I understand, a Miss Cora Bates.'

Her face was drained of colour now and her dark eyes had a hard look. Something in that look told him how much she'd been through in the past.

'You know a lot, don't you?'

'Well' – he smiled – 'it's our job to know a few things. You were in Blackpool, weren't you, in August three years ago?'

'What if I was? You ain't got no hold on me.'

'You admit it.'

'No, I don't; it's a lie. I was never near Blackpool, I wasn't.'

'Strange.' Nye shook his head as if puzzled; he was beginning to enjoy himself. 'I'd have sworn you were one of the hostesses at the Alhambra Palais de Dance.'

'You mean one of these mis'rable girls what gets pushed about by the likes of you at a tanner a time?'

'That's it,' Leonard said, as though he were pleased. 'You put it rather well.'

'You was never in the Palley at Blackpool. Not on your life, you wasn't.' Cora, since her marriage, had begun to speak much better, but now in her anguish she reverted to the language and the accents of her youth.

'I'm not a dancing man,' Nye said. 'I just happened to hear you were there.'

'Who told you?'

'A friend.'

'Does a rat like you have friends?'

'You're right.' Leonard laughed, as if she had paid him a compliment. 'I'm a pretty low type. Nobody loves me. This was more of a professional acquaintance. By the name of Haines. Does that mean anything to you?'

'No, it doesn't. It don't mean a thing.'

'Oh, well, no matter,' Leonard said carelessly. 'It's just that I happened to be with him in court when the judge sentenced you.'

He had saved the punch line for the last. It knocked her cold. All the time she had been hoping, hoping that he knew just a little, not everything. Now all the fight went out of her. She leaned against the door post, her eyes big and dark, darker than ever in her white face, which seemed all at once to have got smaller.

'Why can't you leave us alone?' she said at last, so low he could scarcely hear her. 'I have my feelings, haven't I, the same as anybody else? Why d'you have to come and poke into people's lives?'

'I'm a reporter, dearie.'

'And that means you have the right to show up all human

151

weakness, mis'ry, and suffering? Oh, you're great, you lot, on morals, but what about your own?'

'Now, Cora, there's no harm done . . . not yet.'

'I'm happy, for the first time in my life . . . here . . . with a husband to look after . . .'

'Then he's a lucky man. I don't mind telling you I envy him.' He gave her a look, but she seemed not to take it up. She didn't speak for a long time, then, in a low, indistinct voice, looking at him fixedly, she said:

'What do you want?'

Just for a second Nye felt tempted. She was a damned fetching piece, the house was empty, and the fact that she loathed him made it interesting. But no, he wasn't taking chances – this wasn't pleasure, but business, and important business, too.

'We only want your help, in a manner of speaking, with old man Page,' he said, very easy. 'Just own up when the time comes and that'll be enough.'

Very slowly she said:

'You wouldn't have the face to tell on me, not you.'

'Come now, Cora. It may amount to nothing, in the long run. If we keep our heads, nobody's going to get hurt too badly.'

'I see,' she said, in an indescribable tone. 'You're real good, you are . . . real good.'

There was a long pause, then with her eyes lowered she turned away and slowly shut the door. This time Nye made no effort to stop her. He stood for a moment, almost expecting her to reopen it, but as she did not, he put his notebook in his pocket and went out through the gate. He hadn't taken a dozen paces down the road when he ran straight into young Page. Instinctively David retreated a step, staring at Nye, with his head thrown back.

'What are you doing here?' He found his voice at last.

'Taking a walk,' Nye answered coolly.

'You've been in my house.'

'I wish I had. But it's all been in the open. Never mind. The doctor said sea air was good for me.'

152

'Now look here' – David's cheek had begun to twitch – 'I don't know what you're up to, but I won't have you hanging around.'

'It's a free country.'

'You're not free to annoy my wife.'

'Who annoyed her?'

'You did at the concert yesterday.'

'Good grief,' Nye said, 'I never even spoke a word to her.'

'I'm not going to bandy words with you, sir.' David's voice went up two octaves; his thin figure, pathetic in the buff corduroys, broken-down shoes, and turtle-neck sweater, was shaking all over. 'I merely tell you that if you interfere with my wife I'll . . . I'll break your neck.'

'Look out for your own neck, chum,' Nye told him, then, with a gesture of contempt, he walked away. There was no point in taking the situation further: Leonard did not profess to be a virtuoso of the offensive arts and there was just the chance that in his worked-up state, this young fool might be dangerous.

## VI

DAVID'S HEART KEPT on beating like a hammer as he stood there, overcome, unable to move, watching Nye descend the dusty cliff road.

This sudden meeting had stunned him; Nye had been to the house and Cora had expected him. Beyond that, he could not think clearly; his mind was in a ferment. Awareness that in the face of the other's brash insolence and callous flippancy he had given a poor account of himself – although physically there was no violence he would not have done him – intensified his bitterness and anger.

But at least part of the mystery was solved: Cora and

Nye had known each other in the past, and their association must necessarily have been close. How otherwise explain the extent of Cora's emotion, the promptness with which an assignation had been made, Nye's smug assertiveness towards him? He felt all his body tighten with a cold, sick jealousy. Why did she not take him into her confidence? Her unnatural silence, this pitiable pretence that everything was as it should be dismayed him most of all. Someone less morbidly sensitive would, he knew, have demanded an explanation. But he was not shaped in that normal mould, and the inner voice, which he often heard, forbade it. If Cora did not wish to speak, he would not force her to do so. He must give no sign of having met Nye, must accept and echo her pretence, until she, of her own free will, opened her heart to him. With this intention, he went slowly towards the house.

She was seated by the window that overlooked the garden, gazing into the distance, her features sharpened by the hard light. At first she did not see him, then she started slightly and, with a quick intake of breath, collected herself and got up.

'You had a good walk.' Although her back was towards the light he saw that her eyes were swollen. 'Are you going to work now?'

'I think I shall.'

There was a silence. As though excusing her inactivity, she said:

'I've got nothing done this morning, not a thing.'

'You weren't in the garden?'

'No. At least, not that long.'

Another pause. She averted her eyes.

'I'm even behind with your lunch. So now I shall have to run down to the store.'

'Something you've forgotten?'

'Yes.'

'Let me get it for you.'

'No, no . . . I'd like a breath of air. I shan't be no more than a minute.'

He noticed that in going out she took her purse from the

154

drawer of the Welsh dresser. Since they had a monthly account at the store he was at once aware that she had gone to telephone. The transparency of her action, betraying such ineptitude in deceit, heightened his distress.

He began to pace up and down the room, realizing, for the first time in many months, how completely he depended upon Cora. With his patronizing attitudes and studied indifference he had fallen into the habit of taking her for granted. Now the threat of losing her reawakened all his first feeling for her, with redoubled intensity. She was his . . . his . . . no one must come between them. Yet he must be calm, both for Cora's sake and for his own. Hadn't Dr Evans warned him against any emotional crisis, against allowing a sense of grievance to get hold of him? But how could he suppress his bitterness against Nye? A hard throbbing went through David's head, turned him so giddy that for a moment he had to shut his eyes and grip the edge of the table for support. Striving for control, he went upstairs to the attic, from force of habit put on a record. But immediately he had to switch it off. Today there was no comfort in his favourite Berlioz, only an incitement to greater agitation. He could not even look at the manuscript on his desk. His book, upon which he had built such hopes, now seemed utterly without importance.

He sat down and listened for Cora's return. After what seemed an interminable time the front door opened, the sound of her footsteps came up to him from the hall. Then she went into the kitchen and from time to time he heard her movements as she prepared lunch. Ordinarily she rang the little hand bell punctually at half past twelve, but today she was late and did not summon him till past one o'clock.

Downstairs, he saw that she had freshened her face; her eyes were no longer swollen, but her pallor was more marked – she looked ill. Yet with a sort of desperate persistence she still strove for a note of animation, almost of propitiation, false and quite unlike her. At first her remarks were inconsequential, then, not very cleverly, she brought the conversation to the subject she had raised last night.

155

'You must have thought me silly, David . . . when I spoke of us going away.'

'Not at all.' He had to reply on the same level of pretence. 'It's very natural to want a change.'

'But you couldn't because of your book?'

'The book isn't everything. If you really wished it, I suppose we could go.'

'Do you mean it?' Before he could answer she went on, with a little rush. 'I was reading in a magazine the other day about a man who went out to California and grew oranges. The climate was wonderful, warm and sunny. He made a lot of money, too. Couldn't we do something like that, David?'

'I know nothing about growing oranges.'

'We could learn. I'd work like . . . anything. It might be even better for your health than Sleedon.'

The situation would have been farcical had it not been so pitiful. Although the strain was telling upon David, he tried to keep it within bounds.

'I thought you wanted to see France.'

'That was just for a holiday.'

'And this would be for good?'

She nodded, and was about to speak, when a sudden spasm prevented her. All along, in the effort to be natural, she had been trying to force down some food. Now her stomach revolted; she choked in a fit of nausea, coughed, reached for her glass of water, and burst into tears.

He went over to her. All his resistance broke down. He knew he should not put the question, but he could hold it back no longer.

'For God's sake, Cora, what is the matter?'

What he had dreaded happened: she refused to tell him.

'Nothing. Nothing's the matter.'

'There must be. You're so upset.'

'No, no.' Somehow she managed to stop crying. 'It's just one of these days when everything goes wrong.'

He looked down at her rigidly.

156

'It's more than that; someone is annoying you . . . this fellow Nye.'

'No, no. It's nothing, nothing. I don't know him. I never knew him. He's nothing to me, less than nothing . . .'

'Then why did he come here this morning?'

'He came to ask about your book.' She was almost hysterical. 'I swear to you, David . . . that's the truth. Before today I never even spoke to him in my whole life.'

By this time David was himself in such a state he could barely speak.

'If he's trying to hurt you he'd better look out. I'll go and have it out with him.'

'No, no . . . there's no cause for you to go. We shan't ever see him again.'

'There must be something I can do.'

She took both his arms and pressed them hard. He felt her body trembling. His own nerves were at breaking point.

'Just stay with me, David. And don't let nothing come between us. And it won't either . . . you'll see . . . you'll see.'

## VII

MEANWHILE NYE HAD made his way back to Hedleston. He went slowly, for he had some adjustments to his plans to think over and the gentle flow of air occasioned by the movement of the car was conducive to concentration. His interview with Cora, the fearful agitation and wretchedness he had caused her, gave him not the slightest concern. He had long ago learned the realities of the business and could dishonour himself daily without a qualm.

The journey occupied just under an hour, and by half past eleven he had turned in the car at the garage and was back at the Lion. He found Smith in the deserted lounge, not sitting in his usual corner, but marching up and down by the window. Nye felt rather well pleased with himself and the way things were working out, but it was not his style to show any feeling. He merely said:

'Right. It's exactly as I told you. She's the one.'

'Yes . . . yes,' Smith said, staring straight through Nye as if he were thinking about something else.

'What's the trouble? I tell you Cora is our bird.'

'I know. She telephoned me five minutes ago.'

Nye sat down and looked at him. Why the hell had she done that? Smith was restless and disturbed, couldn't stand still, kept on with his pacing, his big hands bunched in his side pockets.

'She told her husband she had to go shopping and ran to the village phone booth. She was so upset I could scarcely make her out. You must have used her very hard.'

'Smith,' Leonard said, 'I was gentle as a lamb.'

'It's a dirty business.' He shook his head, like a retriever shaking off water. 'A nasty, dirty business. I tell you straight I'm having nothing to do with it.'

'You're crazy,' Nye said. 'We have them exactly where we want them.'

'No. I won't do it. I'm an honest man. At least, I've always lived decent . . . tried to, anyhow.'

'Don't talk such melodramatic crap. You'd think you were back in the old Lyceum. We're only offering a *quid pro quo*. We're not going to pressure Page; the choice is up to him. In any case, who cares?'

'I tell you I won't.'

Leonard had never seen him so jittery; he had known for some weeks that his nerve was going and now it seemed gone. He thought: When a slob like Smith cracks up, it shows a mile wide. But he could handle him.

'All right,' he said. 'She begged you to leave her alone. Let's be a couple of gentle Jesuses and do it, so help me God, amen.'

'Don't take the Lord's name in vain,' Smith interrupted,

almost with a shout. 'I won't have it. You're . . . you're an irreligious dog, Nye.'

'We'll pack our bags,' Leonard went on affably, taking no notice, 'and go back to Somerville. I'll resign. You'll be fired . . . thrown out, right on your fat behind . . . for keeps. After this botch – all the money you've lost up here – you'll never get another job. And I mean never. Your name'll stink all over Fleet Street. You'll be finished.'

Smith stopped his pacing and sat down on the edge of a chair. Leaning forward and biting at his thumb nail, he was trying not to look at Nye. His collar stud had come undone at the back and the collar itself had worked up his neck. At last, he said:

'Greeley would never go along with a thing like this. He's a strict man. He sticks to the law.'

'And so will we . . . we won't put a foot wrong. Anyhow, Greeley's on holiday, digging up ruins. He always goes to Italy this time of year. And Challoner, who looks out for him, is a pushover. When Greeley comes back it'll all be tied up. He'll be delighted.'

'But, Leonard,' Smith protested, 'even if we did . . . what you suggest . . . and persuaded Page to sell, how do we pay him? Somerville is really hard up . . . he's taken a lot of punishment from Mighill lately. After all the money that I've – I mean, that we've – had to spend here, he's not in a position to produce further capital. He'd never do it.'

'What a babe you are, Harold.' Nye smiled coolly but in a companionable manner. 'Don't you see that an outright sale is off the menu now, period? And not only for the reason you mention. A wholesale appropriation of the *Light* would set the entire town against us all over again. No, no, what we'll propose is a friendly amalgamation on a fifty-fifty basis. We've made up our differences; each paper will contribute its goodwill and plant – don't forget we still have the printing hall – Page will retire, and be paid off with a percentage of the net receipts every year. We don't put out a penny of capital.'

As he stared at his companion, carried away by this latest ingenuity, Smith's actuarial eye glistened.

'Why . . . that way we'd be fair enough . . . yet make a most advantageous deal. We'd allow for equal amortization, then calculate Page's percentage on a present-day basis. When the atomic plant comes in, sales will go up . . . No, no' – he recoiled sharply – 'I can't see myself doing it.'

There was a pause. Nye lit a cigarette, making no attempt to break the silence, then, almost pensively, he said:

'I thought you were ambitious, Harold . . . that you wanted to make a position for yourself, on your own home ground.'

Smith didn't answer, he swallowed several times. Nye went on persuasively.

'And haven't you family reasons for wanting to succeed . . . your wife . . . ?'

'Yes, yes . . . there's Minnie. I won't disguise it from you. I'd do a lot to get her back. But this . . .' He was still biting his nail, down to the quick. 'It still doesn't sound right to me.'

Nye saw that he was weakening. He hardened his tone.

'Oh, for Christ's sake, be a realist. What is this game anyway but a bloody cut-throat affair. Mighill's at Somerville's throat. Jotham's at Mighill's. And Vernon would give his eye-teeth to get his knife in either of them. It's kill or be killed. You can't blame yourself. You offered Page a damn sight more than his paper was worth. He should have taken it. But no, he had to fight us. And he mucked us up properly. And now when I make you a present of a certainty for turning the tables on him, you sit there moping like a sick cow. Have some guts, man. I tell you straight, if you pass up this chance you'll regret it all your life.'

Smith's eye slid away, then came back to Nye again. He wet his lip, hesitated, then said:

'This thing has got me down, Len. I could do with a drink. Do you think it would hurt me?'

Stretching out casually, Nye pressed the button on the wall beside him. The waiter brought two double whiskies.

Smith took his, sipped it at first, then drank it in a quick gulp – like he'd just crossed the Sahara, thought Nye.

'I needed that.' He sighed. 'I've not been quite myself lately. And now this . . . so hard to decide . . . it's bowled me over.'

'Have another.'

'Later . . . well, if you insist.'

Nye told the waiter the same again. He brought them.

'You know, Len,' Smith reflected, in a tone that had begun to mellow, 'the trouble with me is that at heart I'm still religious. I taught Sunday school all the years I was in Australia. My poor mother brought me up very strict. As a boy I was well grounded. Before I was eleven years old I could recite the whole of the Thirteenth Chapter of First Corinthians. But when I take another look at the situation. I see it from a better angle. We needn't be too rough. We'll be diplomatic. Page really ought to retire – he's a sick man.'

'You'll be doing him a good turn.'

'As for Cora . . .' He broke off.

'Nothing,' Nye told him quickly. 'Nobody'll know a thing outside the family. The jerk loves her. He'll forgive and forget.'

'Get me another drink. The way you put it, I can't see we have any alternative. It's justifiable . . . that's the word. What d'you suggest as our first move? Phone Page?'

'No. Send a letter by hand. Ask for an appointment.'

Smith thought for a minute, stroking his chin with the back of his hand.

'One thing . . . important. We'll need your friend Haines. You better phone him at once.'

That, Nye told himself, is a smart one for a man, religious at heart, who could formerly recite the Thirteenth Chapter of Corinthians.

'I'd already thought of it,' he said. 'He's still with Mighill. But first the letter.'

He waited while Smith finished his drink, then they got up and went into the waiting room.

# VIII

AT HALF-PAST TWO that afternoon Henry Page left the Northern Counties Club and set out at an easy pace for his office. He had just lunched with Wellsby, who had wanted to discuss details of the coming testimonial dinner now fixed for September 25th. It had been a cheerful meeting and Henry, gently stimulated by the excellent Chablis which his host had insisted upon, was in the best of spirits. He smiled to himself, reflecting on the adroit manner in which Wellsby had announced his Parliamentary intentions – well, Sir Archie would not make a bad candidate; at least as a solid Northumbrian he would, in the local idiom, stick up for the North.

Turning the corner at Park Street, Henry took the shortcut through Rimmer's Lane. As he did so, his eye was caught by a piece of china in the window of Bisset's second-hand shop. He drew up, recognizing it at once as a rare example of his favourite Staffordshire, a beautiful salt-glaze Pecton shell, white in colour and ornamented with size gilding. It was early, too – he could tell at a glance – almost certainly by John Elers, the senior of the Elers brothers who settled in Burslem in 1690 – and the price on the ticket was only five pounds ten.

What a find! And one which might mark the start of a new collection to replace the prized bits and pieces he had sacrificed at the Tynecastle Auction Mart. Of course, Henry could not resist it. He went in, and after some genial bargaining with Bisset, secured it for five guineas. Back in the office, he unwrapped the treasure and was admiring it on his desk when Moffatt came in, bringing a note which she said had just been delivered by hand. She submitted, with an air of humouring him, while Henry explained the design and markings, even put a few amiable questions that indicated a qualified improvement in her opinion of him – although no doubt, in her own mind, she was convinced he had survived only by the merest fluke. Then she left for her own room.

Absently fingering the lovely shell, encouraged by the processes of digestion, Henry fell into a pleasant reverie. After weeks of strain and almost insupportable anxiety, his victory in the struggle forced upon him was an unimaginable relief. A great moral principle had been upheld; his paper could now continue unmolested, stronger, indeed, and more secure than before. At home, too, the others had shared in the general upsurge. Dorothy seemed to show a glimmer of regard for him, even casual signs of respect. And he had hopes that his relations with Alice might be entering a more equable phase. When he saw how much she looked forward to her long-anticipated reception on Thursday and to the public dinner and the testimonial he had consented to accept next week, he blamed himself for his past indifference to this aspect of her life. The naïveté with which she pursued such activities was part of her nature; he had his own peculiarities, why should not he indulge hers? By so doing he might at least promote in her an answering tolerance towards Cora. If only he could create an enduring sense of family unity, his satisfaction would be complete.

At this point he recollected the letter Moffatt had brought in. He took it up, opened it and read it. Then, after a moment with an exclamation of distaste, he tore the sheet up and threw the pieces in the wastepaper basket.

Once in a while the *Light* was the target of an abusive, scurrilous, or threatening letter, almost invariably anonymous. This was not anonymous – it was signed by Harold Smith – yet Henry could not have believed him capable of so stupid or so spiteful a parting shot.

Dismissing the thing as beneath contempt, he got down to work – for the next day's issue he had planned an economic feature on the proposed European Agreement, which, in the

163

light of the recent conferences in Paris, seemed full of promise. But his thoughts would not flow; they kept winging back to this extraordinary letter which, the longer he dwelt upon it, became more inexplicable. He was alone in the office. Almost against his will he bent down, took the torn scraps from the basket, and with some difficulty fitted them together. The very form of the repieced sheet gave to it an air that was vaguely sinister.

*My dear Mr Page,*

*There has come to our knowledge something of very considerable moment which may seriously affect you. In your own interests I advise you to give my colleague and myself an appointment at your earliest convenience so that we may discuss it with you. The matter is urgent and important.*

*Believe me, with all regard,*
*Yours very faithfully,*
*Harold Smith.*

Henry drew a sharp breath. What on earth were they driving at? The vagueness of the phrasing, which suggested careful composition, was in itself enough to create uncertainty and alarm. A sense of insult burned in Henry. Why was the cliché 'something of moment' used – as though hinting at future disclosures of a damaging nature? And didn't these three ambiguous words 'I advise you,' conceal the implication of a threat? But no, he couldn't permit himself to lapse into this train of conjecture. He knew that Smith and his associate were on the point of leaving Hedleston. The letter was no more than a final thrust and, like the last sting of a crushed wasp, was charged with venom. He decided firmly to ignore it, crumpled the scraps and threw them back into the basket.

For the next hour he concentrated well. Then Malcolm Maitland came bustling in to say goodbye. He was having a couple of days off to go down to Nottingham for the Autumn Horse Fair, hoping to buy a young trotter there.

'I've had my eye on a good one for some time,' he told Henry. 'A smart little mare by Spitfire out of Arabian Night. She's a beauty.'

Ever since the *Light* had come out on top he'd been in unusually good form, and he added with a chuckle:

'Now we're solvent again, I feel I can afford it.'

More than ever Henry had become attached to Maitland. Over the past year he had drawn largely upon his knowledge, experience, and accumulated information, as well as on his sincere and vigorous character. Privately, he had often sought his advice, and with the thought of the letter still at the back of his mind, he had a momentary impulse to speak of it to him. But Maitland was, for once, full of his own affairs and eager to be off. Henry had not the heart to impose himself upon him; he decided to let him go.

'Have a good time, then, Malcolm.' He held out his hand, adding feelingly, 'You know how I'll miss you.'

Page's sentimentality bothered Maitland – it was the difference between the two men – and he would no more have dreamed of displaying his own deep regard for Henry than he would of embracing his horse.

'I'll be back,' he said dryly, his lips puckered. Then a smile illuminated his ugly face. 'Keep the presses buzzing while I'm away.'

By four o'clock the article was finished and Hadley – plump, timidly smiling, running as usual about his business – came in with the photographs that were to go with it: some interesting views of new Continental housing developments, airports, bridges, and modern factories. After he had gone, Henry was about to ring for Moffatt when he heard a quiet tap on the door.

'Come in,' he called.

Glancing up, with a queer sense of something unexpected, he saw Cora standing there.

'Am I disturbing you?'

She was wearing a new brown dress he had not seen before and the string of pearls he had given her for Christmas two years ago. He had never known her to look prettier; her eyes were especially brilliant. She went on, a trifle hurriedly, as though excusing herself.

'I had an errand in the town . . . for David, it was . . . and I couldn't think to go home without looking in. But if you're busy, I'll just be off.'

'Don't you dare. Come in and give me your news.'

Although she came seldom to the office, held back by her natural diffidence, her visits always lightened the day for Henry. Now, especially, he was glad to see her, so bright and with such unusual vivacity.

'How are you?' he asked.

'Oh, me . . . I'm never anything but well.'

'You've quite got over your faintness at the concert?'

'It was nothing. I'm not used to crowds any more. And the hall was warm.' There was a pause, then she said, 'The question is . . . how are you?'

'Pretty spry, considering.'

'When did you see the doctor last?'

'A week or so ago . . . I really forget. As a rule, I go once a month.'

'You still have to take your little pills?'

'Well, yes . . . they're a great help.'

As though deploring his reliance upon the nitroglycerine tablets, she shook her head, not at all in her ordinary manner, but like a bad actress trying to simulate regret. Then she came over to the arm of his chair. Her eyes, unusually large, seemed to beg his consideration.

'David and I had a long talk about you last night.'

'Yes?' he said indulgently, gazing up at her. The dark brown dress, matching her eyes, set off the soft texture of her cheek, which now seemed slightly flushed. Under her bright affection he felt an odd sense of strain as she said, with a little rush:

'You know how fond of you we are . . . and we're both ever so worried. We think you've been doing too much, far more than you didn't ought to. In fact, we think that for your own sake' – she drew a quick breath – 'you should have a long rest.'

'How long?' He smiled.

'Well' – again that pained and nervous pause – 'that you should retire.'

Sheer surprise silenced him. Then he said:

'My dear . . . at this late stage . . . are you advising me to give up the paper?'

'It would mean that, I suppose.'

'But I have just put up the fight of my life to keep it.'

'Yes, you've won. That's just it. You've proved yourself. You didn't give in. It was wonderful. And now you're in a position to take advantage. They'd give you ever so much more money now . . . ever so.' She took his hand with a caressing smile that ended prematurely in a slight trembling of the lips. 'Do give over . . . it really would be best . . . for the sake of your health . . . and everything.'

The hidden urgency in her voice, even more than the complete unexpectedness of her appeal, suddenly caused Henry a distinct misgiving. Could some connection exist between her visit and Smith's letter? He looked away, worried. He could not bring himself to speak of the letter, nor would he think ill of Cora, yet he had to put this question:

'You're not in any sort of trouble, are you?'

She started – it might have been from surprise.

'No . . . not me, I'm not.'

'If so, I wish you'd tell me.'

'Of course I'd tell you. But I'm not . . . not me.' A frightened smile came to her lips. 'How could I be?'

'That's all right, then,' Henry said stiffly. 'As for my giving up, I mean to take a holiday fairly soon. And I dare say I shall retire one of these days and David will take over. But it won't be for quite a while.'

There was a constrained silence. The situation was saved for both of them by Moffatt, who, according to her usual routine, brought in the five o'clock mail. Although she apparently found little to admire in her own sex, from the beginning she had been predisposed in Cora's favour. She greeted her warmly and they talked for a few minutes, then Cora said that she must go.

Henry's mood was still disturbed as he came back from seeing her to the door, where, in a few hurried words, she pressed him to reconsider what she had said to him. Her last glance, charged with silent pleading, subdued, pitiful almost, so troubled him that he could not settle to the work in hand. Outside in the street they were relaying the pavement. The noise of the pneumatic drill went through his head, preventing all his efforts to reason things out. At half past five he left the office, hoping to find peace for reflection at home.

But here, immediately he passed through the front door, Alice met him in the hall.

'How clever of you, Henry, to be so early!' she exclaimed. 'You are just the man I want – just in time, before the light goes.'

She was choosing a new distemper for the spare bedroom and, distrustful of the local painter, proposed to create the colour scheme herself. Unable to resist, Henry permitted her to lead him upstairs, where for the next three-quarters of an hour, wearing a blue overall with a raffish air, she mixed and demonstrated a range of colours upon which he was called to offer comment. In the end, after much discussion and ingenuous indecision, having traversed the full circle, she decided on the first shade she had shown him.

Yet this interlude, which might well have aggravated Henry's mood, produced instead the opposite effect. In his wife's preoccupation with the colour of a room there was something familiar and reassuring which soothed him, made his disquiet of the afternoon seem fanciful. Why must he always seek out trouble? Smith was just trying to make a nuisance of himself; Cora had come because she and David were concerned for his health. Between these two events there could be no connection whatsoever.

Next morning at the office everything seemed normal – no defamatory messages, no further communication from Smith. Henry was congratulating himself that his attitude in ignoring the letter had proved effective when, at eleven o'clock, another note, more peremptory than before, was delivered to him.

> *If we do not hear from you within twenty-four hours we shall be forced to make public certain information of a most damaging nature concerning your daughter-in-law which is now in our possession.*

Henry stared at it rigidly, holding it at a distance, as though it burned his hand, repeating to himself, 'Concerning your daughter-in-law.' He might have been dismayed if the tone of the thing had not made his blood boil. The more he studied it, the worse it became. Unsigned, it was of a nature so divorced from the normality of life, at least of his life, that he could barely credit it. That he, Henry Page, should reecive such a threat, in his own office, in the town of Hedleston – it was infamous.

Now, indeed, he could not hesitate; strong and immediate action was imperative. After some reflection he instructed Moffatt to telephone Smith that he would see him at three o'clock that afternoon. Then he thought of Cora: she must, of course, in fairness to herself, be on hand. The cottage was without a telephone; it was not easy to reach her. He wired her to come to the office at the same hour.

## IX

IT TOOK ALL Henry's strength of mind to get through the day, so completely were his thoughts dominated by the coming meeting with Smith. Sustained by a sense of outrage, he was impatient, even eager for it to take place. He did not go out for lunch but instead ate a few biscuits from the tin he kept in his drawer. Restlessly he watched the hands of the office clock move slowly towards the afternoon.

Cora was the first to appear; she came early, at quarter to three. Her look of strained expectancy suggested to him that she had misconstrued his summons. Did she imagine that on reflection he favoured her suggestion of the day before? He gave her no opportunity to reopen the matter. Nor, since he had no wish to alarm her, did he mention why he wished her to be here. Under the pretext of being busy he asked her to wait in Miss Moffatt's room, adding that Moffatt would certainly wish to make her a cup of tea.

The next fifteen minutes passed with intolerable slowness. Although Henry steeled himself to remain composed, he felt his heart beginning to thud . . . harder and harder. He tried to avoid having recourse to the amyl nitrate Bard had given him, the doctor having warned him that its repeated use diminished the effect, yet he was forced to crush one of the ampoules that he carried now, for emergencies, in the little case at the end of his watch chain.

He had barely finished inhaling it, and his face was still flushed from the drug, when Smith arrived, accompanied not only by Nye but by another younger man whom Henry had never seen before. The unlooked-for appearance of this stranger, although he seemed quiet, affable, and altogether presentable, was for some obscure reason a shock to Page – it seemed to invest the proceedings with new and unknown complexities. They stood there, all three, looking down at him, with Fenwick, who had shown them upstairs, remaining in the background. Smith broke the silence.

'You had my letters.' His voice sounded strange, hoarse and almost slurred; he appeared to speak with an effort.

'Both of them,' Henry answered. Then, as he had resolved, above everything, to be calm: 'Will you sit down?'

They sat down, like three automatons, the stranger with a disconcerting impassiveness, Nye with his usual insolent air. He glanced at Fenwick, who had found them chairs.

'Do we need him?'

Page told Fenwick he might go.

'You'll thank me later,' Nye said. He lit a cigarette, adding as a polite afterthought, 'You don't mind?'

A short pause followed, then Smith cleared his throat. His face, normally the shade of suet, had a sweaty pallor, accentuated by his blue unshaven chin and a dark puffiness under the eyes. He seemed acutely ill at ease; his collar was soiled, his necktie loose, his general appearance indicated a kind of feverish disorder. Henry had never before seen him in such a state.

'Mr Page,' he began haltingly, yet as if rehearsed, 'I have no personal animus against you. I respect you and wish to cause you no distress. I even hope that you entertain similar feelings towards myself. At the same time, circumstances can arise in which a man in my position is obliged to take certain steps in his own interest. Mr Page, it's a painful thing to say . . . but information has come into our possession which we feel we must put before you.'

'If I am to believe your letters, it concerns my daughter-in-law.'

'You've said it,' Nye threw in, flicking the ash off his cigarette.

'In that case, though it may strike you as too fine a point of honour, if you have anything to say against her I prefer you to say it in her presence.'

'Wait, Mr Page. You'd better hear us first. We don't want to hurt a woman.'

'Oh, cut it out, Smith,' Nye said. 'For God's sake, come to the point.'

'Very well, then,' Henry said. 'I'll hear you. But I hope you are conversant with the law of slander.'

'Mr Page, it's a difficult thing to say . . .'

'Look here,' Nye broke in. 'Let me take over.' He stubbed out his cigarette and fixed Page with a cold, protruding eye. 'You print a pretty pure paper, don't you? You stand for a clean press, a clean community, a clean everything. You're so lily white inside and out you've probably never heard the word abortion?'

'I . . . I know the word,' Page said, taken aback.

171

'I hoped you might,' Nye sneered. 'It makes things easier. Then you probably know that when a young woman gets in trouble, and isn't married, and wants to save her pretty face, she hies herself to some old bag in a back street who relieves her of her encumbrance. Unfortunately, however, there's a nasty little law known as Offences Against the Person Act, 1861, which says that if a woman unlawfully permits the use of any instrument or other means to procure her own\ miscarriage she is guilty of a felony, for which the offence is penal servitude for life or not less than three years, or imprisonment for not more than two years . . . a pity, isn't it?'

'That's enough,' Smith said thickly. 'Mr Page, it's painful to have to tell you. In August three years ago your daughter-in-law, then Cora Bates, was convicted under that act at the Northern Assizes.'

Henry stared at him, petrified. His entire body seemed fixed and frozen. All sense of his surroundings vanished and nothing remained but the blurred, wavering vision of Smith's somehow misshapen face.

'No . . . no . . . I don't believe it.'

'It's true. And we can prove it.'

'No,' Henry said again, with mechanical insistence. 'It's not true.'

'Oh, pipe down,' Nye said. He pointed to the third man. 'Haines here was on the case . . . followed it from first to last. Isn't that so, Jack?'

'I'm afraid so, sir.' Haines looked at Page with a vague apology, or at least an assumption of regret. 'I was in court all through the trial. I must say the magistrate was very lenient, under the special circumstances. It was a light sentence.'

'Sentence?' Gripping the arms of his chair, Henry could barely speak the word.

'Six months.'

Henry's heart failed him; for a long moment it halted in its beat. He had believed some accusation possible, the raking up and magnifying of some foolish mistake she had made, perhaps a silly affair with this young man Haines, or something having regard to her impoverished background and early struggles, but never this fatal thing, so far beyond the worst of his imaginings that suddenly everything within him rose up in revolt . . . he could not, and would not, accept it.

'It's impossible . . . a lie. She's here . . . she'll deny it.'

'Fetch her in, then,' Nye said, with a cool, off-hand assurance that chilled Page. 'We'll see who's the liar.'

Henry rose to summon her, then sank back in his chair. He could not have her in to answer this horrible accusation.

'Go ahead,' Nye urged. 'Let's settle this once and for all. Ask the little lady how she got in the jug.'

Frozen by doubt, Henry could not decide what to do. While he still hesitated, the side door giving access to Moffatt's room opened. Tired of waiting, Cora had come to see if he were free. Never would he forget her face as, in an instant of comprehension, she took in the scene before her. A mortal stillness fell upon tne room, then, terrified, she gasped:

'Excuse me . . . I didn't know . . .' and started to back out.

'Wait a bit,' Nye said. 'There's a gentleman here has come quite a way to see you.'

She stopped, as if she had no power to resist.

'I think you remember me?' Haines said.

'No . . . I never seen you before.' The reply was so indistinct as to be barely audible.

'I beg your pardon, Miss . . . at least you were Miss Bates then . . . I have the press clippings on me, with the photographs, and the statement you signed in the hospital.'

He felt in his inside pocket. Page thought Cora would fall. She began to cry, a hard, dry sobbing without tears that shook all of her body. He could not bear it.

'That's enough,' he said to Smith. 'For God's sake, leave us.'

'Are you convinced?' Nye said as he got up.

Smith also had risen. He stood by the desk, not looking

173

at Page, his despatch case in his hand, perspiration beading his forehead.

'Now look, Mr Page. Nobody need know a thing about this. We'll keep it as secret as the grave. No harm done. None whatever. The solution's quite simple. I've drafted a little agreement here, all perfectly open and above-board.' He fumbled, opened the despatch case. 'I'm sure you'll want to accept it. Then we'll never print a word of your little bit of trouble. And believe me, my dear Mr Page, there need be no hard feelings on either side.'

'Go, please, all of you. I'll talk with you later.'

Smith put a long Manilla envelope on the desk and led the way towards the door.

When they had gone Page turned towards Cora. He could find nothing to say, absolutely nothing; the words withered in his throat. She was still crying and, with her arms across her face, had leaned blindly against the wall. He tried to find a consoling word, but he could not. It was she who broke the silence. Through her tears, still in that same abandoned attitude, she began to speak.

'It's true . . . true . . . what they told you. But perhaps they didn't tell you everything . . . that ever since I was sixteen, I've been on my own, working mostly in cheap over-the-counter stores. One summer I took a seven-day trip to Blackpool; so help me, I'd saved up for it for months. I went dancing at the Palley. The manager saw me and offered me a job. I took it. He was nice to me and I was lonely. I'd always been lonely. It made me soft, made me want to find somebody to love. I never knew he was married . . . not at first, I didn't. He didn't care about me really, not him; he was a rotter, all right. When he found out I was that way he was furious at me. He treated me real bad. He was afraid his wife would find out. He said he knew what to do. I didn't care much, the way he'd treated me; I let him take me to that place. A woman there did things to me. I was sick, proper sick, I thought I was going to die and I wanted to. She got frightened and fetched a doctor. He put me in the hospital and then it all came out.'

She almost broke down but forced herself to go on. 'I was in the hospital for eight weeks. I had the fever and everything. When they let me out the police took me. They had to, I suppose. They wanted me to turn Queen's evidence against the woman. But she was poor like me, hadn't no friends; somehow I couldn't do it. When my case come up that went bad against me, but the judge let me off with six months. I think he was sorry for me. I wasn't much to look at. They'd cut my hair in the hospital and I was just skin and bone. I didn't care. It wouldn't have made no difference if they'd sent me away for the full stretch. Nothing made any difference. I just couldn't be myself again.'

'Don't Cora . . .' Pity made him rise and go to her. 'You've said enough.'

'I got to tell you, if it kills me. When I came out they wanted me to get a job in Blackpool – the aid society. But I'd had enough of that place. It was summer again. I saw an advert for my sort of job in Scarborough. I went there. The work was easy. It was selling doughnuts and that like, in a stall on the front. But I couldn't get back to myself. I didn't belong anywhere. I had no feeling, except I felt like I was really dead. Every evening when I closed up at six, I'd go for a walk by the harbour. And there, on the end of a bench, I'd usually see him. It was David. There was something about him. One night I couldn't help myself. I stopped and spoke to him.'

Another spasm racked her.

'That was the start, that was. I didn't dare tell him about myself. But he was in the same boat. I knew it just by looking at him. I wanted to help him. And I think I have helped him. I've been a good wife. But if he gets to know, it'll be the end; I don't know what will happen to the both of us.'

A final sob shook her, and, turning convulsively, she came towards him as though, forsaken by all the world, lost and bewildered, yet still with a painful thirst for happiness, she begged for his support.

'Don't cry,' he said, holding her. 'And don't on any

account say anything to David. There must be something we can do about it.'

'I couldn't help myself . . . it happened to me . . . that's all. I can't say more nor less. But what must you think . . . you especially? After all you done for me, I been and brought this on you. Oh, can't you see it . . . you're the one that counts the most.'

As she said these words she stopped short, looked at him wildly and, before he could detain her, broke away and ran out of the room.

He had to let her go. Heavily, he sat down and, bent over the desk with his head between his hands, tried to collect his scattered forces and brace himself against the final shattering disaster. What a mess, he thought, what a frightful mess! His first reaction of anger and disgust was gone, supplanted by compassion. He could not blame her, yet for him, and for the *Light,* the consequences were fatal.

Instinctively, he took up the contract Smith had placed upon his desk and, with a blank face, read it through. It was not a swindling agreement; in fact, of its kind, it was strictly fair – Smith, in his attempts at self-exoneration, had used all his efforts to make it so, justly proportioning the assets of the two papers and assessing their goodwill on the relative sales over the past twelve months. Yet, while the end result might be financially adequate, Page was left with no illusions as to his situation. He was to be dispossessed. If he refused to give up the *Light,* the whole story of Cora's past, linked to its present setting and suitably embellished, would be headlined in Hedleston and in every Somerville paper throughout the country.

A tremor passed over Henry as he envisaged that appalling publicity. How they would scarify him, the uplifter, ex-mayor of Hedleston, due for a testimonial dinner, the man of probity and principle, who stood four-square against corruption. Alice, with her social ambitions, would not be spared, nor David, the deluded husband; even Dorothy would have to take her share – none of them would escape. They would all be dragged through the mud with the skill of hands

long practised in that art. The result for him would undoubtedly be social and political extinction. For David it
would be so much worse he scarcely dared to contemplate
it: this shock would destroy him, send him back into that
confused, tormented hell from which he might never again
emerge.

As for Cora, would she not suffer worst of all? The knowledge that she had brought this trouble upon them, that the
pain and humiliation of her wretched experience must again
be undergone, magnified a hundredfold, that her hard-won
security, her safety and peace of mind, must irretrievably
be shattered, all this would surely break her heart.

He rose suddenly, and began to pace the floor. How could
he see this hurt inflicted on her, and on his family – he must
yield, must give up the *Light*. Even to think this sent a stab
of pain into his side. He tried to tell himself that it was
merely wounded pride from undue attachment to a long-
cherished family possession, that he, Henry Page, was merely
an out-of-date idealist who wrote platitudinous articles and
set exaggerated store upon his ownership of a small provincial newspaper. It would not serve. When he considered the
long, bitter struggle he had waged, and the hard victory he
had won, only to be robbed at the last moment, the blood
mounted to his forehead. The *Light* was his inheritance, his
tradition, his life.

As though compelled, he moved along the corridor to the
little end room where the earliest copies of the *Light* were
preserved, and at random began plucking them from their
racks. Here, in 1785, was the report of Blanchard's pioneer
balloon flight across the English Channel, accomplished on
a Friday 'notwithstanding evil foreboding,' and there, ten
years later, was the first instalment of Paine's *Age of
Reason,* a serialization which had brought on Daniel Page
the threat of government prosecution and had finally dis-
credited Pitt. Here, again, was that famous report of the
mutiny at the Nore in 1797, when the Bank of England
suspended gold payments. Another issue held a society
report from Charles Lamb, sent to Margate to gather news

of the fashionable arrivals, and another, a vivid account of the great Chartist meeting. Feverishly now, irrespective of their sequence, Henry ran through the faded yellow sheets, each with its imprint of England's history: Trafalgar, the fall of Kabul, Balaklava, the attempt in 1842 to assassinate Queen Victoria, the Napoleonic Wars, with terrifying cartoons of the Corsican ogre, the bulletin of Browning's death, the funeral in the Abbey, the South African War, the fund begun by Robert Page to supply the troops with comforts . . . no, he could not bear it. He groaned aloud, pressing his throbbing temples between his palms. The *Light* itself was history; he could not surrender it to an ownership that would irretrievably debase it.

He swung round and, with a new sense of purpose, went back to his office. A glance at the clock showed half past seven – unconscious of the passage of time, he had lost almost three hours. Moffatt must have gone at six as usual, quite unaware that anything was wrong. However, after a search he found a Bradshaw in the drawer of her desk. The night train for London left at seventeen minutes to eight. He had not time to go home and pick up a suitcase. He would have to take a cab directly to the train. Quickly he wrote a note for Moffatt, telling her he had been called unexpectedly to London, and placed it on the hood of her typewriter. Next, he phoned his house; Alice was out, but he left the message with Hannah, saying that, at the most, he would not be away for more than two nights. Then, taking his hat and coat, he left the office, and hurriedly set out for the station.

# X

On the folllowing morning, after a troubled night, David came to the realization that he could no longer endure the silence, constraint, and heartbreaking pretence between Cora and himself. He must find some way out. When he left the house at nine o'clock, ostensibly for his usual walk, he got on to the Hedleston bus which departed from Sleedon at half past nine. Only two other passengers were inside, and as both had places at the front, he seated himself well to the rear, so that, free of the persecution of their stares, he might more clearly define his course of action.

First, he must see his father. Although David did not care to show it and was often compelled by a sense of his own inadequacy to extraordinary moods of pretentiousness, in the depths of his nature he had for Henry both gratitude and affection, and while he could not agree with many of his father's views, he believed implicitly in his goodness and common sense. These were the qualities he most needed now and which, in seeking his father's advice, he would be sure to receive.

The slow, jolting journey, with long stops at Lacey Hummocks and Hurst Green, seemed interminable, but at last the blurred shape of Hedleston became visible through the steamy, chattering windows and presently the ancient vehicle shuddered to a final halt in Victoria Square, the omnibus terminus.

Rain pricked David's forehead as he got out and started walking towards the *Northern Light* offices. To enter this building, consecrated to his father's idealism and regarded by Henry as his logical inheritance, was an ordeal which he habitually shunned. Even today, obsessed by other fears, he felt like an interloper as he climbed the stone staircase and knocked at Page's door.

When he went in, the room was empty; then Moffatt suddenly appeared, viewing him with a surprise which could only be due to the rarity of his visits.

'How are you, Miss Moffatt?' he said, then knowing that with her he must state the obvious: 'I came to see my father.'

'Of course,' she answered, with that proprietary, half-playful manner which she had always adopted towards him ever since those days when she had come to Hanley Drive to look at him in his pram. 'But he's not here.'

'When will he be in?'

'I can't tell. He's gone to London.'

'To London!'

'That's right. Why, I don't know. He went unexpectedly last night and only left a note, saying he'd been called away. I expect it's to do with this Economic Conference.' After a brief pause, she added, 'He can't be away long. There's your mother's reception tomorrow.'

He must have given some indication of being upset by this unforeseen check, for she continued to study him, and with deeper penetration and concern.

'Where's your coat?' You're the most awful chap. You haven't even an umbrella. Don't you know it's pouring cats and dogs? You're half soaked. And your hair . . . here, let me straighten you up.'

As he stood there, rooted and possessed by the problem of what he should do now, she came forward, fastened the top button of his flannel shirt, brushed the raindrops from his jacket and went through the motions of tidying him.

'There now . . . that's better. I'm just making my elevenses. You'll stay for a cup. Your wife had one with me yesterday. She's a nice creature, David. Come along . . . we'll go into my room.'

'No . . . no.' He roused himself. 'You must excuse me . . thank you. I have to go.'

'But David . . . wait just a minute . . .'

He would not, could not, stay. He turned and went down

the stairs with a rush that carried him across the street, just in front of a passing car. Uncaring, he went on, convinced that his father's sudden and unpremeditated absence was linked in some way with this hateful enigma that he could not solve and that, like the spent oil that came sometimes upon the Sleedon beach, seemed insidiously to spread its pollution everywhere.

With an effort he took himself in hand. What must he do now? Useless to go to Hanley Drive to seek advice and enlightenment from his mother. Yet he could not return, defeated, to Sleedon, to further hours of solitary brooding. Only one course lay open to him, and while he knew what exactions this would make upon his nerves, he did not care; sooner or later it was inevitable that he take it.

The Prudential offices were quite near. Crossing the gardens, he arrived at the entrance in less than five minutes. From the indicator outside he saw that the *Chronicle* office was on the third floor. He did not immediately go in, but began to stride up and down outside, schooling himself in what he meant to say, summoning all the resources of mind and body at his command. Conscious of his weakness in a crisis, he resolved that on this occasion he would not be at a loss. Yet the very process of this preparation was its undoing, for as he projected an image of the coming scene, foreseeing the insults he would receive and return, anger began to burn in him, his throat constricted, and his mouth went dry.

He could no longer endure it. With a sharp, unco-ordinated movement he halted, dived into the building, and, ignoring the lift, climbed breathlessly to the third floor. The name, in gilt letters, was on the ground-glass door: DAILY CHRONICLE: EXECUTIVE OFFICE. Without knocking, he went in.

The general air of inactivity and emptiness took him by surprise. A lad of about seventeen was idly typing at a low table placed sideways by the window beside the telephone switchboard. In a voice which he hardly recognized as his own, David told him he wished to see Nye. The youth sat back in his chair, glanced at him across his shoulder.

'He's not here. He's gone to Tynecastle.' Then, at David's quick look of disbelief, he added, 'None of them are here. Mr Smith's at the main Mossburn office.'

So keyed was he to the necessity of seeing the thing through, David still could not believe him. Two doors at the end of a narrow corridor gave access to the other rooms which completed the office suite. Quickly he looked into each room. Both were empty. He returned to the entrance lobby.

'When will he be back?' he asked.

'How should I know?' The boy spoke with an injured air. 'There's nothing doing here now . . . at least not much. It's quite likely he'll be away all day.'

'All day,' David repeated tonelessly, then, after a pause, he turned and went out.

In the street again he hesitated, hands still clenched, body tense with the bitterness of frustration. Nothing had been discovered, nothing settled or achieved. A culminating sense of his own ineffectuality overwhelmed him. It was now the lunch hour, the pavement was thronged, people hurrying in the rain kept pushing against him as he stood there, undecided, his ears still ringing with the pounding of his blood.

At last he moved off towards Victoria Square. Nothing to be done after all, nothing but an inept return to Sleedon. .A bus was on the point of leaving, almost full. He found a place in the middle of the coach, trying to subdue the waves of confused thought that kept breaking over him. It was not long before he convinced himself that the combined stares of the other passengers were directed towards him, part in derision, part in outright hostility. He kept his head down, his eyes fixed upon the floorboard, unable to summon up the blank indifference with which he normally met the provocations of the crowd. Yet he could not find detachment, the turmoil in his breast remained; indeed, it increased all through the journey. Nor, when he reached Sleedon, did the rapid walk he took towards home dispel it.

The house seemed empty as he entered, but in the kitchen

the kettle was steaming on the stove and through the window he saw Cora in the garden, walking on the gravel path. He longed to go to her. Gone now was the attitude of indulgent patronage, the bland acceptance of her service, driven out by jealousy, uncertainty, and the evidence of her suffering. Instead, all the need of her, the physical longing of those early days in Scarborough had been renewed in him. He would have wished at this very moment to go to the bedroom, call her from the window, and when she came, to love her. But no, he must compose himself. She must know nothing of the disorder of his thoughts, nothing of his futile errand, nothing that would augment her own distress. He went upstairs to the attic and sat down at the plain deal table he used as a desk.

As a tranquillizing expedient Dr Evans had told him to take a sheet of paper and write down quickly, automatically, all the thoughts that kept crowding into his mind. He picked up his pen and began this process of liberation.

'The pain of loving too deeply,' he wrote, 'may often surpass the joy . . . and one may give oneself to the hurt with as much abandon as the happiness. My footsteps are in a maze, obscurity presses upon me, but I am not defeated. I can surmount any difficulty, overcome any enemy if my will remains strong. Soon we will be rid of this affliction. Nothing must harm Cora. I will protect her. And now, let me breathe in a sense of rest, of deep quiet . . .'

He had not written more than these few lines before he stopped short, his head on one side, in an attitude of listening.

'A sense of rest, of deep quiet.'

Was it merely tinnitus, the ringing that for months had persisted in his ears, usually as the sound of bells, occasionally as a thin, high-pitched whistle, or did he actually hear a voice, echoing his own words in faint derision as he formed them? Listening intently, he heard nothing, but as he resumed his writing, the voice again picked up the words he was putting on paper: 'When the light broadens and the darkness mitigates . . .' repeating them more loudly, in perfect timing and co-ordination with his pen. By writing slowly, he tried to still the voice, but without avail; then he went faster, dashing the words across the page; the voice swept on, loud, articulate, at breakneck speed.

David dropped the pen as though it were red hot, and gripped the edges of the table hard, trying to steady himself, remembering Dr Evans's sharp advice when he had first told him he heard the voices.

'It's pure fancy. An aural hallucination, we call it. Put it out of your mind. Don't give in to it . . . not for an instant.'

David raised his head slowly. Now, at last, it had gone. Or had it? Rigid, in an attitude of listening, he waited, hoping for silence. But instead, independent of his writing, unconnected with the pen which still lay on the table, he heard, faint yet distinct, a call that seemed to come from the bedroom on the floor below. It was a man's voice, calling out his name. 'Page . . . Page . . . are you there?' Then, with a start of horror, he heard these words:

'Look out for your own neck, chum,' and he recognized the voice of Nye.

He jumped up, as though catapulted from his chair, pressing both forefingers tight into his ears in an effort to exclude all sound. This was imagination, a morbid delusion of his disordered nerves. Yet while he fought against it, the repetition came, loud, insolent, and more distinctly, from the room below.

'So you think you'll break my neck, Page . . . but just look out for your own neck, chum.'

Impossible to be mistaken, he could resist no longer. He opened the door, dashed down the narrow wooden stairs into the bedroom, and began to search – in the two cupboards, under the bed, feeling between the dresses hanging in Cora's wardrobe, in every corner of the room. No one was there.

Limply, his forehead cold and dank, he sat down on the edge of the bed. Was he going mad? The voice, the disembodied presence, both had vanished. As on the previous occasion, his thorough search and the physical proof afforded

184

by it had banished the illusion. He felt weak but more himself again.

With a long sigh he got up and, standing at the mirror on the dressing table, began in a normal manner to brush his hair. Then, reflected in the glass, he saw that Cora was beside him. Here, at least, was substance among the shadows.

'I didn't know you were in,' she said. 'You had a long walk.'

His new mood of quiet lucidity ruled out all thought of dissimulation. He came close to her, took her hand and pressed it.

'I wasn't walking really,' he said. 'I took the bus to Hedleston to see Father.'

'And did you?' He felt her body tighten, then, as he shook his head, suddenly relax.

'He's gone to London. Quite unexpectedly.'

'To London.' She said this slowly, then her expression lifted, warmed with a hopefulness he had not seen for days. 'Oh, David, I'm so pleased. I trust your father. Don't you ask me anything, not now, David . . . but I feel this will be good for us.'

## XI

EARLIER THAT MORNING – to be exact, at quarter past six – Henry Page arrived at King's Cross. His train, delayed at York, was very late and the express from Leeds, pulling in five minutes earlier, had taken most of the taxis off the rank. After a considerable wait in the cold semi-darkness of the station, Henry managed to secure a cab. He was not often in London, and on these infrequent visits he put up at a quiet hotel near the British Museum, the Esmond. Here the night porter recognized him and, although he had no luggage, he was given a room without question.

'Can I have breakfast?' he asked the man.

'I'm sorry, Mr Page. There's no one in the kitchen until seven. Shall I leave your order before I go off duty?'

'No, I'll ring,' Henry said, thinking that he would first try to get some rest. During the journey, huddled in the corner of his compartment, he had slept little, and now, as the grey dawn crept over the grimed roofs and soot-encrusted chimneys and filtered into the narrow, inhospitable room, he lay down on the bed fully dressed and closed his eyes. But his mind was still too charged with active and agitating thoughts to permit of sleep. He simply lay there, feeling so unlike himself it seemed as if he had become the disembodied witness of some unhappy stranger stretched motionless upon the bed.

At seven o'clock he rang for strong black coffee, which, although he had been forbidden it, in his present state he could not do without. They were a long time bringing it and when it did come it was the usual insipid brew, but after three cups and a slice of toast he felt somewhat revived. He washed, then went out to an adjoining barber's and was shaved. From force of habit he bought the morning papers, but could do no more than glance through them, and that with a queer irrational dread that news of his misfortune might already be in print.

It was still too early to give effect to his purpose – Somerville would assuredly not be at his office until ten – but Henry could not bear to delay. He took a bus to the Strand, then walked down Whitehall to Hercules House. So different from his own establishment, the *Gazette* offices, dominating the Embankment, presented to the ancient river, which this morning flowed almost wearily between its bridges, a glittering façade of glass and steel-ribbed cement, cold, impersonal, suggestive of power. In the foyer, with its Corinthian columns and chequered marble floor, one of a group of uniformed commissionaires took Henry's name, transmitted it to the reception desk, then, after some delay, directed him to the express lift. On the topmost floor, at the end of a long corridor, he was received, or rather intercepted, by Somerville's private secretary, a young man in a cutaway and striped trousers who, considering Henry with an air of polite misgiving, remarked:

'Actually, Mr Page, the man you ought to see is Mr Greeley. Unfortunately he is on leave. I suggest you have a talk with his deputy, Mr Challoner.'

'No,' Henry said firmly. 'My business is with Mr Somerville personally.'

'Yes, of course,' the other agreed thoughtfully. 'I'm afraid, however, that he is engaged most of the morning. And he hasn't actually come in yet. Still . . . if you care to . . .'

'I'll wait,' Henry said.

'This way, then, please.'

Of set purpose, Henry had made no appointment, since he judged there would be less chance of a rebuff if he presented himself without notice. He knew he would have to wait – if, indeed, Somerville consented to see him at all – and he did wait, in the small red-carpeted anteroom, furnished with leather armchairs, a cocktail cabinet, and some eighteenth-century English sporting pictures. Here, for more than an hour, he sat gazing dully at a large canvas by John Fernley depicting a meet of the Quorn, which hung on the opposite wall, not seeing the painting at all, but trying to piece together the little he knew of Vernon Somerville.

Unlike two of his competitors, Jotham and Mighill, who had emerged respectively from the back streets of Aberdeen and the wilds of Ulster, he had pursued a more conventional path, by way of Dulwich and the City. After a short spell in Throgmorton Street, his first venture in publishing, the purchase of the expiring *Gazette*, then run down to the verge of extinction, had proved a spectacular success. A fixed determination to succeed, allied to an extraordinary capacity for gauging the popular taste, had enabled him to transform the paper. As sales multiplied and soared, his confidence and natural assertiveness increased. Urged on by a presentiment of further triumphs, he started a smart weekly, *Town Topics*, then, quickly, the *Sunday Argus*. At first these new and hazardous ventures went well. Tasting power, Somerville began prematurely to play the role of the great press lord. A yacht appeared; there were contributions to charity, which, though they fell far short of Mighill's princely benefactions, were nevertheless more fully publicized; a group of four Cotmans, not to be compared with the unique Giorgiones given to the nation by Jotham or the pendant of superb Canalettos donated by Sir Ithiel, still, good sound British paintings, was presented to the Dulwich Gallery. Then came marriage to Blanche Gilliflower, the darling of the gossip columns, Lord Jotham's niece.

Here, the first hint of failure crept in. Apparently the marriage had been unfortunate. Vaguely Henry recollected some gossip of Alice's: that in the year following the wedding Somerville's wife had divorced him to become – after a brief period as a photographer's model advertising shampoos and face cream, and a near marriage to an Austrian baron – fashion editor of the *Globe*, where she now functioned with such success that Mighill, who gave his paper a certain cachet by employing 'society lovelies,' had become paternally attached to her.

By this time the stimulating effects of the coffee had passed; a sick torpor began to settle upon Henry, so that when at last the young man reappeared and with a confidential air summoned him to the inner office, he forgot to swallow the two pills he had promised himself immediately before the interview.

Somerville, wearing carelessly a loose dark grey flannel suit with a red tie and a dark carnation in his buttonhole, was seated at his desk signing letters as Page entered. He continued for a full minute without looking up, then he swivelled his chair, half rose, and held out his hand. Of middle stature, with a short neck and heavy shoulders, the owner of the *Gazette* seemed older than his forty-five years. His complexion was plethoric, accentuated by the tie, the carnation, and by a small but noticeable portwine birthmark on his neck just under the left ear. An injected eye gave indication of the pressures within, and his manner, charged with a restive impatience, was that of a man fully occupied with his affairs, who would not suffer at any price stupidity, incompetence, or interference. Having resumed his seat, he crossed his legs, lay back, and openly studied Page.

Henry, accepting the chair beside the Chippendale desk, found nothing to reassure him in this reception. Somerville seemed waiting for him to begin, then, as though sensing the difficulty of Page's position, he said, driving straight to the point:

'You should have let me know you were coming. We might have lunched together. As it is, may I congratulate you on the excellent fight you've given us. I thought at one time you were going to knock us out. But now I understand we see eye to eye in the matter.'

'No, not quite.' Henry was painfully ill at ease. He could actually feel his legs trembling as he sat there, but the very act of speech helped to restore his courage. 'It's almost two years now since you bought the *Chronicle*. I admit that my attitude then was resentful and prejudiced. You had every right to come to Hedleston and to set up your paper in competition with mine. Since there wasn't room for two of us, it was for the people of the town to choose between us. Well, they've chosen . . . and I'm here to ask you to let that choice stand.'

Somerville did not immediately reply. Then he said:

'Public favour is a variable quantity. It may change overnight. We are still selling the *Chronicle*. We will continue to do so.'

'No.' Henry shook his head. 'Let's be open with one another. You've tried to put me out of business and you've failed. Now, for God's sake, leave the *Northern Light* alone.'

'I don't follow you,' Somerville said curtly. 'After all the work and sweat we've put into Hedleston, are you asking us to walk out with our tails between our legs?'

'I am asking you to suppress a certain item of news.'

'Suppress news! My dear sir, you amaze me. Our first

189

principle, our moral obligation to the public, is never to suppress the news.'

'This is not an important item. It merely concerns my family and myself.'

'My dear sir, I have no knowledge of the matter. I scarcely know what you are talking about. Still, in Hedleston, surely anything that concerns you is important. I imagine my editor up there would take that view.'

Henry felt his lips dry and tighten.

'This is a pitiful story raked up from the past which can only hurt a number of innocent persons.'

'Good God,' Somerville said with sudden roughness, 'what sort of line are you giving me? We're in the middle of the twentieth century. You can't be thin-skinned nowadays. In the rough and tumble of our business there's always some abuse given and received. I cannot personally vet every word that goes into the *Chronicle*. I've every confidence in my editor. I leave it entirely to him.'

Page could not repress a spasm of bitterness.

'And he, of course, proposes to publish this story on moral grounds.'

Somerville made a restive movement, glanced impatiently at his watch as though to terminate the interview.

'My dear sir,' he said, 'why do you come bleating to me? The affair is out of my hands. I've given my people in Hedleston complete authority and must abide by their decisions. This is obviously a purely local thing within the competence of the local staff. You can't expect me to know about it, or to concern myself with it.'

His manner ruthlessly set aside the matter. Page saw that, while he was without scruple, he would never personally descend to the sordid; it would all be done for him. A dark, nervous anger began to kindle in him, a determination not to be disposed of so easily.

'Why do you want the *Northern Light*?'

Somerville, who had begun to arrange some papers on his desk, looked up sharply, suspecting a motive behind the question. Did this little provincial nonentity guess what he was up against . . . fighting pyramiding costs, mounting wage spirals, and powerful amalgamations who would like nothing better than to put him out of business? Jotham and Mighill about to merge . . . in that field practically a monopoly . . . Fleet Street chuckling for weeks over his failure to absorb the *Light*, the *Argus* losing money, *Town Topics* almost moribund . . . he had to expand or go under. Watching Page carefully, he answered:

'For a very simple reason. I need more circulation.'

'You already have a large circulation. The *Gazette* sells at least a million and a quarter.'

'In these days of competition if you don't go forward you go back.'

'And your idea of going forward is to multiply the *Gazette* or its counterpart, the *Chronicle*?' Page, beyond caution and resolved at whatever cost to speak his mind, took a sharp, painful breath. 'In a recent issue of *Survey* there was an article on the press. Did you see it?'

'*Survey* is an excellent publication; I seldom read it.'

'This was a thorough and impartial report. The conclusion reached was that our intelligent and high-principled newspapers are being swamped by the lowest segment of our popular press . . . papers run, not as a public service, but purely as a financial investment, and which had become the trashiest, silliest, most objectionable, most vulgar in the world. The *Gazette* was singled out as the worst.'

Somerville barely smiled, quite unperturbed.

'We have our detractors. A pity. After all, we only try to please the masses . . . to envelop them in . . . shall I say . . . a soothing *ambiance*.'

'By feeding them the garbage of the news?'

'We give them exactly what they want.'

'No.' Page shook his head with nervous violence. 'Humanity is not always as stupid as it seems. You can't write our people off like that. They have great qualities – courage, cheerfulness, warmth of heart, humour – yet because three-quarters of the population are under-educated, they aren't equipped to resist your blandishments.

I won't repeat the obvious. It's not just sex, crime, and sensation, nor yet the stupid trivialities that fill your paper that makes it so pernicious; it's the manner in which the grossest prejudices and appetites are artfully stimulated, while contempt is heaped cynically on all who oppose you. Don't you remember what Balfour said: 'I'd rather sell gin to the poor than poison them that way'? Another fifty years in this direction, with your zymotic bilge, and you will have reduced the masses almost to illiteracy. No one knows better than you what an immensely powerful instrument you have in your hands. Why don't you use it to create? God knows, there never was a time when the country had more need of an intelligent, high-principled press. We were magnificent in the war when we lived in easy intimacy with death. But since then we've suffered a relapse politically, economically, and morally. It's only temporary, I'm convinced, but we've got to shake ourselves out of it. If we don't . . .'

A wave of physical weakness came over Page as he broke off, aware that he had made not the slightest impression on Somerville, realizing, too, the terrifying danger of power without a comparable sense of responsibility. His tongue was thick, his mouth dry. He could find nothing more to say. Somerville, who had been observing Henry with a hard expression in which contempt predominated, was quick to profit by the sudden hopelessness that showed in Page's face.

'My dear fellow,' he said soothingly, 'I understand your feelings. But time grows short; let us keep to the point. We are making you a reasonable offer. You are under no compulsion. Simply tell us if you wish to accept it. Perhaps,' he went on, 'if you decide to sell – and I'm sure you will – you might care to continue on the staff. Your editorials . . . they have an impressive Edwardian quality.'

'No,' Page said heavily. 'I couldn't. It must be all or nothing.'

'Is it to be all, then?'

Henry could not look at him, could not raise his head. He felt beaten down, defeated.

192

'I'll think it over . . . for a few hours. I'll telephone you this afternoon.'

'Good.' Sómerville rose. 'I look forward to hearing from you.'

Somehow Page got out of the room.

A fine, drizzling rain was falling as he left the building and turned slowly up from the river towards Victoria Street. Through his despondency an increasing faintness warned him that he ought quickly to find some refreshment – since noon the day before he had eaten practically nothing. Across the way he saw an A.B.C., but as he made to cross the street, the volume of traffic, with its rush and roar, suddenly struck at him and set his heart beating with incredible rapidity. He hesitated, quite breathless, realizing that he could not trust himself to make the passage. Dizzily, he continued on his own side, looking for another lunch room. At the corner of Ashley Gardens, just by Westminster Cathedral, the pain began. In recent months he had experienced certain symptoms of cardiac spasm, mainly in the nature of shooting pains down his left arm, but this pain was different, covering the entire area of his chest, and of such intensity that his ribs seemed imprisoned and crushed by a colossal vice. Breathing, movement even, was impossible, and with this came a deathly sickness that drew beads of cold perspiration from his brow. The anguish was inhuman, and through it all ran the silly, childish dread that if he did not find some refuge he would make a fool of himself and fall down in the public street. With a great effort he managed to drag himself across the pavement into the adjoining cathedral, where, collapsed upon a row of seats, he lay struggling to regain breath.

At last the agonizing grip began to slacken; he took, with difficulty, a few shallow gasps, managed to fumble in his waistcoat pocket, crushed and inhaled two of the capsules Bard had given him. Then he swallowed a heart pill. Presently his respirations strengthened, and after about twenty minutes he was able to draw himself up to a seated position, bent forward and leaning on the chair in front. The thing had passed, leaving him spent and bruised as though by stones, but it was gone. The miracle seemed to him that he was alive.

The cathedral was empty except for a black-clad, solitary woman, perhaps a nun, immobile before the altar. Something in her attitude of entreaty, seen dimly in the dank, raw brick interior, brought Cora to his mind, in a quick flood of feeling. Quite distinctly, as though close to him, he saw the image of her face, the brow contracted as though troubled, the veined cheeks slightly hollowed, her dark eyes filled with confiding sadness. Well . . . she need no longer be sad and troubled, she would be safe now, would again know happiness and security. At least, out of his defeat he could draw that one deep consolation. Never before had he experienced such an emotion. It was as if, all his life, he had vainly sought an unattainable joy, trying to satisfy needs, yearnings, and aspirations which he could not even put in words, and which now were realized, not in ravishment, but as something close to pain, something, at least, that tasted bitter-sweet.

At last he felt himself sufficiently recovered to get up. With caution, yet fairly surely again, he went out to the street. A taxi took him to the hotel, where he had a tray sent to his room. After he had eaten and rested for half an hour he telephoned Somerville. He was out, but Henry gave the message to his secretary: that he was returning to Hedleston by the night train and would sign the documents in the morning.

Now that the issue was beyond doubt, a faint mist had diffused across that aspect of consciousness, replacing acute emotion with a sort of dulled blackness. But the thought of Sleedon came like a brightness in the prevailing gloom, and he was taken by a sudden longing to be there, less perhaps to see David, who, after all, knew nothing of events, than to be with Cora, dear Cora, to end her anxiety and restore her peace of mind.

# XII

In Hedleston that same Wednesday afternoon, just at the hour when Henry was returning to his hotel, Leonard Nye stepped off the train from Tynecastle, where, with considerable pleasure and apparent profit, he had spent most of the day. In the morning, unaware of Page's departure for London, he had said to Smith, with complete assurance:

'Look, Harold . . . it's a certainty that Page'll phone you some time this afternoon. When he does, go round, soap him up, and get his signature.'

'And what about you?'

'Use your head, man. You know I only put his back up. You're the one he'll want to deal with. Besides, I have to go to Tynecastle.'

'What for?'

'I have a couple of calls to make. Besides, I need a haircut and a manicure.'

Despite this cool show of imperturbability, an attitude upon which Nye particularly prided himself, he had been on edge most of the day, and now as he walked towards the office in the Prudential Building he experienced a tightening of his nerves, which he endeavoured to counteract by pausing to light a cigarette and reducing his pace to a leisurely stroll.

The lift took him to the third floor. Unconsciously, he hurried along the passage to his office.

'Any messages?' he asked Peter – whenever he got in.

'Mr Smith's been on the line several times from Mossburn.'

'Get him.'

Peter went to the phone and plugged in to the private line. For a moment there was no answer. Nye crushed out his half-smoked cigarette, lit another, and took a few quick draws. While he was waiting to get through, Peter said:

'There was a caller, too, Mr Nye. I think it was young Mr Page.'

'So he dropped in?'

'Yes, Mr Nye. Looked very queer indeed.'

'Doesn't he always? Let me know if he shows up again. I'll deal with him.'

'Very good. Hello. Hello. . . . You're through, sir.'

Nye took the receiver.

'Smith . . . Nye here. . . . Any word?'

'Word!' Smith's voice came back charged with suppressed feeling. 'I should think there is. . . . Page left for London last night. He's been in with Somerville this morning. What's happening, I don't know. Greeley's away, Somerville's got a meeting in the City. I've been on and off to head office all afternoon. It's too bad . . . the way you ran out on me. Everything seems at sixes and sevens.'

Nye's expression had changed at this unexpected news. He said sharply:

'Haven't you anything definite?'

'Challoner's the only one who seems to know anything. It seems that Page has promised to let them know today. Challoner thinks it should be all right, but he can't be sure. In the last hour I've done nothing but hang on the wire, waiting for the decision. It's getting on my nerves.'

Nye bit his lip, angered by his own miscalculation and by Smith's recriminating tone. But there was no point in starting a row at this juncture. He reflected for half a minute, frowning at the opposite wall.

'Why don't you come here?' he said. 'We'll stick it out together.'

From the way Smith jumped at the idea Nye guessed accurately the state he was in.

'I'll tell them to switch the call to you, Leonard. Don't move from the phone. I'll be along in twenty minutes.'

Nye turned to Peter.

'You can go now. I shan't need you any more today.'

He waited until the lad had gone, then went into his room

and sat on the edge of his desk, harassed by uneasy thoughts. It took Smith half an hour to get over – he had been obliged to wait for a taxi – and when he came in, Nye saw that his impression had been correct. Smith was in the jitters and, from his patchy flush and fruity breath, had needed a little help to keep himself going.

'Nothing yet?' He read Nye's expression and sank into a chair with his leather briefcase on his knees. 'I can't stand this much longer.'

'Take it easy,' Leonard said. But he wasn't feeling too easy himself; his nerves were screwed up about as tight as they could go. This business had finally got to such a pitch they simply had to come through – not for Somerville or the *Gazette*, but because he had to win or he'd never look himself in the eye again. Now they had come to the last ditch, the final showdown, it must work out the way he intended, he just couldn't bear to miss.

They were both listening for the phone call. Nye lit another cigarette – he'd been chain-smoking all afternoon. Smith broke the silence.

'What do you think, Len?'

'For God's sake, shut up,' Nye snapped at him. 'We've been over it all before. Talk of something else. The weather . . . women . . . gipsy violinists . . . your favourite laxative.'

There was a pause.

'Did you get much done in Tynecastle?' Smith asked, subdued.

'I damn well did. I went round to all the advertisers, sowing the good seed, saw Spencer at the local office of the Northern Mills, called in at the *Echo* and had a long talk with Harrison. He's a sub-editor there, and I used to know him on the *Enquirer*. Everything was working out at last, I told them all; we were hoping for an amicable settlement with Page. I admitted he'd had rather the better of us, but now, because of his health, he wanted to get out. I tell you, I sweated to put it across – it's important. We don't want any suspicion of bad blood; it would hurt us when we take over . . . or should I now say, if we take over?' He drew viciously on the cigarette. 'That's my story. What's yours?'

Smith drew out his handkerchief and dabbed his forehead.

'Well, I was on the wire all day . . . as I told you. But in between . . . I wrote a long letter to Minnie, asking her to join me. I'll post it if all goes well.' He must have caught Nye's expression, for he shook his head heavily. 'It's not so funny. I can't pick up with women, like you; the way you get off with them is a crime. I'll bet you weren't on business all day in Tynecastle. I've . . . I've suffered.'

Suddenly, before he could continue, the phone rang. Simultaneously they started up. Nye got to the switchboard first.

'Hello . . . hello . . . yes, Nye here. . . . Put him through.'

The message from Challoner was brief and to the point. Nye didn't look at Smith until he laid down the receiver. Then, turning with a blankly expressionless face, he gave him a full minute in which to suffer before he said:

'Page is coming up on the night express. He'll sign tomorrow . . . whenever he gets back.'

'Thank God.' Smith sank into a chair. He fumbled for his handkerchief again, failed to find it, and with the back of his hand wiped his damp upper lip. 'You gave me quite a turn there.'

Leonard smiled and put his hand on the other's shoulder, filled, through his own elation, with sudden amiable pity for the poor clot, who couldn't take it either way.

'You need a drink,' he told him. 'Come on down and I'll buy you one.'

'No, no . . . I'm off it from now on . . . for good. I gave my word.'

'Your word? Who to?'

Smith hesitated, then, with a half-defiant glance:

'I promised . . . that's all . . . if the Lord let us come through.'

It showed how good Nye felt – he didn't even laugh at this compact with Heaven.

'Oh, come on,' he said. He did feel good, real good; he was bubbling inside like a magnum of champagne; he could even be friendly with Smith. 'We've got to celebrate. This is a big night for us. Don't be a dog in the manger. We'll have fun together.'

'Well . . .' Smith wavered, his face warming – he wasn't hard to convince. 'Since it's the last time.'

They closed the office, descended in the lift, and walked along Park Street to the hotel. It was a sweet evening, the pavements dry, birds singing in the gardens, the air soft and cool. The last of the sun, shining through a row of copper beeches, which still had not shed their leaves, lit up the street and put a burnished sheen upon the buildings. Nye did not usually notice these things, but now he did. Hedleston wasn't such a bad spot after all; he had misjudged it in the beginning, but now he conceded its good points. Convenient for Tynecastle, too, where he had established that nice discreet connection. He kept feeling better and better, as though he owned the town. Perhaps he would one day. He was pretty sick of bumming around the globe. At thirty-five he wasn't the juvenile lead any longer, and he was getting a little tired of playing the angles, of walking the tightrope between one job and another. There might be something in this settling-down idea. An incredible wave of magnanimity swept over him as he considered that he might get Aunt Liz to sell the shop and come up and keep his house – no matrimony for him, leave that to Smith. Suddenly he saw himself as mayor, with a chain round his neck, opening . . . what? . . . well, say, a home for delinquent girls. He even heard himself making the speech, and parodied it instinctively: 'Ladies and gentlemen, friends and fellow citizens of our royal borough of Hedleston, the worthy purpose of this home is to keep these delinquent girls . . . in fact, to keep them permanently delinquent . . .' He felt like laughing out loud.

When they got to the Red Lion, Smith took his letter from his inside pocket and posted it carefully in the mail box, noting the time of the next collection. The letter was a fat one – he'd written reams in the last few weeks. Nye believed that if he hadn't been there Smith would have kissed it.

199

They went into the lounge and found a couple of armchairs by the window.

'What'll it be?'

'Well, if you insist, double Scotch.'

Smith still had the briefcase; he put it down tenderly, beside him. Nye felt sure he'd go to bed with it.

'I've brought the triplicate contracts from Mossburn; I had the seals put on this morning; in fact, I've been carrying them around all day. In spite of everything. I must have had a premonition he'd sign,' Smith said.

'He will, Harold . . . he will.'

They had their drinks and Nye signalled to the waiter for the same again. When he came back he brought the menu. Leonard ordered the dinner and a magnum of Pol Roger, to put on ice.

'You know,' Smith said solemnly, 'it's wonderful the way we've come out on top, in spite of everything. Yet I can't somehow get Page out of my mind . . . that look in his eyes . . . I like the man.'

Nye hadn't had much lunch, only a snack at the station bar, and the Scotch, on an empty stomach, was giving him a lift, too. He extemporized:

> 'You like little Page,
> His coat is so warm,
> But we haven't hurt him;
> He'll come to no harm.'

'No, seriously, Len.' Smith eyed the other censoriously. 'It's not a joking matter. I mean . . . well . . . if it had come to the bit, I don't believe I'd have gone along with you . . .'

'On what?'

'Printing the dirt.'

'For Christ's sake!' Nye looked at him, realizing that he was a bit over the eight – he must really have been soaking it up all day – still, it was sickening to hear him try to exonerate himself. 'Don't you know that's what we live on

. . . dirt . . . sensation . . . murder . . . sudden death. It's like feeding the animals at the zoo. We've got to serve the meat red, raw, and tainted. Haven't you ever in your sweet life heard the newsboys shout? "Horrible murder in Holloway . . . girl raped and strangled." That's news, brother. "Gor blimey, 'e 'ad it, before she 'ad it." '

'Still' – Smith blinked at Nye owlishly – 'I think Page had a point. We need to improve the eth – the eth – uh, excuse me – the ethical standards of journalism.'

'How?'

'Some sort of board of control.'

'You can't control the freedom of the press – not in a democracy. Damn it all, that's censorship. Besides, if the people don't want what we offer them, why the hell do they buy it? Who is it wants to know whether the condemned man ate a hearty breakfast? There was an electrocution at Sing-Sing when I was in New York, Jesus Christ, you should have seen what appeared in one of the tabloids . . . their reporter had smuggled in a microfilm camera and there was a whole spread of pictures of the poor bastard strapped to the chair in the death cell, with the electrodes on him, being officially bumped off. Next year the same bright newsboy won the Homer Gluck Prize for his pictures of a lynching.'

'Horrible, Leonard, frankly horrible. It proves my argument. We have to edu . . .teach the masses.'

'And go right out of business? Don't talk inflated drivel. The people need their daily dose of opium these days; otherwise this bloody world – which is going to be blown to smithereens in any case – is too tough a place to live in. We're the real humanitarians, not those would-be do-gooders like your friend Page.'

'All right, all right, Leonard. No offence, not the slightest. I'm only glad I'm on the business side. You know me. I have feelings . . . deep. You understand. I feel deeply . . . love my wife . . . a family man. To do your stuff, it would cut me to the heart.'

'Oh, go fry an egg,' Nye said. 'You can't have a heart in this game. I learned my lesson early. When I was a young

201

reporter, green and innocent, if you can believe it, with an American syndicate, they gave me an assignment to cover a stunt parachute jumper, a young Austrian, Rudi Scher-mann, the Human Eagle, they called him. He went around doing his act at country fairs and such like, and I went with him. He was a simple sort of fellow blond, clear-skinned, with a nice wife and kid, and as brave as they come – I needn't tell you his stunts were as dangerous as hell. I got to like him – I still could like people in those days – and I sent in photos and snippits until he had quite a build-up. I knew the risks he was taking and kept telling him to get out while he was still in one piece. So did his wife. But he would smile and shake his head. He wanted to make enough to retire to a little farm in the Tyrol, with some ducks and chickens and a cow – he was just that simple.

'Well, one day it happened. Rudi took off at ten thousand feet, let out his smoke signal amid the "oohs" and "aahs" of the crowd of mucking bumpkins in the field below, and prepared to soar. But something went wrong. He didn't soar. He began to plummet. He pulled his first ripcord, but the parachute didn't open. I saw him struggling with his tangled harness. He couldn't free it. He was down now to fifteen hundred feet. He tried his second chute, real desperate now, but it was caught in the tangle too. It opened slightly, but not enough. He hit the ground not thirty feet from me, with the most sickening goddam awful thud. He was alive and no more when I picked him up; I'll never forget the way he looked at me. He died a few seconds later, in my arms. I had feelings in those days. Yes, it's a laugh all right, just to think of it, but the tears were running down my cheeks. Somehow I got to a phone booth. I phoned my editor. I was shaking all over. Do you know what the S.O.B. said? "Fine," he said. "We'll give him the whole front page. I want all the wordage you can let me have and lots of photographs. Be sure and get a good one of the body." ' Nye looked at Smith and took a long drink. 'If you want to know, that's when I lost my journalistic virginity. Where the hell is that waiter? We'll have another round, then we'll go and eat.'

# XIII

THE KNOCKING ON his door finally roused Smith. Dimly, through the muddle of sleep, he heard the boots' voice.

'It's seven-thirty, Mr Smith. You wanted to be called, sir.'

Smith opened his eyes with difficulty, then hurriedly closed them. The light, filtering beneath the blind, hurt him. His lips were sticky and gummed together and there was a pounding in his head. But he managed to say:

'All right.'

'Very good, sir. Your hot water's outside. And your shoes. Quite a nice morning.'

When the man had gone, Smith lay for a while with his arm across his face, overcome with remorse for having allowed Nye to persuade him into the celebration on the previous evening. He couldn't recollect how much they'd drunk, but from the way he felt now, it had been too much. When he gave way, awakening next morning was the worst of it – not just the headache and the foul taste in the mouth, although these were bad enough, for liquor never did suit him, but the sick sense of self-reproach that made him blame himself for a weak-kneed fool. Now, as he forced his eyes open, he felt especially bad. That champagne, he thought with a shudder, trying to break wind. Yet perhaps there was some excuse for him. These last few days, with all the strain and uncertainty, he'd had to keep himself going somehow. Now that it was settled, he swore he'd keep off the stuff for good.

He rolled over in bed, struggled into his bathrobe, and rang for his morning tea. When the maid brought it she seemed to look at him in a queer sort of way, but perhaps that was only his fancy, he wasn't seeing things too clearly yet. She was a pert little piece whom he didn't approve of at all – he'd often heard her giggling with Nye in his room. When she'd drawn the curtains he had the impression she wanted to say something, but he took no notice. The tea made him feel better, but when he got on his feet again he was still inclined to be shaky, so he went to the wardrobe, where he kept an emergency bottle of Scotch, and took one short drink to steady himself. That, he told himself, is positively the last.

It took him longer than usual to dress; his things were scattered all over the place, and he had trouble getting on his elastic stockings. Smith was sensitive on the point and never spoke of it, but he suffered from varicose veins, and when he indulged the swelling became worse. However, he was ready by half-past eight. On the way to breakfast he looked in on Nye. As he'd expected, Leonard was still asleep. Although Smith shook him several times, he couldn't rouse him. Last night in the lounge he had been very intemperate, and cynical, too – Smith hadn't liked it at all. He left him and went downstairs.

In the coffee room where the breakfasts were served he ordered porridge and a kipper. He wasn't exactly hungry – after rinsing out his mouth several times it still felt like a garbage can – yet he fancied something tasty. Although the hotel food was good he had become tired of it. Often he had thought of moving to a private lodging where he might be more comfortable, but without Minnie, and as he had never known when a settlement with Page might be reached, he had stayed on at the Lion. Now, however, he could afford to take a house, a nice dignified property, with a good garden, a conservatory where he could grow tomatoes, and perhaps a lodge at the entrance to the drive. Minnie would be bound to like that. There ought to be something really nice out Hanley Drive way; he must look over that district next week. It might even be that Page would wish to give up his house and move to another locality. The thought of settling down in Hanley Drive gave him a bit of a lift, took the edge off his depression.

When the waiter brought his kipper he placed the morning papers on the table as usual. Smith always ran through them before he went to the office. But at the moment he was too busy planning the day that lay ahead of him to bother with the news. Page, having taken the night train home, would be tired, might possibly have gone to bed for a few hours, so he would not disturb him too early. If he made their appointment for eleven o'clock it ought to suit him reasonably well. He had all the documents prepared and ready – very different, of course, from the original papers which he had brought with him nearly two years ago. If only Page had accepted then, Smith reflected sombrely, what an immense amount of strife, enmity and grief, to say nothing of the expense, might have been saved on both sides.

The thought of Page began to get him down again. He was not exactly looking forward to the coming meeting. He would have to hide his feelings and harden himself, be businesslike, and abrupt – that obviously was the only way to deal with a painful situation . . . get it over quickly. A good stiff drink might help him through, and in the circumstances he'd be justified in taking it.

By this time he had finished breakfast and was about to leave when George, the waiter, wandered back to the table.

'Everything all right, sir?'

'Fine,' Smith said. George was a good sort, agreeable and attentive, but he was a talker and Smith was in no mood for conversation.

'Can I get you another kipper?'

'No, thanks.' He was on the point of rising when George gave him a sidelong glance which somehow put him in mind of the chambermaid's expression earlier on. Then the waiter, rocking on his heels, hands clasped behind his back, remarked:

'I suppose you've seen the *Globe*, sir.'

The *Globe*, which was Mighill's paper, Smith did not normally go through very particularly, but it came in with the other three dailies and now, as he looked down, he saw that it lay on the top of the pile, folded small, no doubt by

George, so as to expose a two-column spread on the middle of the back page. He picked it up, then, stunned, as though hit by a hammer, he almost dropped it. There, before his shocked and unbelieving eyes, was the heading: FEMALE EX-PRISONER MAKES GOOD. The opening lines danced up and down in a jumbled maze as he tried to take them in.

*Cora Page, who, as Cora Bates, in 1954 was convicted of an unnatural and criminal offence was unexpectedly run to earth by our Northern reporter – the same who saw her sentenced to six months at the Northern Assizes . . .*

Smith's stomach turned over as he skimmed sickeningly through the double column. It was all there. Written apparently as a story of regeneration, more or less the way Nye had intended, nothing had been hidden; every painful fact was revealed in a manner as damaging as if Leonard had composed the thing himself.

Smith rose from the table. Ignoring George, who was saying something he scarcely heard, he made instinctively for Nye's room. Leonard was up, standing half-dressed before the mirror, shaving with his electric razor.

'Read that,' he said, 'quick.'

Nye threw him a nasty look, charged with a morning-after surliness, but Smith's tone made him switch off the current. He took the *Globe* and sat down on the edge of his bed. Smith couldn't contain himself.

'It must be Haines,' he said. 'He's used the story himself.'

'Shut up.' Nye had turned a dirty grey. In his slack singlet and drooping underpants, with one side of his face unshaven, he looked grotesque. He pressed his knuckles against his forehead.

'Let me think.'

'Why should Haines . . . ?'

'Can't you see it, you infernal fool? It's not really Haines. He was just smart enough to leak the story to the head office. This is Mighill himself. He knows how much Vernon needs this pitch. He's got on to our scheme and gone out

206

of his way to wreck it.' He bit his lip hard. 'Why didn't I think of this? God's truth. God's bloody truth. He's cut the ground from under us. What time is it?'

'Just after nine.'

'We've got to work fast.' Galvanized to action, he began pulling on his clothes, talking in quick, jerky sentences. 'If Page sees this before he signs we're done. But there's a good chance he hasn't. The night train got in at five-thirty this morning . . . before the papers. He'd almost certainly go straight home. Now listen to me. Get the contract and take a taxi to his house. It's my guess he'll be there. Lay on a line of soft soap. You wanted to make it easy for him, all very private and so forth. Get him to sign. Do you hear me? We've bloody well got to get his signature. I'll check at the *Light* building. If he's not at his house, call me at the office.'

Smith hurried to his room, picked up his briefcase, and plunged downstairs. In the morning it was difficult to get a taxi, but luck favoured him: as he came through the swing doors of the hotel, one of Hedleston's antique cabs rattled up to discharge a passenger. There was a pack of luggage that looked like stock samples to be unloaded, which made Smith fume at the delay, but within four minutes he was being driven towards Hanley Drive. As the cab edged through the traffic of the Cornmarket he noticed on the corner newsstand a row of the yellow *Globe* posters, far in excess of the number usually displayed. He thought: They've flooded the town with this edition. He must get to Page at once. Now more than ever. The possibility that, at this final moment, their plans might break down, that everything he had hoped for would be lost, made him so desperate he kept pressing on the floorboards, trying to drive the old cab on with his feet.

Still, the chances were in his favour – as he approached Page's villa it was not yet half-past nine. He stopped the driver some fifty yards down the road and told him to wait. Straightening his hat, which a lurch of the taxi had displaced, and with the briefcase under his arm, he entered the drive, trying not to seem in a hurry, and was immediately confronted by a gang of workmen busy erecting a large green-and-white striped tent on the front lawn. For an instant Smith stared at them, stupefied, unable to believe his eyes, then it dawned upon him that the marquee must be for the reception, the garden party he'd vaguely heard of, and the fact that everything seemed to be proceeding normally gave him a sudden spurt of hope. The front door was open and he was about to mount the steps and ring when he saw a woman come round the side of the house. He recognized her at once – Mrs Page. She wore a wide-brimmed garden hat that shaded her face and carried a wicker basket of flowers. Immediately, from her manner, condescending, yet moderately pleasant, he knew that so far nothing of the disaster had reached her.

'Good mornnig,' she began, before he could speak. 'Have you been waiting long?'

'No . . . not at all,' he stammered.

'I've been cutting chrysanthemums, as you see. Aren't they lovely? I want them for my marquee. This is our big day, you know. I do hope it will keep up.' She looked up at the sky. 'What do you think?'

'I think, I hope it will be fine. But, Mrs Page . . .'

Misunderstanding his confusion, she gave him a meaning, half-playful smile.

'I didn't think to send you an invitation . . . but, perhaps . . . well, if you'd care to come . . .'

'Mrs Page . . .'

'I'm sure there's no ill-feeling . . . at least nót on our side. I rather liked your paper, you know. Especially at the beginning when Dorothy won the guineas. And as you're leaving the town it would be nice if you and Mr . . . well, if you both joined with us and our friends that afternoon. You see . . .'

'Forgive me, Mrs Page.' He managed to break in at last. 'I must speak with your husband.'

'My husband? Henry?' Her voice lost its overtones of

polite society and took on a note of asperity. 'You will be lucky indeed to get hold of *him*.'

'But I must see him. It's a matter of the utmost importance.'

'I dare say. There are several important matters awaiting Henry. However, two days ago he chose to run off to London.'

'Yes, Mrs Page,' Smith said hurriedly, beginning to sweat, 'but his . . . his business in London finished yesterday. And we've been assured that he took the night train home.'

'He did?' She considered Smith with a foolish expression. 'Well, I can assure you of another thing. He's not here.'

'Not here?' Smith repeated, then went on with a rush. 'Listen to me, Mrs Page. The train came in at half-past five this morning. We know he was on it. Now suppose your husband didn't want to disturb you . . . wake up the household at that hour . . . where do you think he might have gone?'

She thought this over with a prim expression that drove him frantic.

'Well,' she said, with sudden pique, 'he might have gone to my son's place. At Sleedon. There's no accounting for Henry. He has a mania for Sleedon.'

This possibility sent Smith's hopes up again, with a sudden lift of relief. Sleedon! . . . That was it. Since Page's main concern would be to reassure Cora with the least possible delay, it was more than likely, in fact almost certain, that he would go direct to Sleedon from the station. Yes, it was evident how strong would be his desire to tell her that he had saved her. Hurriedly, Smith excused himself and retreated to the taxi. As he set off for Sleedon he told himself that in this turn of events luck was with him again – there seemed little likelihood that the news would have reached such a small, isolated community on the coast. He pressed the driver on to greater speed until the vehicle, which, like most of the local taxis, was a prewar model, creaked and bounced all over the road.

Suddenly, when he was no more than two miles from his

destination, the car took an extra swerve and, with a jarring of brakes, bumped to a stop. Even before the driver climbed out of his seat Smith knew that a tyre had gone. With almost insupportable impatience he waited, pacing up and down, while the man jacked up the rear axle and changed the wheel. All the while he kept grumbling that it was not his fault, that his machine had never been built to go careering across country at fifty miles an hour. He himself was not young and, hampered by an old tweed coat and elbow-length gauntlets which he did not remove, his movements were maddeningly deliberate. Smith kept looking down the road, hoping for a car that might give him a lift, but the only conveyance that passed was the local bus going in the opposite direction towards Hedleston. To make matters worse, the air had turned sultry and a thick bank of cloud, dark and threatening, had rolled up from the north. He felt sure they were in for a storm. At last the job was done and, pacified by the promise of a larger tip, the man drove off again at reduced speed.

If Smith had looked at his watch once he'd done so a dozen times. Now it showed half-past ten as he entered the village, which, as though half asleep, wore a reassuring air of calm. He had some idea of the location of young Page's house on the cliff walk, and it did not take long to find it. When he got out of the car he took a deep breath to clear his lungs, but his head still felt stuffy and his nerves were strung to breaking pitch as he approached the front door. The next few minutes must be decisive.

He pulled the bell, with anxious moderation, and waited. There was no answer. Had it sounded in the house? He fancied he had heard the peal, yet in his present state he could not be certain. He pulled again, more loudly, but without result. For the third time he rang, almost dragging the bell handle from its socket, plainly hearing the loud jangling within, and still there was no answer.

He tried the front door, turning the handle hard, both ways, but without result. Through the windows no movement was visible. What on earth was the matter? Surely someone must be at home. Then it occurred to him that Page might be sleeping upstairs – it seemed altogether feasible. And if he were Smith could not hold back, he simply had to get to him.

The taxi-driver at the gate was now viewing Smith with sharp suspicion, but he ignored him and took the narrow gravel path that ran round the side of the cottage. As he expected, it led him to the back door. This he found to be ajar. Quietly, he pushed it open, entered the scullery, went through to the kitchen. And there, seated at the table, was Cora.

Even when he came close to her, she did not move; she seemed to be oblivious, or at least quite heedless, of his presence. Her eyes remained averted, as though held by some far-off, paralysing vision. The change in her outward look since he had last seen her at the concert, only a few days before, was truly fearful. She seemed aged by ten years, sunk into herself, stripped bare of all joy, of all the life that had been in her. But he had no time to pity her. He had to get hold of Page, and he told her so.

She did not answer.

'Look,' Smith said, bending over, as though talking to a child. 'It's Henry Page I want. I must talk to him.'

She was so long in replying he thought she had not heard.

Then, slowly, she turned. Her face was of a marble pallor, almost expressionless, as though fixed by an interior anguish so deep it numbed all sensation.

'He's not here,' she said.

'But . . . I was told . .'

'He's not here,' she repeated, in that same frozen tone. 'He changed his mind late last night. He wired us that he'd travel up today.'

'But, we were advised . . .'

'The telegram's there . . . by the mantelpiece.'

Smith read the telegram. It was to Cora, reassuring her, stating that he had decided to sleep in the hotel, and return the following afternoon.

'Oh, no . . .' Smith cried out.

'What does it matter anyway?' she said.

All at once, looking beyond her, he saw, on the table, an open copy of the *Globe*. Her dead eyes, following his, rested upon it.

'Yes, that's it. You're satisfied, I hope. The first time you only done for *me*. Now you've done for all of us.'

Instinctively Smith started to protest. He wanted to clear himself, to say it hadn't been his doing, then he broke off. He was in it as much as anybody, and more. Besides, she was right. It was useless now. As she had said, they were all done for, words and actions alike were useless. And at the sight of her, seated there, crushed, turned to stone, the dregs of last night churned up in his stomach; he felt deathly sick. In a sudden turn-around of feeling he saw, for the first time, the fearful thing that had been done. All the harm and hurt ever inflicted by a callous and ruthless press seemed concentrated in this broken human creature.

'How did you get the paper?' he asked her.

'David . . . my husband.'

'But where?'

His words seemed to reach her from a long way off and her answer, delayed, travelled back an equal distance.

'Every morning he takes a walk on the pier. At the news-stand . . . he saw the poster . . . they'd plastered them all over . . . he brought the paper home . . .' A dry shudder passed over her, shaking her rigid body. 'It's the very thing I tried to stop. I knew what it would do to him. I never saw him look the way he did. And to leave me, without a word.'

'Where did he go?' Smith asked.

'I don't know . . . I can't tell. I tried to stop him, but it wasn't no use. I can't do no more. I'm done for . . . it's the end.'

What could he say to her? He could think of nothing, absolutely nothing. At last he said, in feeble consolation:

'It won't be as bad as you think. He'll come back to you.'

No.' She raised her eyes slowly to his, and in her voice there was something that chilled him. 'Not to me, he won't.'

There was nothing more that he could get from her; a

212

fresh access of despair had turned her dumb. He tried to tell himself that later, perhaps, relief might come in a burst of tears. Then he turned and went out of the house.

Back towards the cab he went – slowly – there was no need for hurry now. In the distance the storm had broken and thunder had begun among the Eldon hills. Even here the sky was like lead and the air more stifling than ever. In his shaken state there was something frightening in these detonations rolling in heavy waves like gunfire through the sultry air. As he got into the taxi a single splash of rain fell upon his hand, heavy and hot as blood.

He told the man to return to Hedleston – there was no alternative. He had now abandoned all idea of finding Page. He was not here, he was in the train, perhaps still in London. In either case, he must have learned the worst. He would never sign now, never surrender the *Light*. Nothing remained for Nye and himself but to give up and get out. But logic alone did not account for this sudden desire for withdrawal that had taken hold of Smith. The situation he had created with Nye and the forces they had loosed now thoroughly alarmed him. He felt weak inside, he would have given anything for a drink. He must get away. Whether or not he lost his job had become relatively unimportant. All that mattered was that he should get out of Hedleston, without further delay.

The need of support threw him back on Nye. Leonard had said that he would be at the office, and as they approached the outskirts of the town, Smith asked the driver to take him to the Prudential Building. A deluge of rain was now falling and a high wind had sprung up which lashed torrents of water against the windscreen. The streets were almost empty except for a few people hurrying for shelter, bent forward under their umbrellas. But suddenly, as they swung out of Victoria Street into the Cornmarket, they ran into a thick traffic jam. Smith lowered the window and looked out. The narrow street was solidly blocked – mainly with those trucks and lorries that dealt with the produce from the central market. He thought a water main had burst, or that the street was flooded. He couldn't wait, it wasn't far to the office. He pushed some notes into the driver's hand and got out.

Then, as he turned the corner and hurried up Park Street, he became aware of a big crowd of people on the pavement. In spite of the rain, there they were, standing tightly packed, craning their necks, swaying this way and that as they pressed towards the doorway of a building. Smith's heart missed a beat as he saw that it was the entrance of the Prudential offices. There's been trouble, he thought, they've smashed up our office. He was afraid, but he had to find out. He ran forward. At that instant, he heard the wail of a siren and in the gardens across the way, coming along the beach avenue that was normally closed to cars, he made out the white blur of an ambulance.

A sick terror took hold of Smith as he pushed and elbowed his way through the crowd. He kept repeating who he was, that they must let him pass. When he got to the entrance the policeman recognized him and allowed him to go in. He stood in the hallway, breathing heavily, afraid to go further. He made himself press the lift button. Nothing happened. It was not working, the indicator showed that it was stationary on the third floor. Suddenly he heard someone running down the stairs. He turned. It was Peter, the telephone boy. He saw Smith, and flung himself against him, gripping hold of his arm.

'Mr Smith . . . oh, sir . . . sir.'

'What's the matter?'

He clutched at Smith hysterically, moaning to himself.

'I want to go home. It's terrible, terrible . . . and I saw it.'

'What?' Smith shook him hard. 'For God's sake . . . what?'

Peter looked up, his head fallen slackly back. His voice rose shrilly.

'Young Mr Page . . . he shot at Mr Nye . . . Mr Nye fell down . . . then he shot himself.' He choked for breath, his voice rose higher. 'The doctor says he's dead.'

'Who?' Smith faltered.

'David . . . young Mr Page.'

Smith leaned against the wall, drained of everything but a hollow nausea. Behind him, he heard the whine of the descending lift. A moment later, Nye stepped out, accompanied by the office doctor. Nye looked shaken, and under his coat, which was draped over his shoulders, a wad of bandage bound up his left arm, but stuck in the corner of his pale lips there was a cigarette.

'Crazy young bastard,' he said to Smith, in passing.

In a daze Smith saw the two get into the front compartment of the ambulance. Summoning all his forces, he was about to move when from the back of the lift two attendants edged their way out, carrying between them a sheeted stretcher. Smith tried to close his eyes. He could not. He watched it go past. They slid it into the body of the ambulance. Through the open doorway, against the background of the silent, gaping crowd, Smith saw, bent on one knee in a professional attitude, a man with a camera, taking pictures.


# XIV


THESE LAST FOUR days, after the thunderstorm of Thursday, had brought a spell of unusually fine weather, a real Indian summer. Malcolm Maitland, walking sombrely through the Cornmarket to the *Light* building, felt it right warm, the more so as the dark suit he'd put on had got a bit tight for him. At the inquest the Town Hall had been stifling, he had never known it so crowded – it was at least a relief to be out in the air. His seat near the side exit had allowed him to get away early, and as he came up the stairs to his office he thought he would be the first back. But Moffatt was before him. Through the open door of her room he saw her pushing up her window. He stopped.

'Well, it's over,' he said.

She did not immediately answer. Then, grimly, she agreed. 'Yes . . . it's over.'

Dressed entirely in black, her face grey from the heat, Moffatt looked thoroughly exhausted, and her expression was particularly forbidding, but the need to talk drew Malcolm in.

'Henry came through it not too badly,' he said, after a pause.

'Better than I expected,' she admitted. 'The Coroner helped . . . for once he was half human. But, oh' – she took off her hat, stabbed it with her hatpins, and hooked it forcibly on the back of the door – 'these poor young people. What a waste, what a pitiful waste! If that poor crazed fellow had only done what he meant to, it all wouldn't have been so useless. When I saw Nye in the box, bold as brass, I could have done for him myself. But it was just like David to bungle it.'

'Better that he did,' Maitland said slowly, 'for Henry's sake. I'm sure that's the general opinion. The town is still with him. When all's said and done, the *Light* has come out of the mess better than we could have hoped.'

'Maybe,' she said, frowning. 'But it took . . . well, what it took . . . to do it. Believe me, if it hadn't happened this way our name would still be in the mud. I've no doubt Henry'll put it all down to the milk of human kindness.' Her tone sharpened. 'What it really means is that one sensation has been knocked out by a bigger one.' She turned, and with a jab, plugged in her electric kettle. 'I'm going to make a cup of tea. It's the only thing on a day like this. And what a day! Will you have one?'

'I could do with it,' Maitland said, watching her as she rattled down the cups from behind the filing cabinet and took out the lump sugar and the tin canister of tea she kept in her desk drawer. Then, from its resting-place on the cold-water pipe, she produced a half-bottle of milk. This she inspected doubtfully, murmuring fretfully to herself, 'It's not today's, but we'll have to put up with it.'

'Of course,' she went on, her mind still dwelling on the inquest, 'Smith was the one who really turned me. When he said he ought to have stayed with Cora in the cottage and not left her alone, then broke down, it was abject. Even before that he'd begun to look mealy-eyed . . . when the woman in the store, Mrs Dale, was telling how she saw Cora run down the pier, and called out to stop her and couldn't. To think of the likes of him blubbering over Cora – I could have hit him.'

'Poor devil,' Malcolm said. 'He tried to blame himself for everything. I couldn't help feeling sorry for him.'

'You needn't be,' she said, with that tightening of the lips Maitland knew so well. 'I've a bit of news for you on Smith.'

'Yes?'

'Henry's given him a job.'

'What!'

'Balmer's. He's on the staff. Our new advertising manager.'

'Good Lord.' Malcolm thought for a bit, then he said, 'You may say what you like. Page is the nearest thing to a good man I've ever met up with in this most ungodly world.'

She shook her head and began to infuse the tea.

'He's soft-hearted, that's all. His father would never have done such a thing. He'd have thrown Smith out of his office the minute he set eyes on him.'

'You're much too hard on Henry. You always are.' He took the cup she offered him. 'Look what he's come through these last couple of years . . . with his bad heart and all. Then this, on top of everything. You know how bound up he was in David.'

'Yes,' she agreed gloomily. 'My dear David.' Then, sipping her tea, she shot a dark glance at Maitland over the rim of the cup. 'But Cora's the one he'll really miss.'

Before Malcolm could interpose, she went on. 'He mayn't have known it, but he was in love with her. Oh, I don't blame him for it. In fact it's one of the few things about him I could admire. Cora was a real woman, warm and human She needed to be loved and David didn't quite fill the bill. Especially when he began to go queer again, making her read those highbrow books, treating her like something in a glass case. She never said a word of it to me, but I could tell. I understood her through and through. I admit she was fond of David, devoted to him, sorry for him . . . but it wasn't enough.'

'You're talking nonsense,' Maitland interrupted curtly. 'And this isn't the time for it.'

'Perhaps not. But I've known it for long enough. Henry liked Sleedon, but he never liked it so much, or went there so often, until Cora was there. He would have done anything for her . . . even have given up the *Light*. I was with him in the office yesterday when Bob Lewis brought word that they'd found her body washed up on the North Shore. I wish you'd seen his face. And do you know what he said? "Was she harmed?" he said. "Disfigured in any way?" And when Bob said, "No, sir, not at all," he said, "Thank God . . . thank God for that."'

Malcolm stared at her, between annoyance and a kind of irritated curiosity, and suddenly he found himself saying:

'Moffatt, why are you so against Henry? And always by comparison with his father.'

She did not answer immediately.

'I'm not really against him,' she said at last. 'He's just not my idea of the editor of the *Light*. Too gentle, too inclined to put up with things instead of driving right through them. His father wasn't that way. He was a real man.'

'You admired him?'

'Yes, I did.' She spoke with sudden defiance. 'Not only for what he was, but for what he did for me. I suppose they've told you that he bought me my little house.'

'I did hear something,' Maitland said temperately.

But Moffatt, lifted out of herself by the events of the day, was not to be deterred.

'Yes,' she continued, 'he knew I liked to be out of the town, with a bit of a garden, and one day . . . I'll never forget it . . . he just handed me the title deeds. When I offered to pay him out of my wages, all he did was laugh and say, "Bring me a bunch of flowers occasionally." That's why I still bring them.' She paused, forgetful of Maitland's presence. 'And after his wife died, he'd drop over of a Saturday afternoon and smoke a pipe and drink a glass of ale. Burton he favoured; I always kept it for him.' She broke off and, suddenly conscious of Malcolm's gaze upon her, coloured deeply. It was the only time he had ever seen her flush.

Neither of them spoke for several minutes. The silence was becoming awkward, when Maitland rose to his feet.

'Well,' he said, 'I suppose we ought to be getting on. No slacking while the boss is away. What we all need now is work, and plenty of it. We'll have the staff meeting at noon today. Tell the others. Thanks for the tea.'

He went to his own room, sat down, and began to think over his plans for the next three months, when, in Henry's absence, much of the responsibility must fall on him. Presently there was a knock on the door, and Fenwick appeared, with a teletype strip.

'Here's an item that just came in on the A.P.'

'Yes?' Maitland looked up inquiringly.

'They seem to have changed their minds about the atomic site on Utley.'

'What!' Malcolm exclaimed, in sharp surprise. 'You mean . . . they're not coming here after all?'

'Apparently not. They're considering the Highlands now . . . Sutherlandshire. The Under-Secretary made an announcement in the House yesterday.'

He handed over the strip.

'Can you beat that?' Malcolm said, when he'd read it. 'I hope to heaven he'll stick to it.'

'It seems likely. He indicated that Sutherland is a much more suitable site.'

'Thank goodness!' Maitland exclaimed, with emphasis, showing signs of satisfaction. 'It means we'll be left alone . . . down here.' Under his breath, he added, 'At least for a bit longer.'

When Fenwick had gone Malcolm sat thinking on all that

had happened simply because a government department had, in the first instance, been unable to make up its mind. But for the abortive Utley project they would never have known these two years of useless strife and the tragedy that had ended it.

With an effort he turned his mind towards the future and began to jot down the agenda for the staff meeting. He had worked steadily for about half an hour when, from the corridor, a familiar sound caused him to raise his head. He remained motionless and uncertain, telling himself that he could not have recognized Henry's footstep, then, to his surprise, the door opened and Page came in.

Maitland immediately got up.

'Why, Henry,' he exclaimed, as lightly as he could, 'I thought you were supposed to go straight to bed.'

'I'm only here for a few minutes . . . the car's waiting outside,' Page said, bracing himself against the edge of the desk. He was paler than usual and there was a fixed look of endurance on his face, yet the change in him over the past few days, while marked, was less annihilating than Maitland had feared. What was it, Malcolm asked himself, that enabled this little man to stand fast, despite his physical handicap, without the show and symbols of courage? A lifetime of faithfulness and honour, regard for his neighbour and respect for the pledged word – these insistent, inescapable, exemplary values of upright behaviour were the things that held him together when another stronger in body, would have crumbled.

'I shan't see you for quite a while, Malcolm,' Page went on, when he had recovered his breath. 'Apparently, when they let me up, I'm to have a long sea voyage. Alice has always wanted to visit Hawaii, so we shall go there. . . . But first, I want you to know that I am taking you in with me on the *Northern Light*. I've asked Paton to draw up the deeds of partnership. I'll sign them before I leave.'

Maitland remained perfectly still, but his homely face lost its ruddiness momentarily, then was slowly flooded by a deeper colour. After all the years of steady unrewarded plodding, this offer, quite unlooked for, was so overwhelming he could not completely master himself. In a voice which, despite the grip he kept upon himself, shook slightly, he said:

'There's precious little I can say, Henry . . . only . . . thank you.'

'That's settled, then,' Page said, then continued seriously, 'There's just one thing more on my mind. It may surprise you – I shouldn't perhaps speak of it – but in these last four days, well, the sympathy and kindness shown me, not only completely unexpected, but unmerited . . . it has been just another example of the fundamental charity of our people here.'

If Maitland was reminded of Moffatt's recent sarcastic prediction, he gave no sign of it. He waited, as Page went on.

'I wondered if I could break my rule and do something personal, just this once. You may know what's in my mind. A message from myself to our readers . . . a reaffirmation of my personal faith . . . an appreciation of their loyalty and support, an assurance that in spite of all that's happened to us, the paper will go on.' He paused, searching Maitland's face. 'Do you think I might write something along these lines? Or would it be in bad taste?'

'Write it, Henry,' Maitland said firmly, permitting himself not the slightest hesitation. 'It'll do you good. And everybody else.'

Almost imperceptibly Page's expression lightened.

'I will, then,' he said. 'Thank you, Malcolm.'

When he had gone Maitland waited a few minutes, then he moved off to go to the copy room. As he walked along the corridor past Henry's open door he saw him, already at his desk, bowed a little, his head supported by one hand, but writing, writing steadily, writing ·his personal message for tomorrow's *Northern Light*.

# A SONG OF SIXPENCE

## A. J. Cronin

Scotland at the century's turn.

In the still heat of late afternoon, a young boy waits at the station for his father. A plume of steam, white against the purple heathered hills, marks the train. Beyond, blooming along the shoreline, the flowers of high summer, as a tall-funnelled paddle steamer beats and froths down the wide Clyde estuary . . .

A magical, closely-observed story of the senses and the half-understood complexities of growing up.

'brilliantly written' *Sunday Times*

'A. J. Cronin at his best' *Daily Express*

**NEW ENGLISH LIBRARY**